Swift
Edge

ALSO BY LAURA DiSILVERIO

Swift Justice

Swift Edge

LAURA DiSILVERIO

Minotaur Books

A Thomas Dunne Book

New York

A THOMAS DUNNE BOOK FOR MINOTAUR BOOKS.
An imprint of St. Martin's Publishing Group.

www.thomasdunnebooks.com
www.minotaurbooks.com

LIBRARY OF CONGRESS CATALOGING-IN-PUBLICATION DATA

DiSilverio, Laura A. H.
    Swift edge : a mystery / Laura DiSilverio.—1st ed.
        p. cm.
    ISBN 978-0-312-62444-6
    1. Women private investigators—Fiction.   2. Figure skaters—Crimes against—Fiction.   I. Title.
    PS3604.I85S93 2011
    813'.6—dc23

                                                                    2011026759

First Edition: December 2011

10 9 8 7 6 5 4 3 2 1

For my husband, Thomas:

Your presence makes the sunny days brighter and the gloomy ones lighter. Our life together is a gift I could never deserve and I am overwhelmingly thankful for you every day.

Acknowledgments

Since my experience as an ice-skater is limited to a couple of tailbone-bruising outings back in my youth and to TV viewing, I could not have written this book without help. Many, many thanks to John LeFevre, president of the Broadmoor Skating Club and former executive director of U.S. Figure Skating, and to Carolyn Braley, a skater herself and mother of a former competitive figure skater, for sharing their knowledge and anecdotes with me. They get credit for all the accurate data about figure skating; I'll accept the blame for errors, misunderstandings, or license taken for plot needs.

As always, thanks to my agent, Paige Wheeler, my editor, Toni Plummer, and all the folks at Folio and Thomas Dunne/Minotaur, as well as to all those involved in the book distributing and book selling businesses. Thank you, Joan, Marie, Lin, and Amy, for your insightful reading and comments on early drafts. Extra-special thanks go to the readers who enjoy Charlie and Gigi and make it possible and fun to continue writing their adventures.

Swift
Edge

1

Mondays suck, especially when they happen on Thursdays.

And this Thursday was shaping up to be the Monday from hell.

I'd had a flat tire on the way to my office, Swift Investigations, and changed it on the shoulder, crouched in two inches of grimy snow left over from the storm we'd had on New Year's Eve, and pelted by the slush and grit kicked up by passing cars. I'd missed my eight o'clock appointment. Now that I'm unwillingly splitting the firm's meager profits with a partner, Gigi Goldman, I couldn't afford to alienate a potential client, even one who wanted me to tail his daughter and her boyfriend to make sure they weren't "doing the nasty" (his words). I'd reluctantly agreed to meet with the man even though he sounded nuttier than a squirrel convention, but he was gone when I parked my Subaru Outback in front of my office at eight twenty. I sighed and unlocked the door, recoiling at the smell of burned coffee. Not again.

Flipping the lights on, I saw that Kendall Goldman, my

partner's fourteen-year-old daughter and our part-time receptionist during Christmas vacation, had neglected to turn off the coffeepot for the third time in as many weeks. A half inch of tarry sludge caked the bottom of the carafe. Grrr. The replacement cost was coming out of Kendall's wages, I decided, mentally overriding the objections Gigi would make. Better yet . . . I stalked across the room and yanked the coffeemaker's cord out of the wall. Picking up the whole contraption, I dropped it from shoulder height into the trash can. *Clang.* I didn't drink coffee anyway. With grim satisfaction, I opened the minifridge behind my desk and yanked a can of Pepsi from the door. It exploded when I popped the top, raining caramel-colored spots on my white turtleneck and the papers on my desk.

"Shit, shit, double shit!" I yelled, trying to slurp Pepsi from the lid of the can before more of it bubbled over.

"Is this a bad time?" A voice from the doorway stopped me in midslurp.

"Not at all," I said, forcing a smile. I hoped I didn't have a Pepsi mustache. "Just give me a moment." I blotted my face, blouse, and desk with paper towels from the small bathroom and shook hands with my visitor. She was young—late teens or early twenties—with dark hair pulled into a high ponytail. She had an air of confidence as glossy as her hair. Huge blue eyes, so dark they looked navy, dominated her heart-shaped face. Shorter than my five foot three, she looked ethereal at first glance, but her handshake was firm, and the slim legs showing beneath a short denim skirt had an athlete's muscle definition. Clunky Ugg boots were her only concession to the January weather. She wrinkled her nose and sniffed.

I gestured to the trash can. "I'm afraid I can't offer you coffee." Not that I would have anyway. I don't like to encourage clients to linger and had objected when Gigi installed the coffeemaker.

"Not a problem. Coach wants me to limit my caffeine, anyway."

Aha! I was right: She was an athlete. I hoped she was also a paying client.

"I'm Charlotte Swift," I said, motioning her to the chair in front of my desk. "How can I help you, Ms.—?"

"I'm Dara Peterson."

She paused as if expecting me to comment. When I merely raised my brows, she continued, slightly disconcerted. "My partner is missing. Your Web page says you specialize in missing persons, and I want to hire you to find him."

The Web page was new—Gigi's brainchild—but I had to admit it was paying off. Mr. "Nasty" had also found Swift Investigations online. "I do," I told Ms. Peterson, turning to an un-Pepsied page in my legal pad. "Tell me about your partner. How long has he been missing?"

"Five days. I haven't seen him, he hasn't been in touch, since Saturday."

I made a note. "And when you say 'partner'—he's your boyfriend? Business partner?" I was betting on boyfriend. She looked too young to be running a business.

"He's Dmitri Fane," she said, with an undertone of "duh" in her voice. "Peterson and Fane?"

Clearly, she thought I should recognize the names, but I didn't. Maybe they were singers, like Sonny and Cher or the Captain and Tennille. I didn't really know what young adults were listening to these days. My mind cycled through other famous pairs: Rowan and Martin, Starsky and Hutch, Siegfried and Roy. She didn't strike me as the animal trainer type.

I resorted to honesty, always the best policy except when a lie will work better. "Never heard of you."

A wrinkle appeared between her brows. "Really? We're skaters. We're the reigning world champions—we've held the title for three years. We were junior world champs the two years before that."

"So you're like Torvill and Dean?" I asked, proudly dredging up the only skating names I knew besides Dorothy Hamill and Scott Hamilton (who I was pretty sure didn't skate together).

"They're ice *dancers*." She rolled her eyes contemptuously, whether at my ignorance or ice dancers, I wasn't sure. "We're *pair* skaters. Much more dangerous."

Puh-leeze. Scuba diving with great whites is dangerous. Teaching high school is dangerous. Ice-skating? Hardly. "I'll take your word for it. So, you haven't seen your partner in five days. Is that unusual?"

"We're in training! I mean, the Olympics are right around the corner! He wouldn't disappear like this, not now. Something's happened to him."

What appeared to be genuine worry smudged her self-confidence. She chewed away the pink lip gloss from her lower lip. "The police won't do anything. They say he's a grown man and he's entitled to take a few days off if he wants. They treated me like I was a jealous girlfriend." She crossed her arms over her chest, seething.

"Are you?"

My question startled her. "Me and Dmitri? Not hardly. He's gay."

"I assume you've talked to his friends, maybe his parents? Has anyone else heard from him?"

She shook her head, setting her ponytail swinging. "Nobody.

His dad died in a car crash a couple months ago, and his mom's in Detroit. I called her—nada. Yuliya—our coach, Yuliya Bobrova—was royally pissed when he didn't show on Monday. Ice time isn't free, you know. I called a couple of his friends, but no one's seen him. I'm really worried, Miss Swift—"

"Charlie."

"Do you think you can find him?"

"I can't guarantee anything, but I'll do my best." I figured this case would be relatively easy. A high-profile athlete would find it difficult to stay hidden for long. Maybe he'd checked himself into an addiction treatment center, or maybe he'd gone off with a boyfriend Dara didn't know about. Maybe he was burned out and I'd find him holed up at a resort in Aspen or on the beach in Cancún. Either way, it shouldn't be too hard to pick up his trail.

I grilled Dara for another half hour on Dmitri's friends, habits, and background and accepted her retainer check. "Try not to worry," I said, shaking her hand. She'd remained tense throughout our conversation, and I wanted to reassure her. "Hopefully, I'll have something positive to report in a few days."

Her eyes narrowed. "If he's not back by the start of Nationals next week, he'd better just stay gone because I'll kill him if we don't make the team."

"Team?"

She gusted a put-upon sigh. "The Olympics?"

So sue me. I'm not that into sports, and even though the Olympic Training Center is here in Colorado Springs, I probably couldn't name four Olympic athletes. I couldn't tell you where the Super Bowl was being played this year or who won the World Series, either. I know where the Kentucky Derby is, though, because I'd gone with a friend one year and echoes of the mint julep hangover I'd suffered made my head hurt whenever anyone mentioned the state.

"The U.S. Figure Skating Championships here in the Springs next week doubles as the team trials for the Olympics. I've been working for this since I was eight. If we don't make the team because Dmitri's pulling a—"

"Pulling a what?" I prompted her when she stopped.

"Nothing," she muttered. She slung her purse over her shoulder and crossed to the door. "Just find him, okay?"

———

I was studying the notes I'd taken and making a list of who I wanted to interview and in what order when the door swung open and my partner blew in on a gust of cold air. Georgia Goldman, Gigi for short, stamped her feet on the mat and shivered with a dramatic "Brrrr." Clumps of snow fell off her quilted fuchsia parka.

"Is it snowing?" I peered out the wooden blinds by my desk but didn't see any flakes.

"No." She shook her blond head and unzipped the parka. "That very rude man I served up in Monument was clearing his driveway. When I handed him the summons, he turned the snowblower on me!" Indignation flushed her cheeks, and her southern accent thickened as it always did when she was excited or angry.

I bit back a smile. Swift Investigations had started process serving in August as a way of bumping up our cash flow, and Gigi got dumped on—literally—at least once a week. Last week had been syrup. She said she was never serving someone at an IHOP again. The week before that it was hair mousse because she'd tracked the defendant down at a salon. This week, apparently, it was snow. Her dry-cleaning bills were phenomenal because she wasn't willing to schlep around in casual attire to deliver summonses. Despite all evidence to the contrary, she refused to accept that her designer clothes wouldn't shield her from people's hostility when she served them.

"But it's Michael Kors," she said, wide-eyed, the first time I pointed this out to her. "They have to respect Kors."

The data suggested process recipients didn't respect Kors or Blass or Lagerfeld or Wang. Today's outfit was typical. Her cashmere sweater undoubtedly bore a designer label, but it made me wince to look at it. Huge red and green squares, each embroidered with a holiday item—an ornament, a Santa, a menorah—magnified her thirty extra pounds, and the black boots she wore beneath a conservative (for her) red wool skirt hugged her chubby calves. She patted the beigey-blond hair so many well-off women in their fifties affected and sank into the chair behind her desk with a soft "whew," stowing her Marc Jacobs purse—a red leather satchel big enough to say Samsonite on the label—under her desk.

Gigi's desk is to the left of the door, while mine runs perpendicular to it in the back right corner of the office. Our different styles have resulted in a schizophrenic decor. Think Oscar and Felix, or maybe even Turner and Hooch. Her desk is littered with kitschy doodads, while mine is organized, uncluttered, and clean. She has a poster of kittens hanging behind her and a life-sized plastic and fake fur bison head named Bernie, a memento from her first undercover job with Swift Investigations. I have a window with wooden blinds. I missed the no-nonsense air the office exuded before I was forced to accept Gigi as a partner five months ago but had to admit the place seemed warmer somehow.

"Where's Kendall?" Gigi asked, apparently noticing her daughter's absence from the card table we'd set up as her desk.

"Not here." And thank God for that. School would start up again a week from today, and I was counting the minutes. I was also busy thinking up reasons why the girl couldn't work here over the summer.

Gigi dialed the phone and reached her daughter, issuing a gentle command to "Hurry in to the office, sugah. Did your alarm not go off again?"

That would put the fear of God into a lazy teen, all right. I refrained from rolling my eyes and switched on my computer to see what it could tell me about Dmitri Fane. When I'd asked Dara Peterson for a picture of Dmitri, she'd said, "Can't you Google him?"

Apparently, I could. Hundreds of articles and photos popped up. I clicked on one at random and studied the photo of a handsome man—Dara had told me he was seven years her senior at twenty-six—with dark hair and a blazing white smile. Tall, with broad shoulders and slim hips in his form-fitting skating costume, he balanced Dara over his head with one hand. She didn't even look scared. Okay, maybe pair skating was more dangerous than I'd realized. Personally, I'd've been scared just to gad about in public in a gauze and sequins costume like the red one spray-painted on Dara.

I skimmed the article, which seemed to be about a judging controversy, but didn't learn any more about Fane than Dara had already told me. He was born in Russia, she'd said. His mother was a figure skater and he didn't know who his father was. He got the name Fane when his mother married an American skater, Stuart Fane, who adopted the four-year-old Dmitri and moved them all to Detroit. Irena and Stuart Fane opened a skating school, and young Dmitri was an early standout. His first partner wasn't up to his level, though, and he agreed to give Dara a tryout when her coach approached him. He moved to Colorado Springs at age eighteen to train with the eleven-year-old Dara. Their success as a pair team was the stuff of legend (according to Dara). An Olympic gold would be the icing on the cake (and bring in big sponsorship bucks, Dara admitted). Dmitri worked part-time as a waiter and bartender for a catering company to help fund his training costs.

I'd start by interviewing the coach, Yuliya Bobrova, I decided, then follow that up with a swing past Fane's condo—maybe he'd answer the bell when I rang—and a conversation with his employers, Czarina Catering. Sounded Russian. If none of that gave me a lead, I'd call up Mama Fane and see if maybe Dmitri had returned to the family homestead. Detroit in January sounded miserable, so I hoped I wouldn't have to travel there to hunt for the skater.

I had tucked my notepad into my purse and was reaching for my jacket when the door opened and Little Miss Tardy sauntered in, wiping pink booted feet on the mat.

"Kendall, baby, I was worried," Gigi said, coming around her desk to give the petite blonde a hug.

Kendall avoided the hug by shrugging out of her coat. She mumbled something that might have been "Whatever" and plopped into the folding chair set up at her card table desk. Her skintight jeans and tight pink sweater made her look older than fifteen. "Something stinks," she observed.

"That would be the coffeemaker you ruined," I said, gesturing toward the trash can.

My acid tone got me narrowed eyes from Kendall and a reproachful look from Gigi. "I'm sure it was an accident," the latter said.

"Yeah, the third accident in three weeks."

"I don't like coffee anyway," Kendall said.

"It was for the clients, sugah," Gigi said.

"Haven't seen too many of those." Snide triumph colored her voice.

"As a matter of fact, we got a new client this morning," I told Gigi, turning my back on Kendall.

Gigi clapped her hands together but stopped short of saying, "Oh, goody!" "What's the case?" she asked instead, grabbing up her steno pad.

"I'm—we're—looking for a man named Fane," I said. "He's an ice-skater."

"*An* ice-skater?"

The exclamation came from behind me, and I turned to face an animated Kendall, a version of the girl I hadn't seen before. Her pretty blue eyes were alight with interest, and her porcelain complexion—no zits for this teen—was becomingly tinged with pink. She was going to be a heartbreaker when she lost the braces and the attitude.

"Calling Dmitri Fane *an* ice-skater's like saying Miley Cyrus is just *a* singer or"—she paused, obviously grasping for a comparison someone as old and dim as I might get—"Eisenhower's just *a* scientist. He's—"

"I think you mean Einstein."

"Kendall has a poster of him on her wall," Gigi put in.

"Einstein?" I couldn't resist.

"Mo-om." Kendall tossed her long blond hair. "He's like the most awesome pair skater *ever*!"

"He gets some help from Dara Peterson, doesn't he?" I asked, amused by her reaction.

"She's a bitch."

"Kendall!" Gigi gasped. "I don't like to hear—"

"She's our client," I said. "Where do you know—" Then I remembered. Kendall was a figure skater, and a pretty good one, according to Gigi. She trained at the World Arena Ice Hall, where Dara had said she and Dmitri practiced. "Do you know them?" I asked.

"Of course." Only a teenager talking to an adult could infuse two words with that much scorn. A speculative look crossed her face. "I know someone who will be happy if Dmitri stays gone, too."

"Who?"

"Trevor Anthony," Kendall said. "He was Dara's partner before Dmitri came on the scene. Dmitri totally stole her away. He skates with Angel Pfeffer now, but she falls all the time on the throw triple salchow. They'll make the U.S. team, though, if Peterson and Fane aren't at Nationals." Changing tactics, the girl smiled at me—a first—revealing pink and white bands on her braces. "Can I help with the case?"

"No," her mother and I said in unison.

"It might be dangerous," Gigi added.

To our reputation, I thought. "I've got to get going or I'll be late for my interview," I said, happy to cede Gigi the task of quelling her daughter's newly found ambition to be a PI. "I'm meeting Fane's coach in half an hour."

"Bobrova?" Kendall's smirk was knowing. "Good luck with that."

2

A skater clad in leggings, a turtleneck, and gloves twirled in the middle of the ice when I arrived at the World Arena Ice Hall, where the Broadmoor Skating Club trained. A low building with squat sculptures of Zamboni ice-making machines out front, it had a reception area with a cheery fireplace, a reception desk—unoccupied—and a store selling skating gear and souvenirs. I'd turned right out of the reception area and found a rink, only to be told by a hulking skater with a Jason mask and a hockey stick that I needed the Olympic rink. Silly me, thinking an ice rink was an ice rink. Finding the correct rink on the other side of the lobby, I'd circled around to a swinging gate that barred access to the ice. Now, gazing across the sheet of blue-white ice in the arena smelling of cold metal and damp, shivering, I watched the skater reach behind her to grab the blade of her skate and pull her foot up toward her head. Ow. Auburn pigtails stuck out from either side of her head, making her look like Pippi Longstocking. She couldn't have been more than twelve. She was amazing.

"Dat is not a spin! Dat is a disaster," croaked a Russian-accented voice.

The skater returned her foot to the ice, slowed, and hung her head as a dumpy figure stomped toward her across the ice, leaning heavily on a cane. What seemed to be a black cape obscured most of her shape and swirled around calves that disappeared into fur-trimmed ankle boots.

"Lengthen your spine, so." She prodded the girl in the back with the tip of her cane. The girl stood up straighter. "Your line must be elegant. Elegant! Again, from the transition."

The girl nodded and skated toward the far corner of the ice. Seizing the opportunity, I called over to Bobrova. "Excuse me, I'm—"

She turned her head and glared. Her eyes seemed black from this distance, set under heavy, almost straight brows, drawn together in a frown. "Dis is a private training session. You go." She turned back to study the skater, now gliding on one foot with the other leg stretched out behind her, never doubting that I'd obey. Well, she might be Empress of the Ice Rink, but she wasn't the boss of me, so I pushed through the metal gate and made my way onto the ice. Whoa! My right foot threatened to slip out from under me and I windmilled my arms to balance myself. When I felt steadier, I slid one foot forward cautiously, then the other. In this shuffle-step manner I made it to within a couple of feet of Bobrova. She was turned away from me, focused on the skater who was doing some fancy footwork on a diagonal line across the rink.

"Deeper knees," Bobrova called, thumping her cane for emphasis.

Resisting the temptation to say "Boo," I got her attention with a moderate "Ms. Bobrova?"

She pivoted to face me, scowling. "I told you to go." Up close, her face was deeply lined and framed by hair as gray as a Moscow winter cut bluntly at jaw length and threaded with white. She was about Dara Peterson's height, but stout around the middle with short arms and legs. I was pretty sure she was a hobbit, only not so happy, and that her flat-heeled boots hid hairy toes. My imagination couldn't stretch far enough to see her in spandex and sequins, doing loop-de-loops around the ice with a handsome partner. Yet Dara had told me in an awed voice that Bobrova and Petrov had dominated pair skating in the sixties and seventies and that Bobrova had trained more world and Olympic champions than any other coach in the business.

I tried a smile. "My name's Charlotte Swift. I'm a private investigator. I'm here about Dmitri Fane."

She ignored my proffered hand, saying only, "Bah!" Having assessed me with one acute look, she returned her gaze to the young skater.

I let my hand fall. "Does that mean you're not worried about him?"

"Why should I worry about Dmitri?" A trace of her native Russia gave the words a guttural feel, but her English was excellent.

"Hasn't he been missing since Saturday?"

She shrugged. "He is a grown man. It is not for me to keep track of him. What's the saying? It is not my day to watch him."

Despite her words, I caught an undertone of tension in her voice and the tautness of her jaw. I wished she would look at me so I could read her expression, but she kept her eyes fixed on the skater.

"You seem strangely unconcerned about the possibility of him missing the Olympic trials next week," I said.

"Dmitri will be here. He always turns up. I told Dara not to worry, but that girl does not listen. On the ice—nerves of steel. Off it—" She made a fluttering gesture with a surprisingly dainty hand.

Dara hadn't seemed nervous or flighty to me. In fact, she'd come across as determined and at least as angry as she was worried. "When you say 'He always turns up,' does that mean he's gone missing before?" I asked.

"Outside edge," Bobrova called to the skater, who landed a jump so close that bits of ice sprayed my brown wool trousers. "Sometimes a man has things to take care of," she said. "Merely because he is out of touch for a few days does not mean he is missing."

"What kind of things does Dmitri have to take care of?"

"*Da, da!* The Ina Bauer is beautiful, Nicole," she said, swiveling to keep the skater in view as she glided across the ice with her front knee bent and her foot turned to the left with the other leg behind her, the foot facing right. Her back arced deeply. My ankles ached just watching her. Suddenly, my ankle hurt for real as something whacked it, knocking me off balance. As I fell, I caught a glimpse of Bobrova's cane and the swirl of her cape's hem as she stepped back so I wouldn't take her down with me. I landed on my tailbone with a crack that jolted up my spine to my head. Fighting to keep back tears, I lay still for a moment, until the cold and wet seeping through my clothes prompted movement. Gingerly, I pushed myself to a sitting position. Damn, I felt shaky.

"I am so sorry. Such an unfortunate accident," Bobrova said, shaking her cane as if to punish it. "Here." She reached down her free hand and hauled me to my feet with a strong grip for a seventy-year-old. "Did you hit your head?" She peered into my eyes, looking for signs of concussion.

I let go of her hand as Nicole skated to a stop beside me. "Are you okay?" the girl asked with far more concern than Bobrova. "Let me help you to the side."

"*Nyet,*" Bobrova said. "Your short program needs work."

Nicole looked at me, then at her coach, clearly torn. A gentle swell of breasts under her turtleneck told me she was closer to Kendall's age than the twelve I originally took her for, but she seemed kind, totally lacking the attitude and insecurity of Gigi's daughter.

"I'm fine," I told her. I took two steps to demonstrate. "But thank you. Should I have heard of you?" I asked before she could skate away.

With a shy smile, she said, "I'm Nicole Lewis."

"Current world junior ladies champion," Bobrova said, shooing Nicole away with a brisk flick of her hand. "Soon to be U.S. senior ladies gold medalist if she will focus, focus, focus." Her voice rose on each repetition, and the girl ducked her head as the words bombarded her.

"You go now," Bobrova told me. Without waiting to see if I complied, she stalked across the ice toward Nicole, as sure-footed as a polar bear on the slick surface—and just about as friendly.

3

Sitting in my Subaru Outback an hour later, studying the facade of Dmitri Fane's condo, I drank a Pepsi and shifted from one butt cheek to the other, trying to find a comfortable position that didn't aggravate my bruised tailbone. I made some notes from my conversation—if you could call it that—with Bobrova. Two things seemed clear. One, Yuliya Bobrova knew more about Dmitri's disappearance than she was saying. Two, my accidental fall was no accident. She'd deliberately tripped me with her cane, and I wondered why. Was she just a nasty old witch who enjoyed inflicting pain? Her treatment of Nicole Lewis supported that theory. Or was she hiding something and wanted to get rid of me? If she was hiding something, what was it? I drained the last of the Pepsi from the can and opened the door. Maybe I could find something in the condo that would put me on the right track. Wincing as I swung my legs out of the car, I stood and looked around the parking lot. Only one other car, a white RAV4, occupied a slot near the big Westhaven Condominiums sign near the entrance.

Westhaven advertised itself as being "*the* resort-style, no-maintenance housing choice" for young professionals, and the lack of people and cars in the middle of the day testified that most of the inhabitants were at work. Good. I'd need to talk to Dmitri's neighbors later, but for now I wanted a look at his living quarters, and if I made an unorthodox entry—through a window, say—it was better to be unobserved. Nosy neighbors are both a blessing and a curse for private investigators.

Marching up the sidewalk as if I belonged there, I approached Dmitri's condo. Each step jarred my tailbone, and I cursed Bobrova. Dmitri lived in a two-story unit in a block of four. The building was pseudo Cape Cod with gables and weathered shingles. Dark green shutters flanked multipaned windows. A covered carport with four slots, numbered and unoccupied, was across from the unit. I knew from Dara Peterson that Dmitri drove a silver Mustang, and I kept an eye out for the car but didn't see it. I made a mental note to check with my CSPD friend, Detective Connor Montgomery, to see if the car had been ticketed or towed recently.

My steps slowed as I came level with Dmitri's unit. Should I knock or slink around to the back and see if I could gain access through a window? I glanced around: fenced, multilevel pool, drained for the winter; management office almost out of sight on the far side of the complex; FOR SALE sign in the window of the connecting unit. No dog walkers or landscapers or delivery people. Wishing I had the lockpicks Gigi had bought on eBay, I approached the door and plied the brass knocker twice. Dmitri didn't answer. Shocker. Automatically, I tried the doorknob. It turned easily and the door inched open. Surprised and wary of my luck, I glanced casually over my shoulder. Still no observers. Pulling latex gloves out of my pocket, I slipped them on, rubbed my fingerprints off the doorknob with the hem of my sweater, and pushed the door wider.

Finding myself in a small, wood-floored foyer, I shut the door on the nippy breeze and looked around. To my right was a living room–dining room combination, and to my left a flight of stairs rose to the second floor. I decided to start with the ground floor and leave the bedrooms for last. I gave myself ten minutes—staying longer would increase the chance of discovery—and set my watch alarm. Enough light filtered through the closed blinds that I didn't need to turn on a light as I stepped into the living room. It had all the warmth of an ice rink, outfitted with a white leather sofa and recliner, a big-screen TV, and glass-topped tables with chrome legs. The dining room lacked a table but had a black metal computer desk complete with printer, fax machine–copier combo, laminating machine, and stereo components, but no computer. Two things struck me as I stood in the middle of the room, conscious of the chill in the air that said the heater hadn't run for days. The decor and electronics were high-end, and I wondered how Dmitri afforded them. Surely, part-time catering and ice-skating didn't add up to custom-made sofas and state-of-the art plasma televisions. My second observation raised even more questions than the first: Either Dmitri Fane was a slob, or someone else had searched his condo.

The doors on the entertainment center cabinets gaped wide, and the stack of DVDs inside was jumbled. A thin layer of loose papers obscured the floor around the computer desk. The sofa cushions were askew, and a red silk pillow, the only shot of color in the room, languished under the coffee table next to the remote. Reaching for it, I turned on the TV, and a soccer game flickered to life on ESPN. I turned it off.

In the kitchen, I found the same disarray. Drawers and

cabinet doors were slightly open, and shards of glass on the floor testified to someone's carelessness. I peeked into the cabinets and even the freezer but found nothing more interesting than plastic utensils, a drawer full of takeout menus, and a bottle of vodka. I deduced that Dmitri wasn't much of a cook but liked to sip an icy Stoli while watching the sports event du jour. That didn't get me very far in figuring out where he was.

I returned to his desk, looking for an address book, a calendar, doodles—anything that might give me a hint as to his location. Nada. He probably stored everything on his computer, and it was missing. I wondered if he had taken it with him, or if the earlier searcher had made off with it. Dara could probably tell me if Dmitri was in the habit of carrying a laptop around. There was likewise no phone in sight, and I figured he was one of those people who used his cell phone exclusively.

A scritch of sound made me look up. I listened carefully but heard nothing further. Probably the wind, I decided, watching aspen limbs dance outside the dining room window. I checked my watch—only two minutes left of the ten I'd allotted myself. I needed to speed things up. Maybe Dmitri's bedroom would yield some clues. I climbed the Berber-carpeted stairs and found myself in a short hall with a room on each end. The room on the right was empty except for a twin bed—not made up—and a chest of drawers, all empty. Ditto for the closet.

The master bedroom held more potential. The door stood open, and a window on the west side of the room framed a striking view of Pikes Peak. A closet with sliding doors ran the length of the south wall. A king-sized bed draped with a navy and white comforter and a mound of pillows faced the window. Did the tidily made bed mean Dmitri had planned his absence, or was he just a neat freak? Neatness was not a character flaw, no matter what my new partner thought. The last time I'd left my bed unmade had been in response to a fire alarm when I lived in the dorms at Lackland Air Force Base. A sergeant down the hall had been using a lighter to melt shoe polish to gloss her boots and dropped it when the Kiwi tin heated up and singed her fingers.

I began my search. The bedside table nearest the door held a box of condoms, two raunchy magazines, and a gun. I stared at the snub-nosed .38 but didn't touch it. Why did an ice-skater need a gun? For protection against burglars? It didn't seem likely that a twenty-six-year-old man would feel unsafe living alone in an upscale community like this. Maybe he was the nervous type, or maybe he just liked guns. I slid the drawer closed and moved to the bathroom as the timer on my watch went off. Damn! I'd push my luck and take an extra couple of minutes.

The bathroom, an expanse of black and white checkerboard tile with black toilet and sink and a serviceable black shower curtain drawn around the tub, smelled faintly of some spicy aftershave. It was cleaner than I had expected of a young man living alone. The generalization might sound sexist, but I'd done enough searches, both as an Office of Special Investigations agent in the air force and as a PI, to know that a single man's bathroom was likely to be far less sanitary than a single woman's. I'd told my OSI boss we should be issued hazmat gear before searching a man's quarters. Besides the generic mildew and filth resulting from an inability to aim, I'd once come across a tub full of dirt planted with marijuana, and another time found red goo that turned out to be strawberry Jell-O rimming the toilet and tub. I never asked. Some things you don't want to know.

Nothing that interesting here. A single white towel, dry, hung from a rack. I didn't see a comb or razor on the sink; it was looking more and more like Mr. Fane had planned his departure. I'd check for a suitcase when I rifled the closet. Opening the medicine cabinet, I heard a rustle and caught a glimpse of movement in the mirror.

I spun, but not quickly enough. An impression of surging blackness and an upraised arm blurred in my peripheral vision before something hard came down on my forehead. I fell back, striking my head against the sink, and everything went dark.

4

I regained consciousness slowly, aware of a throbbing head, the coldness of tile beneath my cheek, and a shroud draped over me. It smelled mildewy. I clawed at the fabric, feeling trapped, finally batting enough of it away that I could see again. A glance at my watch showed me that only three minutes had passed since I was attacked. The "shroud" was the shower curtain, complete with tension rod, which the intruder must have dragged down when he leaped from his hiding place in the tub. I cursed myself for not having considered the possibility that the searcher was still in the condo. I'd been careless and paid the price with an aching head and an assortment of bruises to go with my cracked tailbone. This was not turning out to be my day—it's Mondayness was still screwing things up.

Holding on to the sink, I staggered to my feet and surveyed the damage in the mirror. Blood trickled from a cut over my eye where a lump the size of a Ping-Pong ball would soon turn purple. Great. I'm not particularly vain, but I didn't want to scare small children when I walked down the street, either. With my fingertips, I probed under my hair at the back of my skull and found another lump where I'd smacked my head on the sink. At least it didn't seem to be bleeding. I helped myself to some Tylenol from the medicine cabinet and scanned the rest of its contents from habit. Nothing more interesting than prescription bottles of oxycodone and Vicodin, along with shaving cream, deodorant, and a sunless tan gel. Dampening Dmitri's white washcloth, I dabbed at the cut on my forehead, then held the cold cloth to the lump as I looked around. I didn't see the attacker's weapon, but when I bundled the shower curtain into the tub, a long-handled back brush fell out. Clearly, he'd used the first weapon that came to hand. I was lucky it wasn't the gun in the bedside table.

On the thought, I hurried back into the bedroom and opened the drawer. The gun was gone. Mega-shit. Now my attacker was armed. I sank onto the bed and closed my eyes, trying to see him in my mind's eye. I had an impression of height—the back brush had clearly descended down onto my forehead—and the blurred image of a white face. I couldn't focus on a hair color—maybe he'd worn a hat? There'd been a smell, too, something familiar, but I couldn't place it. I gave it up after a moment.

With effort, I pulled myself free of the bed's embrace and stood, feeling wobbly. As I took a step toward the door, the unmistakable sound of footsteps sounded on the stairs. What was this place—Grand Central Station? Wishing I'd had the foresight to bring my H&K 9 mm, I ducked into the closet. With no time to slide the door closed, I wiggled my way backward through a layer of hanging clothes until my back pressed against the wall. Just in time. The footsteps paused at the doorway. The door squeaked wider. I felt rather than heard the vibrations of footsteps crossing the room.

Soft cottons and scratchy wools pressed against me in my

hiding place. The scents of mothballs and Dmitri's aftershave tickled my nose. I breathed shallowly, afraid a deep breath would set the wire hangers jangling and betray me. I strained my ears to hear. The footsteps had stopped. What was the newcomer doing? Maybe it was the old intruder, come back to finish me off. A sighing sound puzzled me until I realized it was the same sound the mattress made when I sat on it. Who the hell broke into someone's house to take a nap? Goldilocks?

I stretched cautiously to the right, trying to see into the bedroom. From my vantage point, all I could see was the end of the bed and a slice of window. My neck was getting a crick from the strange angle, but as I watched, a pair of legs, visible only from midshin down, settled onto the bed. Wait a minute . . . I knew those pink cowboy boots. I had seen them earlier that morning. Uncaring of the noise I made now, I pushed past the jangling hangers and popped out of the closet.

"What the hell are you doing here?"

Kendall Goldman sat upright with a shriek. Both hands went to her mouth, but she lowered them when she recognized me. "I was . . . I was just . . ."

I glared at her, partly because she'd scared me and partly because I knew she must have gone through the notes I'd made after my conversation with Dara Peterson. I'd created a Fane folder and stuck them in there.

"I got the address from the file," she admitted, swinging her legs off the bed, "and I came over here thinking I could help, that maybe he'd be here."

"How is it helping to break in and snuggle up on his bed?"

"The door was open!" she said.

She didn't try to explain lolling on Fane's bed, and I realized she must have a crush on the skater as big (and unrequited, if Dara was right about his sexual preferences) as the one I had on Tom Cruise when I was her age. I was his from the moment he rocked out in his Fruit of the Looms in *Risky Business*. "Unlocked?"

"No, standing wide open."

My attacker must have been in a real hurry after he bopped me with the back scrubber. "How'd you get here?" I asked. "Is your mom outside?" Just what I needed—Gigi camped out front in her yellow Hummer, the equivalent of a flashing neon sign to draw attention to the condo and our illicit presence.

"Nah. Dex dropped me."

Dexter, Gigi's seventeen-year-old son, did not commonly go out of his way to help anyone. I raised my brows.

"I paid him five bucks," Kendall admitted. Her sheepishness gave way to a narrow-eyed stare as she regained her sangfroid. "How did *you* get in? And what happened to your face?"

I ignored the first question. "I was in the bathroom"—I didn't mention the part about pawing through the medicine cabinet—"and someone jumped out of the tub and hit me."

"Here?" Kendall squeaked. She looked toward the bathroom as if expecting a dripping ax murderer to emerge with a hatchet.

"He's gone," I said, "and we'd better follow suit. I'll give you a ride back to the office." On the way we could have a nice chat about how she was never, ever to peek at a client folder again, much less use the information to stalk the object of her adolescent desires. I smiled grimly.

Perhaps catching the intent behind my smile, Kendall sidled past me to the bedroom door. "Dexter's waiting for me at the 7-Eleven on the corner. He'll give me a lift back. Bye."

She disappeared down the stairs before I could frame a response. Chances were, she'd grab the opportunity to play hooky from the office. Fine with me. I sighed, feeling achy and old, and started to follow her. It made me feel even older to realize she could be my daughter if I'd started at twenty-three. Good God. At twenty-three I'd been an air force cop for five years, had completed my degree at night school, and earned a commission as a second lieutenant. I was still a year away from marrying the fighter pilot who couldn't spell monogamy with the help of a dictionary, and having a baby had never crossed my mind. The only bright side to this incident, I decided, was that it gave me a rock-solid reason for refusing to hire Kendall for the summer.

Slightly cheered by the thought, I decided to do a quick search of the closet while I was there. Surely it couldn't keep being Monday, could it? I was due some good luck after all the day's mishaps. Skipping the handful of shirts, I turned out the pockets of Dmitri's four or five pairs of slacks, finding nothing but lint and a couple of receipts. I shoved those in my pocket. It didn't look like the other searcher had bothered, so maybe he'd already found what he wanted, or maybe it wasn't something small enough to fit in a pocket. Maybe I'd interrupted him before he'd had the chance to search the closet. That thought spurred me on, but the collection of skating costumes at the back of the closet were useless, mostly skintight spandex or romantic pirate garb without a pocket in sight, and the shoe boxes on the floor contained only shoes. I didn't come across a suitcase. Emerging from the closet with a lock of dark hair hanging in front of my eyes, I brushed it back and looked at my watch. I'd been here almost half an hour, what with letting intruders use my head for batting practice and arguing with infatuated teens. Past time to go.

Stripping off the latex gloves, I tucked them in my pocket. My eyes swept the room one more time, lingering on the dresser, but I knew I couldn't afford the time to search it. I left the room and started down the stairs, the draft telling me Kendall had left the door as she'd found it—wide open. The wind had swirled a few dead leaves into the hall and I bent to pick them up. As I straightened, I found myself staring into the barrel of a gun held at arm's length by a stern-looking policeman.

"Freeze," he said.

5

I talked my way out of a possible arrest by telling the officer that I was a friend of Dmitri's who had happened to stop by. Finding the door open, I had rushed in, afraid Dmitri might be ill or injured. Thanking God I'd already removed the incriminating latex gloves, I produced ID for the cop's inspection, mentioned my good friend Detective Connor Montgomery (who would make me pay when he heard this story), and displayed my forehead with its lurid mogul. I was brutally attacked, I said, by a criminal ransacking Dmitri's condo. Thank goodness the police had responded so quickly, I added dramatically.

Young Officer Knowlton, a compact five foot ten with a sandy crew cut, put his weapon away and took copious notes, looking disappointed by my meager description of my assailant. He called in the incident, then asked if I could tell if anything was missing. I hadn't had time to look around, I lied, and probably wouldn't know anyway, since I wasn't all that familiar with the place. Did I have a number they could use to get in touch with Mr. Fane? I wrote down the cell phone number Dara had given me.

As I was edging away from the condo, congratulating myself on getting out of a tight corner, an unmarked Buick pulled up and a familiar figure got out. An involuntary tingle shot through me at the sight of Connor Montgomery's long legs, broad shoulders, and handsome face. Too handsome, I reminded myself for the umpteenth time. The man couldn't have been more than thirty-two or -three, several years my junior, and the devil-may-care glint in his eye reminded me too much of my ex-husband and his fighter pilot brethren. I walked to meet him, bracing myself for an interrogation I knew would be far more suspicious than Officer Knowlton's.

"Charlie," he said with a crooked smile. "Imagine my surprise to hear that you were at the scene of a B and E. What prompted you to break into this place, may I ask?"

"I merely entered," I said, my expression challenging him to prove otherwise.

"Sir, she's the victim of an assault," Officer Knowlton put in helpfully. "The perp got away."

"An assault?" Connor reached out one finger and lightly traced the bump on my forehead. "Are you okay, Charlie? Need a doctor?"

His unexpected gentleness confounded me, and it was a moment before I could speak. In my defense, I'll reiterate that it had been a hard day. "It's nothing," I said.

"I could kiss it and make it all better," he offered in a low voice, "and then we could—"

I suppressed the surge of warmth his offer elicited and manufactured a glare. "I'm fine."

He put an arm around my shoulders and steered me down the sidewalk, out of Knowlton's hearing. "Want to tell me about it?" he asked, in a tone that said I'd better. "Don't feed me whatever fairy tale you dished out to Knowlton, either."

I gave him a wounded look but filled him in on everything except Kendall's appearance. "Dmitri Fane," he said when I'd finished, a thoughtful look in his eyes. "That name's familiar."

"He's an Olympic skater," I said.

"Yeah, but there's something else. It'll come to me."

"Could you let me know if there've been any John Does admitted to local hospitals recently? Or the morgue?"

"Anything else?" He raised a mocking brow.

"Yeah, the car. Can you check and see if a silver Mustang's been ticketed or towed? I'll get you the plate number."

"I can get it," he said. By this time we had reached my car, and he backed me up against it, his body almost, but not quite, pressed against mine. The frozen metal of the car against my back made an unbearable contrast with the heat pulsing between Montgomery and me. "Now, what do I get in return for all this information, not to mention for not running you in and charging you with breaking and entering?"

"My undying gratitude?"

He pretended to consider that. The scent of soap and spice and warm skin coming off him was driving me crazy, and I fought the urge to pull him against me. "I think something more substantial's in order," he said, his eyes darkening as they lingered on my lips.

My breath caught in my chest as he lowered his head. His lips grazed mine, very lightly, and lingered for a moment. "Let me know when." He pushed himself back, gave me a two-fingered salute, and headed back toward Fane's condo and the gaping Officer Knowlton. I slid into my Subaru and started it with shaking fingers. Damn the man. He always managed to slip under my guard.

I deliberately banished Connor Montgomery from my thoughts as I headed back to the office. Pondering Officer

Knowlton's appearance at the condo, I wondered who had called him. It could have been a neighbor, of course, someone who had noticed the open door and been disinclined to investigate on his own. The timing was awfully coincidental, though. My fingers tapped the steering wheel. It was time to explain the facts of life, Swift style, to Kendall Goldman.

～m～

"We've got new neighbors next door," Gigi said when I walked back into the office. She bounced in her chair.

"Whoop-de-doo." I beelined for my fridge and the Pepsi I needed desperately.

"Next door" was the retail space that had formerly housed Ecolo-Toys, a shop marketing ecologically sound toys for politically correct youngsters to "engage" with. There'd been an incident a couple of months back with a Goliath bird-eating spider—a hairy sucker as big as a dinner plate—leaping out of a toy chest made from some kind of wood I'd never heard of and imported from Belize. The environmentally sensitive purchasers had reduced the critter to spider mush with a diaper pail without a thought as to whether or not the species was endangered. Tsk. The resulting publicity had closed down the store faster than Simon Cowell could hurl an insult.

"What are they selling?" I broke down and asked after swallowing half my soda.

"I don't know," Gigi admitted, "but I saw a woman going in there. She must own the place, because she had the key. Maybe she's Domenica?"

For the past two weeks, carpenters had been refitting the space, and a sign painter had applied a discreet DOMENICA'S in gold script on the door. Closed blinds kept the shop's contents hidden.

"We should take her cookies or muffins as a house-warming gift," Gigi said, making a note.

I stared at her. "It's not a house. It's a business. And we're not neighbors—we're strangers who happen to have an office in the same strip mall."

"Being neighbors is an attitude, not a location," Gigi said. "I think—"

"Has Kendall come back?" I interrupted.

"No," Gigi said, looking apprehensive. "Why?"

Sparing no details, I filled her in on her daughter's activities, including my suspicion that she'd called the cops on me.

"Maybe she was worried that the man who attacked you was still there?" Gigi suggested doubtfully.

I snorted.

"Well," she tried again, "I think it's super that she's taking such an interest in the business. I've been trying to encourage a stronger work ethic—why, when I was her age I was already doing my friends' hair and some of their moms', too. It looks like it's finally paying off. I've been worried, you know, because generally I can't even get her to put her bowl in the sink after breakfast. Maybe this summer—"

"No."

"But she—"

"Hell, no."

"You don't need to curse." Gigi gave me that sad puppy look.

"She's not interested in the PI business, Gigi," I said, exasperated. "She's gaga over Dmitri Fane. She was draped all over his bed, for God's sake!"

"His bed?" Gigi's mouth fell open.

"It's beside the point. The point is that Kendall can't rifle through our files and use the information for her own purposes."

My anger finally got through to Gigi. "I'll talk to her," she said. She made another note. Her list must now say: 1. Bake cookies. 2. Chastise daughter.

"Do more than talk," I said. "Ground her. Better yet, fire her."

Gigi sat up straighter and said with dignity, "I said I'd talk to her."

I held my tongue, but I didn't place much faith in Kendall giving a damn about one of Gigi's talks. However, I had a case to solve and a paying customer to satisfy, so I let it drop. For now.

"I'm going over to Czarina Catering to see what they can tell me about Fane," I told Gigi. "What have you got going this afternoon?"

"Another process to serve," she said, waving the paperwork in the air. "Then I thought I'd do some background research on Fane in the databases, check out his financials."

"Good idea." The courses Gigi had attended since joining me in the business, especially the one on computer searches, had been money well spent. She was still a disaster at surveillance, but she'd done some skip-tracing via computer that had resulted in some nice fees. Even though I still wasn't thrilled that she'd horned in on Swift Investigations when her husband, my silent partner, had abandoned her for a love nest in Costa Rica, leaving her no choice (she said) but to make the partnership an active one and drain my profits by pulling a salary, I had to admit she was almost pulling her weight.

"Albertine has invited us down for a drink after work," Gigi said as I pulled on my navy peacoat.

"Can't."

Gigi's eyes lit up. "Do you have a date?"

I rolled my eyes. For some reason, Gigi and Albertine, my

friend who owned the eponymous Cajun restaurant at the south end of our strip mall, were convinced that my love life was lacking. They kept trying to fix me up and practically applauded any time I had a date—which wasn't often. "No date. Just helping Dan with a project."

Gigi slumped back in her chair, looking disappointed. Father Dan Allgood was the priest who was my closest neighbor. He lived in the rectory belonging to St. Paul's, the Episcopal church on the corner, and we were buds. "Tell Albertine I'll take a rain check."

My cell phone rang, and I recognized Montgomery's number. Maybe he'd found Dmitri, or at least his car. "Swift."

"I know why the name Dmitri Fane seemed familiar," he said. "He's pulled this before, four years ago."

"Pulled what?"

"A disappearing act. He went missing for nine days last time. It was a big deal. Some evidence suggested he'd been kidnapped, although there was never a ransom demand. His skating partner, Dana Something—"

"Dara Peterson."

"That's it. She insisted he was the victim of a serial killer. He turned up on his own after nine days. Said he'd been in the Bahamas, 'taking a breather,' and hadn't paid any attention to the news, had no idea people were looking for him. Cost the taxpayers thousands."

My fingers tightened on the phone. I didn't like being played for a fool. "Did you believe him?" Gigi looked at me curiously.

"Hell, no. It wasn't my case, but Jensen, the lead detective, told me it was a publicity stunt from start to finish."

"Thanks, Montgomery. I owe you." I hung up before he could suggest a way for me to work off my debt.

I told the waiting Gigi what Montgomery had said, pacing the small office as I talked.

"I remember that," she said when I finished.

I glared at her. "You might have mentioned it before."

"I didn't remember it before. I only remembered it now." She twiddled with a gold button on her sweater. "Kendall had just started training with the BSC—the Broadmoor Skating Club—and we hadn't actually met Dmitri and Dara then, but people were talking about it. Every time we went to the Ice Hall, there was a new theory floating around: He was kidnapped, he eloped, he was in an accident and got amnesia and didn't know who he was, he cracked under the pressure and went home to Detroit. That was the summer that Dexter got arrested for shoplifting—"

Not to be confused with the summer he got arrested for DUI or the fall he got suspended for paying a buddy to hack into the school's computer and change his grade. His comp sci grade. His teacher probably would've given him an A instead of suspension if he'd been able to do the hacking himself.

"—so we had other things on our minds," Gigi finished. "Thank goodness he was okay. It turned out he was taking a little vacation and hadn't told anyone. So thoughtless of him, not to realize people would worry. Well, that's how kids are."

"Yeah, right," I muttered under my breath. I wasn't as willing as Gigi to extend the benefit of the doubt. Maybe if she weren't so inclined to give others the benefit of the doubt, her husband, Les, might not have found it so easy to run off to Costa Rica with all their money and his personal trainer.

"What are you going to do?"

"Have a come-to-Jesus meeting with Dara Peterson," I said,

dialing her number as I strode toward the door. Clients lie. All of them. If I only accepted clients who told the truth, the whole truth, and nothing but the truth, I might as well declare bankruptcy right now. Still, I like to discourage the practice.

6

Somewhat to my surprise, Dara Peterson had a part-time job. It irritated me that I hadn't stopped to wonder where a nineteen-year-old got the money to pay for a private investigator. She worked at Maggie Moo's in the Shops at Briargate, an outdoor shopping plaza mere minutes from my office. Over the phone, she said she couldn't leave but that it was quiet at the moment and we could probably talk. I hadn't told her what I wanted, and the hope in her voice told me she thought I'd located Fane already.

The store was small and, as promised, deserted when I walked in. Ignoring the turquoise and hot pink board advertising ice cream treats and the cow motif on the walls, I stood in front of the refrigerated cases holding gallons of ice cream in flavors ranging from Cotton Candy—a sickly blue—to Piña Cowlada (I kid you not). Dara appeared from a back room seconds after I walked in. She looked younger and more innocent in the Maggie Moo's crisp cotton uniform with her dark hair pulled back by a pink headband. "Did you find out something?" she asked, her eyes bright.

I skipped the preliminaries. "Why didn't you tell me Dmitri had gone missing before?" I asked.

"I didn't think it mattered." She tried to brazen it out but couldn't hold my gaze.

I let my silence and raised brows tell her what I thought of that.

"This is different," she insisted.

"How?"

"It just is! I was only fifteen when Dmitri went off to the Bahamas and I was naive about some stuff."

"Like?"

"Like now I think Dmitri disappeared back then to get some private time with a lover," she said, her dark blue eyes meeting mine squarely.

"What if that's what he's doing now?" I let my skepticism show.

"It's not. I know him better and I'm older and it doesn't *feel* the same. Something's happened to him."

"So why didn't you tell me about the earlier incident?"

"I was afraid you wouldn't take the case," she admitted. "That's why the police practically tossed me out of the precinct when I reported Dmitri missing. They think it's a publicity stunt of some kind, but it's not."

"You've lied to me—by omission," I countered the objection forming on her lips, "and Dmitri has a habit of disappearing without letting people who care about him know that he's going. He's probably snuggling with a new boyfriend in a cabana on the beach in Belize or Bimini as we speak. So why should I keep looking for him?"

"Because I'm paying you?"

Good answer.

The cowbell over the door tinkled, and a mom with two

kids, aged about three and six, walked in. The older boy, dressed in jeans, cowboy boots, and a miniature Raiders jersey, dashed toward the display cases and promptly pressed his dirty fingers and nose against the glass. The younger boy, not to be outdone, joined him and actually licked the glass.

"Cole!" the mother said wearily.

Dara moved down the counter toward the mom. "Can I help you?" Her tone and expression led me to believe she was not cut out for a life in customer service.

"I want Cotton Candy with gummi bears," the first boy said. "Lots of 'em. But no red ones. The red ones are icky."

"'nilla! I want 'nilla," the younger boy shouted, wiping his snotty nose on the sleeve of a Batman T-shirt.

"Vanilla is for babies," his brother informed him, giving him a little push.

"Is not!"

"Is too!"

"Not." But doubt twisted the little face.

"Where's my Cotton Candy? Give me a big scoop. Put it in a waffle cone," the older boy ordered Dara. He'd make a good prison guard in a few years. "Now," he added.

When the mother didn't say a word about his manners, I took great pleasure in telling him sweetly, "I'm afraid you'll have to wait your turn. I was here first."

I took my time ordering a scoop of Dark Chocolate—in a cup, no a cone, no a waffle cone, no a cup—from a grinning Dara.

~~~

Czarina Catering occupied a restored Victorian house on the southern edge of downtown Colorado Springs. A confection of gables and spires painted champagne with lime trim and a pink door, the house served as advertising for the business since Czarina Catering did a lot of weddings and was known for their creative (and expensive) cakes. Most of my information had come from food critic articles on the Internet and Czarina's own Web page. I certainly had never used their services and couldn't foresee an occasion when I'd cough up the funds for a catered affair.

I parked in the postage stamp lot behind the house, next to a van painted in colors to match the house with CZARINA CATERING swirled along the side panel. Walking around to the front, I knocked once on the pink door and pushed it open. The foyer featured a Chinese rug and a chandelier with hundreds of small crystals refracting rainbows onto the walls. A snug office opened to my right, giving an impression of warm woods and Oriental-looking vases, but it was empty.

"Hello?" I called.

"In here," came a man's voice from the back of the house.

Following the voice, I found myself in the kitchen, a much more utilitarian space. No frou-frou colors or decorative items here; everything was gleaming white or stainless steel. Yeasty, cinnamony smells wafted from the bank of ovens, and my mouth watered, reminding me I hadn't eaten yet today. The air was warm and humid from the efforts of an industrial dishwasher sloshing under a small window that would have given a Victorian-era scullery wench a glimpse of what was now the parking lot. Two chefs—one male and one female—in jeans and T-shirts covered by white aprons wrestled with what looked like six or eight cake layers frosted with pale blue icing. I watched in awe as they assembled the layers with pillars in between, making the engineering feat of the pyramids seem like a piece of cake—hah!—by comparison.

"For a baptism," said a man at my elbow, regarding me with amusement.

"A baptism?" I was incredulous. The magnificent cake looked more appropriate for a fiftieth wedding anniversary or a huge birthday party than a baptism. Would they freeze a piece of cake for the infant to eat on his first birthday?

"I'm Gary Chemerkin. What can I help you with today?" the man asked, a hint of let's-get-on-with-it in his voice. Despite the name, he had no hint of an accent. He was medium height and slim, with blond hair beginning to show gray at the temples. A closely barbered beard disguised a receding chin. Round glasses gave him a scholarly air. I put him in his mid-fifties. Unlike the cake wranglers, he wore gray suit slacks, a starched white shirt, and a silk tie that was a pastiche of champagne, pink, and lime green. I wondered if he'd had it custom made to match the business.

"Wedding this evening," he explained, catching me eyeing his clothes. "We're serving a five-course sit-down dinner for two hundred."

"Wow." I could maybe manage a sit-down dinner for two, on a good day, if the weather was nice enough to barbecue.

"Let's talk in the office," he said, turning and leading me out of the kitchen. "Our brochures are in there. What kind of event are you thinking of? Not a wedding."

I was slightly insulted that he seemed so sure about that, but he was probably in the habit of checking out ring fingers. Either that or he had bride radar that keyed in on dewy flushed cheeks and the urge to spend enough money to keep a third-world nation solvent for years on the opportunity to be princess for a day, complete with swan ice sculptures and a cake modeled after Neuschwanstein. All financed by Daddy, of course.

"Actually," I said, settling into one of a pair of club chairs that faced the desk in the office, "I'm not throwing a party. I'm here about one of your employees, Dmitri Fane." Over his shoulder, I could see a group photo of seven people, the happy Czarina Catering family, I deduced. Chemerkin stood front and center, beaming, one arm casually draped over Dmitri's shoulders and the other around a dark-haired woman's waist. All wore white aprons or chef's jackets or white shirts with black bow ties.

Chemerkin steepled his fingers. "Ah. And what is your interest, if I may ask, in Dmitri? You don't look like his type, if you know what I mean?"

I was taken aback by his thinly veiled hostility. "I'm a private investigator," I said, handing over my card. "I'm trying to locate him for a client. When was the last time you saw him?"

Chemerkin took his time answering, inspecting my card closely. "He was scheduled to work a party on Sunday," he said finally, "but he didn't show. I had to fill in as bartender at the last minute."

"Was that out of character? Was he usually reliable?"

"Usually," Chemerkin conceded, "although his skating commitments got in the way occasionally. Nothing mattered more to him than skating, and he traveled quite a bit, but he let me know up front when he was going to be gone so I wouldn't schedule him."

"What exactly did Dmitri do for you? You mentioned bartending?"

"He bartended, he waited tables, managed events on-site. He did pretty much everything except cook. He's been with me for almost seven years—ever since he moved to Colorado. I was hoping that maybe one day he'd join me full-time." He shrugged. "With him it was always skating."

"Do you have any idea why he's gone missing? Was he upset about something? Was there an emergency of some sort?"

The man hesitated, pursing his lips. "Well . . ."

"What?"

"There was an incident," he said reluctantly. "Friday night. He was bartending for a party and there was . . . an incident."

"What kind?" This was like pulling teeth.

"Apparently, the daughter of the couple hosting the party offered Dmitri a joint, and he refused. Women were always coming on to Dmitri," Chemerkin said in a resigned tone. "Anyway, this one got in a snit, and accusations were tossed around."

"Accusations?"

"Her parents threw Dmitri out and accused him of dealing drugs. I had to offer them a catered dinner for eight to keep them from calling the police."

"Generous," I observed.

"Nationals are next week—Dmitri didn't need the stress interfering with his performance."

Chemerkin didn't need rumors of drug dealing cutting into his business, either. "Any possibility Dmitri or one of your other employees was dealing?"

"Absolutely not. All my employees are bonded. Most of them have been with me for years. The little madam was just getting back at Dmitri for turning her down."

"He told you that, I suppose?"

Chemerkin flushed red, and I read imminent ejection in his eyes. I changed tacks. "Was Dmitri especially friendly with any of your other employees?"

Chemerkin combed his beard with his fingers as he thought. "He was closest to Fiona," he said finally. "Fiona Campbell."

"Where can I find her?"

He jerked his head. "In the kitchen. She's decorating the cake."

※

Chemerkin said he didn't mind if I talked to Fiona, so I headed back to the kitchen when he answered the phone. The cake was assembled, a multi-tiered edifice of glossy blue, decorated with real flowers and icing ones. It was hard to tell which was which. Both bakers, however, had disappeared. Damn. A chilly draft caught my attention, and I noticed the back door, the one leading to the lot where I'd parked my car, was cracked. A hint of cigarette smoke drew me to the door, and I found Fiona Campbell leaning against the brick wall of the small courtyard, smoking. She had shed her apron and was clothed in only jeans and a mulberry T-shirt that revealed a waifish build and set off the black hair framing her face in a wispy pixie cut. Gooseflesh pimpled her arms, but she seemed oblivious as she raised the cigarette to her lips and drew nicotine and sludge into her lungs. She ignored me, probably assuming I was headed for my car, until I spoke her name. "Fiona Campbell?"

She didn't move, but her eyes slid toward me, assessing. She took another pull on the cigarette. "Yeah?" Her voice sounded like cognac tastes, deep and rich, with an edge. It was incongruous coming from her thin frame. If she sang, she'd sound like Edith Piaf.

"I'm Charlie Swift," I said, crossing the cobblestone courtyard so I could face her. "I'm a private investigator."

"Yeah?" Not a hint of interest sounded in her voice.

"I've been hired to find Dmitri Fane."

A slight pause and a blink of her eyes this time before she said, "Yeah?"

"Yeah." I stared at her, determined to let curiosity work on her taciturnity. She caved after a full minute.

"Who wants to find the shitbird?" She dropped her cigarette and crushed it with the toe of her black boot. Then she raised her eyes—an unusual bluish gray with a dark, almost purple rim around the iris—and looked me straight in the face for the first time, her expression a blend of defiance, anger, and something I couldn't identify.

"Gary said you were close," I said, hiding my surprise.

"Were."

"What happened?"

"What the hell business is it of yours?"

"It's not, unless it plays into his disappearance. When did you last see him?"

She pulled another cigarette from a packet, more to give her hands something to do, I thought, than because she wanted a smoke. She didn't light it. "Saturday morning. He came by here early to pick up his paycheck. I was here, decorating the cake for the Smith-Larsh wedding."

"What did he say? Did he mention leaving town, an emergency of some kind maybe?"

She looked at me from under her lashes. "Gary tell you what happened Friday night?"

I nodded, wrapping my arms around myself as wind gusted into the courtyard. It was getting colder.

"I heard him tell Gary he was quitting. They argued."

"About what?" Funny that Chemerkin hadn't mentioned either Dmitri's quitting or their argument. I'd have to look at Mr. Czarina Catering more closely, see what else he might be hiding.

"I don't know. I was in the kitchen and they were in the office. After Dmitri said he was quitting, they closed the door and all

I could hear was muffled shouting. I couldn't make out the words."

"What happened then?"

"I don't know. I had to deliver the cake, and by the time I got back they were both gone." She had peeled the paper off the cigarette as she talked, and now she scattered the tobacco shreds, letting the wind take them. Worry lurked in her eyes. "D'you think he's okay?"

"Why wouldn't he be?"

"No reason."

When I didn't say anything, she ran her hands up and down her arms. "It's cold."

I still didn't say anything, and she burst out, "Saturday was my birthday. He was supposed to take me and Tanya to dinner—we were going to Giuseppe's—but he never showed up. He never even called! We waited an hour and a half. I finally made Tanya a PBJ."

I understood why she'd called him a shitbird. He'd stood her up. "Tanya?"

"My daughter. She's five." Some of her tension eased as she thought about her kid. "She loves Dmitri."

"Is he—?"

Real amusement flared in her eyes, making them look more blue than gray. "Tanya's father? Nah, he plays for the other team, if you know what I mean. He's been real good to Tanya, though. He was teaching her to skate. And he's my best friend." She said it wistfully, and I could see she was feeling guilty about being mad at Dmitri for standing her up. "When he didn't show for the job Sunday night, either, I got really pissed at him, you know? I should have known something was wrong, that he wouldn't flake out like that without a good reason. God, what kind of a friend am I?"

Now that she'd gotten over being mad at Dmitri, she was embracing self-flagellation with a passion. I inserted a question to stem the tide. "Can you think of any place he might be? Does he have a friend he might be staying with, or a special place he likes to go?"

"You got something to write on?"

I passed her my notebook, and she scribbled a couple of names before handing it back. "I can't think of any special place—"

The sound of an approaching motor made us both look up. The Czarina Catering van negotiated the tight turn into the parking lot and idled. A man got out, opened the double doors at the back of the van, and disappeared into the kitchen without so much as looking in our direction. "I've got to get back to work," Fiona said. "Y'know, Boyce might know of a spot." She lifted her chin toward the kitchen. "He and Dmitri went off for a weekend, once. Fishing, I think. Maybe he—"

She broke off as the man emerged from the kitchen, pushing a rolling cart with a large white box perched atop it. "Hey, Boyce," Fiona called. He looked up, all mousy hair and pasty skin, as we walked in his direction. "This woman's a detective, and she wants to talk to you—"

Panic flared in his eyes, and he shoved the cart toward us, hard. Boyce took off down the alley, the green hood of his fleece pullover flapping behind him. The cart careened toward us. I reached out a hand to stop it, but one wheel lodged between two cobblestones and it jolted to a stop. The box, however, obeying some law of physics about items in motion staying in motion, didn't stop. It slid off the stainless steel top of the cart and landed heavily but upright at our feet, the box splitting open to reveal the cake, still largely intact. As I watched, the top layer teetered on its pedestals. Fiona lunged for it. It slid away from her grasp and the whole cake collapsed as if dynamited, splattering white cake, blue icing, and gooey filling onto my shoes.

"Oh, shit," Fiona and I said in unison.

7

With Bavarian cream filling squishing in my shoes, I climbed the stairs to Boyce Edgerton's third-floor apartment off of Cascade Avenue in the heart of Colorado College country, my tailbone shrieking with every step. Fiona, furious with him, had given me his full name and the name of his complex.

"The Burtons are going to shit a brick," she'd observed, picking one bruised carnation out of the cake muck at our feet. "The baptism will be ruined."

I was pretty sure that baptisms "took" whether or not there was designer cake, and said as much. Fiona gave me a look that said I was dimmer than a night-light. "But the Burtons won't pay us. Plus they'll want their deposit back. I'd better get Gary—"

She disappeared inside the house, tracking cake the whole way, while I jumped in my Subaru and headed after Boyce. I'd found his reaction interesting, to say the least. Very few people took to their heels upon hearing I wanted to talk to them. A fair number of people didn't want to talk to me a second time, for some reason or other, but I'm not that off-putting at first glance. Boyce's flight was evidence of a guilty conscience, I deduced. Whether or not it was related to Dmitri Fane remained to be seen.

The building Boyce lived in was a beautiful old home converted to apartments. A wide walkway led to three shallow steps and an unlocked outer door. Didn't these people know crime was rampant? One of the mail slots in the foyer said B. EDGERTON and gave the apartment number as 3A. I climbed. Arriving on an expansive landing with lovely, wide-planked hardwood floors, now scuffed by careless tenants dragging bicycles and strollers and furniture up and down, I knocked on the only door in sight. I had figured Boyce would scurry home—most critters run for their dens when panicked.

I was right. He pulled the door wide and then, when he saw me standing there, tried to shut it. I blocked it with a stiff arm. Unable to flee, he resorted to shouting.

"If that bitch Vanessa says I violated the TRO, she's lying her head off. I haven't been near her, Detective." Anger mottled his fair skin an ugly puce.

The penny dropped. He thought I was a cop. I was not above taking advantage of his misconception. "I'm not here about the restraining order, Edgerton," I said.

"You're not?" Surprise dropped his arm from the door, and I walked in.

The apartment smelled vaguely of dirty laundry, stale pizza, and marijuana. Hm. All the windows were closed, and it was uncomfortably warm. I shrugged out of my peacoat but held on to it, unwilling to drape it on the only piece of furniture, a tatty futon stippled with cat hair. Ugh. A sheet-cum-curtain obscured the only window. A small kitchenette opened directly off the living area and featured a two-burner stove, a fridge, and a recycling bin piled high with Budweiser and Mountain Dew cans. Edgerton looked to be in his late twenties, but he'd apparently never outgrown his taste for frat boy life, or he'd reverted after he and the bitchy Vanessa broke up.

"I'm interested in Dmitri Fane," I said in my most coplike voice.

Looking confused, Edgerton closed the door and gangled over to me. He wasn't fat, but he looked soft, and I figured running away from Czarina Catering was the most exercise he'd gotten in a month. "What about Dmitri?"

"Have you seen him recently?"

"Hey, is this about what happened Friday night? I had nothing to do with it!"

"I haven't accused you of anything, Edgerton," I said. My tone said I still might. "Tell me about Dmitri. Were you friends?"

"We hung out sometimes. I stayed with him for a couple weeks after Van kicked me out, until I found this place." One large hand gestured at our palatial surroundings.

"Ms. Campbell said you and he went away for a weekend. Where did you go?"

"Fly-fishing," Edgerton said. His eyes, a surprisingly attractive hazel, lit up. "It was sweet. I caught a rainbow this big." He measured air with his hands.

"Congratulations. Where did you stay?"

"A cabin outside of Estes Park. We fished the Big Thompson."

My pulse quickened. A mountain cabin sounded like a great place for a guy to disappear to. "Did Fane own the cabin? Do you have the address?"

"I could find it, but I don't know the address. It was off of Route 7."

A clinking sound from the kitchen made me turn. One of the beer cans toppled off the recycling bin and rolled across the linoleum. "What—?" I started. Then I saw a pointy nose wiggle behind the trash can. "Rat!" I yelped, pointing.

"Don't shoot," Edgerton shouted, zipping around me and holding up his arms as if to block me. "It's only Sadie."

I gaped at him. "Shoot? I'm not armed."

"You're not?" His eyes narrowed and his arms dropped to his side. Just then, a rodent slinked over to sniff at his jeans leg, and Edgerton bent down to pick it up. "She's a ferret," he said, holding the creature out to me. It looked like a skinny mink with a raccoony face, complete with black mask. It wrinkled its nose and drew back its lip, making a hissing sound.

Stroking the rodent, Edgerton looked me up and down suspiciously. "Aren't cops supposed to wear their guns all the time?"

"I never said I was a cop."

"Fiona said you were a detective! I thought—"

"I'm a private detective," I said, offering him one of my cards. "About that cabin—"

"You lied to me." He advanced toward me, the weasel egging him on from a perch on his shoulder.

I held my ground, wondering uneasily what he'd done to Vanessa to earn a restraining order. "I did not. You assumed," I said. "Look, we're on the same side here. We're both concerned about Dmitri, right? If you'd—"

"Out." He stalked past me and yanked the door open. "Now."

I slipped my arms into my coat. "Give me a call if you think of anything else," I said as if he weren't glaring at me and practically shoving me out the door. "Especially about Dmitri's cabin."

"I don't think it was his." Edgerton relented in the face of my imminent departure. "I think it was his aunt's."

I stopped on the threshold. "His aunt's?"

"Yeah, you know, that coach woman. What's her name? I only met her once. Julie Bublova?"

—⁓⁓—

Could Boyce Edgerton be right? I asked myself as I drove away from his apartment. Was it possible that Yuliya Bobrova was related to Dmitri Fane? Dara Peterson certainly hadn't mentioned it. I dialed her number on my cell phone and punched up the heat in my car a couple of notches.

I recapped my investigation when Dara answered, then asked about Fane and Bobrova's relationship.

"His aunt?" Her voice was skeptical. "Neither of them ever said anything about that, and she treats him like she treats the rest of us . . . like dirt."

Assuring her I'd keep her posted, I hung up and headed for the office. Gigi was out, and I spent the afternoon doing paperwork on a couple of recently completed cases. Early winter dusk was falling as I headed home, and I flicked on the Subaru's lights. I'd been counting on getting some skiing in this weekend, but it looked like this case would keep me tied to the city. My mood darkened along with the sky. I'd spent last weekend tiling my powder room instead of skiing, and now it looked like I'd have to pass on the slopes again. Plus, my head and tailbone ached, and I was not feeling up to helping Father Dan with whatever project he wanted to tackle. When he'd phoned this morning before I left for the office, he only said he needed my help with something. Since he'd admired my remodeled bathroom greatly, I thought he might want some help with a tiling project.

Rounding the corner onto Tudor Road, I automatically looked toward the Dumpster in St. Paul's parking lot. I'd seen a bear there late this summer—the same bear, I was pretty sure, who wrecked my bird feeders to dine on my birdseed—but he was hibernating at this time of year, though, and I continued past the church and the rectory where Dan lived to my house. Parking in my driveway, I let the peace of the quiet area drape itself over me. A great horned owl hooted as she set out on her night's hunting. The scent of pine trees drifted on the chilly wind. It smelled like snow, and I reminded myself to check the weather forecast.

I looked longingly at the hot tub on my deck as I changed into a comfy pair of sweats and stuffed my cake-speckled slacks and Pepsi-stained turtleneck in the hamper. Something crackled in my slacks pocket, and I withdrew a handful of receipts. I stared at them, puzzled, then remembered: They'd come from Dmitri Fane's closet. I tossed them on my dresser to look at tomorrow. I'd told Dan I'd come over, so I put off sinking into the steaming water and trudged through the hundred yards of young pines and scrub oaks that separated our houses, comfortable on the familiar terrain even without a light.

"Feed me," I said when he opened the door. Six foot five with shoulders to match and thick blond hair, Dan didn't look like an Episcopalian priest.

"Here." He thrust a glass of Scotch into my hand before I'd even stepped into the warm foyer, his large hand wrapped around the glass seeming more suited to handling a rifle or power tools than a communion host.

"Marry me." I took a sip of the Scotch and closed my eyes, letting the liquid burn its way down my throat to my stomach.

He smiled. "You're too easy." He led the way back to his kitchen, where I could smell something delicious.

"Am not." I scuffed off my boots and padded after him, hoisted myself onto a red leatherette bar stool, one of two drawn up to his counter, and watched him stir whatever was bubbling on the stove. Dan's broad back blocked my view of dinner.

"Venison stew," he answered my unspoken question.

"Have you been out shooting Bambi?" I knew Dan had a couple of guns and that he was quite the marksman. We'd gone to the range together once or twice. I didn't know he hunted.

"A parishioner got Bambi with a crossbow and shared the wealth." He turned around, and his smile faded. "Good God, Charlie, what happened to you?" He crossed the kitchen in two strides and cupped my face in his large hand, tilting it so the light illuminated my forehead.

I'd almost forgotten the lump. It was probably a lovely mix of purples by now. His palm felt hard and callused against my cheek. The calluses reminded me that Dan hadn't always been a priest, that he'd only been ordained ten years ago, and I wondered (not for the first time) what he'd done before answering "the call." Something about the way his body stilled when he concentrated, his fierce intelligence, and the way he kept himself fit told me he hadn't been an actuary or a shoe salesman. I twisted my face away from his hand, which felt a bit too good against my skin. "Um, I got conked on the head while rifling a famous figure skater's bathroom."

"Of course," he said sardonically. Light from the overhead fixture glinted off his blond hair. "So the figure skater came home and smacked you? Who can blame her?"

"Him. He's the one I'm looking for. Someone else hit me while I was going through his condo, looking for a clue as to where he might be hiding out."

"Start at the beginning," Dan ordered, sliding onto the bar stool beside me.

I filled him in on the case.

"So what do you think's going on?" he asked. "Did Fane leave under his own steam, or is he in trouble?"

"Both, maybe," I suggested. "I don't know. I think he left on his own, but I'm damned if I know why. Everyone agrees that skating is his life, so it seems odd that he'd run off right before the Olympic trials."

"Damn odd," Dan agreed, getting up to dish the stew into stoneware bowls. He pulled a loaf of crusty bread out of the oven, sliced it, and slid it onto the counter. "Here okay?"

"Sure." I was pleasantly relaxed and didn't feel like getting up to move to the dining room.

"So what's your next move?" Dan rejoined me, his hip bumping mine as he settled onto the bar stool.

"Talk to the coach again. Dara says she's usually at the rink by five and the first skater arrives at five fifteen. Barbaric. I'll get there early and see if I can't have a real conversation with Comrade Bobrova." Using my teeth, I ripped a bite of bread from the chunk in my hand and chewed hard.

"Do you think she's really Fane's aunt?"

"I don't know, and I'm not sure it matters one way or the other. Maybe she is and they kept it secret so the other skaters wouldn't whine about favoritism. Maybe she's not and Boyce is confused. Totally possible. His pad reeked of MJ. Did I tell you he keeps a weasel in the house?"

I swiveled my stool away from the counter so I could hop off it. "You cooked, so I'll clean up," I said, motioning him to stay seated. "Tell me what you want my help with. Are you going to redo your bathroom?"

He looked confused for a moment, automatically sliding our bowls and plates toward me as I ran water in the sink. "My bathroom? No. I want your help finding a missing kid."

"That I can do," I said, relieved that he didn't want manual labor. I wasn't up to it after getting beaten up by a psychotic skating coach and a mysterious intruder. "Who?" I squirted citrusy dish soap into the sink and made it bubble up by running the water hard.

"He goes by Kungfu."

"That's a name?"

Dan shrugged. "Nickname. He's an Asian kid, maybe sixteen."

I looked at him suspiciously. "Is this one of your runaways?" Dan volunteered at a nonprofit downtown, Dellert House, that provided temporary lodging for homeless men and teens, some of whom were runaways. He did counseling with the boys. "Your runaway ran away?"

"Something like that," he admitted with a crooked smile.

"How do you know he didn't go back home?" I scrubbed at a stubborn spot on the stew pan.

Dan shook his head. "He didn't."

The expression on his face persuaded me. "Okay. Do you have a picture? When did you last see him?"

"Saturday morning." Dan pulled a square of paper from his pocket and unfolded it. Four teens mugged for the camera, holding hammers and pliers and screwdrivers. "This was taken a week ago, the morning we took the guys to work on the Habitat house. That's him," Dan said, tapping the kid second from the left.

I studied him. He looked ordinary, with straight black hair long enough to tuck behind his ears, almond-shaped eyes, and crooked teeth displayed in a wide grin. "What makes you think he didn't just move on?"

"Because I hired him to do some custodial work at the church," Dan said, a line between his brows. "He needed the money. He hinted that he was saving for something big but wouldn't say what. He worked last Friday and half a day Saturday but didn't show up on Tuesday like he was supposed to. I asked around Dellert's, but no one's seen him. His stuff is still there."

I dried my hands on a paper towel and chucked it toward the trash. I'd done pro bono work for Dan before, but this case seemed like a loser from the word go. A kid who'd run away from home wouldn't hesitate to ditch a halfway house he found confining. Or maybe he'd had a run-in with the law. I'd check.

"Why this kid, Dan? Don't runaways drift in and out of Dellert's all the time?" I studied his face. He seemed tired, his skin a little gray under the perpetual tan, the lines at the corners of his eyes a bit deeper. I usually guessed his age as being early forties to early fifties; tonight, he looked like he belonged on the latter end of that scale.

"I don't know," Dan admitted, rubbing a hand down his face. "He seemed like he could make it, brighter than most, with a real plan. Maybe he reminds me of someone I used to know. Shit."

"C'mon," I said, taking his hand. "You need a half hour in a hot tub. That's Dr. Charlie's prescription for what ails you. And another Scotch." I grabbed the Lagavulin bottle in my other hand and dragged him toward the door.

"What ails me?" he asked with half a smile.

I set down the Scotch and framed him between my hands, like a movie director setting up a shot. "An inability to solve all the world's problems and a deep sadness that you can't save the youth of Colorado Springs from their abusive parents or their own stupid choices," I intoned in the voice of a film narrator. "Either that or you're worried about the middle-aged man's trio of fears: hair loss, erectile dysfunction, and high cholesterol." I ticked them off on my fingers.

"Middle-aged!"

"Only one thing will cure all that."

"Prayer."

He didn't even make it a question. No wonder he was a priest.

"No, Scotch and water. Hot water, that is, as in hot tub. Get your suit."

8

Parked outside the Ice Hall Friday morning, I cursed the makers of Scotch and my own stupidity. Relaxing with Dan in the hot tub, I'd drunk more than I intended to. That happened more often than it should when I drank with Dan because the man could put away more alcohol than the Scottish national rugby team. A headache pounded behind my eyes despite the handful of aspirin I'd swallowed with my first Pepsi of the day at four thirty. That's A.M. Even the birds knew there was no point to being up this early, especially in the winter. I'd left the air force mostly because they overdo the whole teamwork thing—rugged individualism was good enough for the pioneers and it's good enough for me—but also because the emphasis on starting the day BCOD (before the crack of dawn) went against nature—mine at any rate. When I stepped out of my car, the bitter cold made it seem even darker. I plunged my hands into my coat pockets, grateful for the black cowl-necked sweater that swathed my neck. My wool ski cap kept my head warm, even though I'd have hat-head later in the day. I wore an old pair of soccer cleats on my feet in anticipation of having to meet Bobrova on her home turf: ice. There was only one other vehicle in the lot, a late-model Volvo I assumed was Bobrova's.

I made my way to the side door Dara had assured me would be open. It was. The only illumination came from the EXIT sign over my head that shed a reddish glow. I started down the hall, calling softly, "Coach Bobrova?"

No answer. I tried a couple of doors, but they were locked. Okay, this was a little spooky. If it hadn't been for the van in the lot and the open door, I'd've assumed the place was deserted. It was quieter than a high school on Sunday with thin carpet muffling my footsteps. Some light would improve the atmosphere tremendously, I decided, running my hand along the wall in search of a switch. No dice. I almost wished Gigi were here; she'd have a flashlight in the saddlebag she called a purse.

A hiss of sound I couldn't identify came from in front of me, from the rink, if I wasn't mistaken. I walked more purposefully toward the double doors and pushed them open. It seemed lighter in here, with the flat sheet of ice reflecting the ambient light from windows set high in the walls and a dim glow coming from a vending machine in the corner, but it was still a dark twilight. As I listened, trying to orient myself, a door clicked closed on the far side of the rink.

"Coach Bobrova?" I was getting pissed. Okay, I didn't have an appointment, but Dara had said Bobrova was here by five every morning. She must have heard me calling her name. If the door closing was her ducking out to avoid me, I was going to haunt her until she talked to me about her putative nephew. Maybe I'd even take a skating class so I could follow her around on the ice. Hah! I looked at my illuminated watch dial. Five ten.

Her first students would be here in five minutes and I'd lose the opportunity to speak with her.

"Help . . ."

The throaty whisper drifted from the middle of the ice. As my eyes adjusted to the dimness, I could barely make out a darker shape on the ice. Bobrova had fallen—she was hurt. The woman had to be seventy, after all, and probably had osteoporosis. Maybe she'd broken her hip. "Just a sec," I called to her, feeling my way to the gate.

My tailbone twitched as I shuffle-stepped across the ice in my cleats, reminding me of yesterday's fall. Reaching the still figure, I crouched beside her, feeling for her hand. I brushed the hem of her cape and let my hand travel up it until I encountered her hip and then her shoulder. My hand was damp, and I wondered how long she'd been lying here, unable to summon help. She was probably soaked to the skin and freezing.

"Where does it hurt?" I asked, reaching for my cell phone.

"Dmitri—" she croaked.

"Why's it so dark?" a young voice asked.

The overhead lights sprang to life, glaring down on the ice and the old woman crumpled there, red blood oozing from her head and making a halo around the matted gray hair. She'd lapsed into unconsciousness after the one word, and I couldn't find a pulse. The dent in her forehead and the bloodied cane lying two feet away gave me some idea what had happened.

Screams bounced off the ice and echoed shrilly in the cavernous space as the young skater who'd turned on the lights skidded to a stop several feet away. Her blades stuttering on the ice triggered a memory: That was the sound I'd heard before entering the rink—something sliding across the ice.

I looked around and saw a trail scuffed into the ice, a trail made by shuffling shoes, not skates. It led to the far side of the rink. The first several feet of the marks glimmered red, and I felt sick. This was not a good morning to be hungover.

Swallowing, I looked up at the bug-eyed face of the skinny girl backing away from me. "Can you—"

"Help! Mom! She killed her," the girl shrieked, spinning and speed-skating for the gate where she'd entered. She thudded into it and let out a squawk.

Running footsteps sounded in the hallway. "Jessica," a woman's frantic voice called. Mom. "Are you hurt?"

I ignored Jessica's boo-hooing, dialing 911. As I waited on the line at the operator's request, I couldn't stop shivering, chilled as much by the brutality as by the frigid air.

9

~~~

"You look awful, Charlie," Montgomery said some hours later, following the arrival and departure of the ambulance with Yuliya Bobrova, the influx of crime scene techs and police, and the endless questioning about what I was doing there and what I'd seen and heard. The first cops who responded had aimed guns at me, primed with Jessica's hysterical assertions that I killed her coach. Montgomery and I were seated in the first tier of spectator seats, cold metal bleachers impressing ridges into my behind and thighs. Yellow crime scene tape roped off the rink, and cops had been posted to send skaters home as they arrived for classes and training sessions. Ice Hall officials hovered on the edge of the action, wanting to know if the hockey practices scheduled for the evening could still go on.

"Nice shiner." His long finger gently traced the swollen area above my eye.

I resisted the urge to close my eyes. "You wouldn't happen to have any aspirin, would you?" I asked. I felt beat-up and stained. Despite the twenty minutes I'd spent over the bathroom sink scrubbing at my hands and coat, Bobrova's blood rimmed my nails and splotched my coat and the hem of my slacks. The fabric was dark enough I could hardly see it, but I knew it was there.

He handed me two Tylenols, and I swallowed them dry. "Is it Monday again?"

"No, it's Friday. Did you bang your head? Let me see your pupils."

"I don't have a concussion." I pushed his hand away.

"Let's go over it again," he said.

I rolled my eyes at him. "I need food." The two Pepsis and the variety pack of headache medicines I'd consumed roiled in my stomach.

"Come on. I'll take you to breakfast." Montgomery helped me to my feet with a hand under my elbow and guided me down the hall that had seemed so spooky earlier. Now it was awash with light and activity. I carried my stained peacoat, not wanting to put it on, and the wind knifed through me when Montgomery opened the door. He guided me over to his car and put the heat on high for me.

Minutes later, I clutched a half-eaten bear claw from a nearby doughnut place while Montgomery stirred creamer into his coffee. Between bites, I ran through my story again. "What do you think happened?" I turned the tables on Montgomery before he could think up any more questions.

"Attempted murder," he said. "Whoever clobbered her wasn't messing around. If you hadn't come in when you did, she'd be dead. Are you sure you didn't see anyone or anything?"

I shook my head and regretted it. "No. I told you. I heard someone on the ice and a door closing, but that was it. I saw nada." Sugar poured into my bloodstream, and I began to feel almost human. "I don't think it was premeditated," I mused, "because the attacker used a weapon of opportunity—Bobrova's cane. Wouldn't he—or she—have brought a gun, a knife, a rope, a candlestick if he intended to kill her?"

Montgomery shrugged. "Maybe, maybe not. Whoever it was clearly knew Bobrova would be there alone. He probably also knew about the cane. Everyone we spoke to this morning said she carried it everywhere."

"I wonder if this is connected with Dmitri's disappearance."

"I wonder if Dmitri beat her," Montgomery said, finishing his coffee. "Maybe her saying 'Dmitri' to you was an accusation."

"Maybe." I needed to think about it some more.

Montgomery caught the glint in my eye. "This is a police investigation now, Charlie. You stay away from it." He put his forearms on the table and leaned toward me. He smelled like coffee and spicy aftershave. Irresistible. If I hadn't been hungover.

"Of course," I said. "I wouldn't dream of intruding on police territory." I licked sugary goo off my fingers.

He snorted.

"I do have an obligation to my client, however, to continue investigating the disappearance of her partner." I smiled at him and got to my feet. "So could you take me back to my car now?"

———

I'd been planning to swing by Dellert's on my way back from the Ice Hall to get started on Dan's missing kid, but the attack on Bobrova had changed things. Gigi could handle the initial interviews at Dellert's while I pursued Dmitri. I pulled into the office lot, not surprised to see Gigi's yellow Hummer parked out front since it was already after nine. I felt like I'd been up for two days. I found both Gigi and Kendall at their desks when I went in. Gigi had on a pink turtleneck, stretched to capacity by her ample bosom, and a purple velvet jacket. A bigger-than-life-sized sea horse brooch of purple, teal, and green crystals glinted on her lapel. Her jaw-length champagne-colored hair was immaculate as usual, and she greeted me with a smile that faded as she took in the particulars of my appearance.

"Oh, Charlie. Were you doing some process serving this morning? I could've told you not to try it at a breakfast place. Luckily, syrup is easy to get out. Soak your coat in warm water and—"

"It's blood," I said and marched to the fridge for a Pepsi. I stuffed the coat under my desk and pulled out the gym bag where I kept a change of clothes.

"Are you hurt?" Gigi asked at the same time Kendall said, "Why are you wearing cleats?"

"No," I told Gigi, then turned to face the teenager. Apparently, she wasn't feeling guilty about trying to get me arrested yesterday, because there wasn't a trace of self-consciousness on her face. "I wore the cleats so I wouldn't slip on the ice."

"You wore cleats on the ice? At the Ice Hall?" Kendall sounded appalled, as if I'd admitted to swindling sweet grannies out of their life savings or having sex with giraffes. "That is *so* verboten!"

"Believe me, a few cleat marks on the ice is the least of their worries today."

I told them about Bobrova.

They sat in stunned silence for a moment when I finished. Finally, Gigi said, "I know you probably feel badly that you didn't get there earlier, Charlie, but I'm grateful you didn't surprise the attacker. Why, he might have killed you, too."

I shot Gigi a surprised look. I *had* been blaming myself for not moving quicker, for not finding Bobrova in time to prevent the attack, but how could Gigi know that?

Kendall had a more predictable response. "What will her students do? Nationals are next week, and the Olympics are in February. They can't switch coaches now!"

"I think they'll have to," I said, finishing my Pepsi. "No way will Bobrova be doing any coaching in the next couple of months, even if she lives."

"You mean she might *die*?" Kendall stared at me open-mouthed, obviously shocked by the idea.

Was there actually a film of tears in her eyes? Maybe she wasn't as heartless as I thought. The girl sank back into her chair, playing abstractedly with a strand of golden hair, and I briefed Gigi on Dan's case. As was her habit, she took copious notes.

"I should start by talking to some of his friends at the half-way house, don't you think?" she asked when I finished.

"Yeah. I think he's probably moved on for good, but I told Dan we'd look into it. Do you know where Dellert's is?" I gave her directions to the house in Old Colorado City, west of I-25 and downtown proper, watching with amusement as she tucked the notebook into today's purse, a purple suede creation large enough to hold the complete works of Barbara Cartland, one of her favorite authors.

"Kendall, you're with me," I said, startling the girl.

"What?" Gigi and Kendall asked together.

"You're going to tell me everything there is to know about the international skating scene," I said, "with a particular emphasis on gossip about Dmitri Fane, Dara Peterson, and Yuliya Bobrova."

"Does that mean I'm like an expert witness?" She tried to sound blasé, but her interest peeped through.

"More like a consultant."

"How much do consultants get paid?"

"The same as part-time receptionists who show up late and ruin coffeepots."

She pouted, but I could tell she was intrigued by the idea and a bit proud to think that her knowledge was valuable. "Let me change," I said, "and we'll hit the road."

10

~~~

Gigi Goldman looked around at the scattering of men and teens in the Dellert House dining room. The room was simply furnished with a trestle-style table and mismatched chairs, obviously donated or rescued from Goodwill bins. No two looked alike, and there'd been a brief squabble between two teens for the most comfortable chair, a wing chair with rose-covered upholstery over thick padding. The housemaster, Roger Nutt, a short man in his early sixties, broke it up. Gigi was glad he stayed, his shoulders propped against the doorjamb, surveying his charges with paternal tolerance. Pale sunlight filtered through miniblinds that could have used a good dusting, but it failed to warm the atmosphere in the room. The four inhabitants chilled the space with their expressions. Ranging in age from maybe seventeen to late twenties, they surveyed her with varying degrees of boredom or hostility. All wore jeans and chips on their shoulders. Gigi, feeling overdressed and out of her league, nervously patted her hair. Why had she thought she could connect with these boys—men, really—just because she had a seventeen-year-old son?

"Well," she started brightly. "I'm Georgia Goldman, but you can call me Gigi. G. G. for Georgia Goldman . . . get it?"

Total silence.

She cleared her throat. "I'm here because one of the inmates here . . . I mean, customers . . . er, boarders has gone missing and people are concerned."

A rude noise came from the slim black teen seated closest to the door.

"Did you say something?" Gigi asked.

The teenager eyed her, debating whether or not to favor her with an answer. "Ain't no one gives a shit about us," he said finally.

"Now, William, how can that be true?" Roger Nutt asked from the doorway. A smile curved the full lips half hidden by a gray mustache and beard. "When you live in a luxurious spot like this?" He gestured to the shabby room.

Loud hoots greeted the gentle attempt at humor, and Gigi smiled her thanks at Roger.

"Who's missing, then?" asked William, leaning forward with his hands hanging between his knees. "Brothers come and brothers go . . . how come one's more missing than another?"

"A boy called Kungfu," Gigi said, not sure she followed William's logic but grateful for his willingness to engage. "He had a job working for Father Dan Allgood at St. Paul's, but he hasn't been there all week."

"Father Dan's cool," one of the twenty-something men offered. He had buzz-cut brown hair and tattoos of dragons coiling around arms bared by a leather vest. A scar disfigured his face, and Gigi fought not to stare at it.

"Did any of you hang with Kungfu?" Gigi asked, hoping she'd used "hang" correctly; she'd heard Dexter say things like "I'm going to hang with Jesse and Dillon at the skate park."

The man with the dragons chewed a hangnail on his thumb; he seemed young for his age. The teen sitting farthest away had his eyes closed and his head resting on the chair back. The other man eyed William but said nothing. William answered for them all. "Nah. Dude was a loner, man."

This was hopeless, Gigi thought, not having felt so uncomfortable in a group since she first married Les and attended a dinner party given by one of his stuck-up clients who clearly despised a girl who spoke with a Georgia accent and did nails and hair for a living. She'd heard the phrase "white trash" whispered more than once that evening.

"How about drugs?" she asked.

"What kind you want?" William asked with a laugh. The others joined in.

"Not me!" Gigi's voice squeaked. "I mean, did Kungfu—"

"They're all clean," Roger Nutt put in from the doorway. One raised brow quelled the laughter. "They agree to weekly drug tests while they're here, and if they fail one they're gone. No exceptions, no second chances."

Gigi shifted from foot to foot. "Well, thanks for talking to me, guys." She'd almost said "boys" but caught herself in time. "If you think of anything, anything at all, that might help us find Kungfu, please let me know." She passed business cards to each of the teens and men. They filtered out of the room until only the man with the tattoo was left, neatly pushing the chairs under the table.

"Thanks, Jerome," Roger Nutt said. He gestured for Gigi to precede him out the door.

Gigi smiled at the man, wondering about the burn scar that disfigured his face from cheekbone to jaw and the air of apprehension that clung to him, despite the tough-seeming tattoo and leather clothes.

"Kungfu had a . . ." His voice trailed off so Gigi couldn't hear him. His hand drifted to his cheek, as if to hide the scar.

"What, sugah?"

He cleared his throat. "Kungfu was getting a tattoo," he said. "Is that the kind of thing you want to know?" He blinked several times.

"Exactly," Gigi said warmly, wanting to hug him—he wasn't that much older than Dexter. "How do you know? Did Kungfu mention it?"

"I saw him at Tattoo4U. That's where I got Saracen and Scimitar."

"Who?"

"My dragons." He flexed his biceps so the dragon tattoos seemed to writhe.

Gigi fought to control her distaste. Who named his tattoos? "Uh, they're very pretty," she offered.

Jerome frowned. "Fierce. They're fierce. They protect me." He stepped toward Gigi, neck poking forward.

Gigi sent a "help me" look to Roger Nutt, who made a calming motion. Jerome nodded jerkily and stepped back. "I'm cool, I'm cool."

"When did you see him?" Gigi asked. She dug a roll of Life Savers out of her purse. "Want one?" Jerome took three and popped them all in his mouth. She offered them to Roger, and he shook his head. Letting a lime Life Saver melt on her tongue, Gigi waited for Jerome to think.

"Monday," he said. "Yeah, it was Monday. I was thinking about getting another tat, but I can't really afford it. Kungfu came in as I was leaving." He juddered from foot to foot and edged toward the door.

"You've been very, very helpful, Jerome," Gigi said. "Thank you so much."

"You're on lunch duty this week, aren't you?" Nutt asked the man. "Better scoot."

Jerome slipped away without another word, and Gigi watched him until he disappeared through a swinging door at the far end of the corridor. The smell of spaghetti drifted into the hall.

"So sad," she murmured.

"That burn on his face is from a curling iron," Nutt said, his voice grim. "His mother . . . He's been here off and on since he was fifteen." He shook his head. "You said you wanted to see the stuff Kungfu left. C'mon."

He led the way up a wide staircase to the second floor of the old house. A hallway branched off to either side of the stairs. "We have room for four in each room," Nutt said, "but we're only half full now. Minors on this wing, men over there." He gestured left and then right.

"How many live here?"

"We can hold a max of sixteen," he said. "We've got nine right now; most of them are at work. Sometimes they rotate out quickly—they go back home or they don't like to follow our rules. We're pretty strict. Other times, like with Jerome, they hang here longer."

He ushered Gigi into a room with two sets of bunk beds neatly made with white sheets and army blankets. Milk crates stacked at the ends of the beds held personal belongings, while clothes hung from multicolored pegs along the walls. "That's Kungfu's stuff," Nutt said, pointing to a blue milk crate and the blue pegs.

It was a pitifully small collection. A pair of jeans and a sweatshirt hung from the pegs, and Gigi quickly patted the pockets. Nothing. A couple of pairs of socks and a pair of BVDs were neatly folded in the milk crate along with a battered paperback stamped with the name of a used-book store. A five-dollar bill fell out of the book when Gigi held it upside down and riffled the pages. "Would Kungfu have left without this?" Gigi asked Nutt, waving the bill.

He stroked his beard and shrugged. "Hard to know. Maybe he forgot it was there."

"If you're down to your last few bucks, you don't forget it's there," Gigi said, thinking of the hundred dollars she had squirreled away in her lingerie drawer and the sixty-three dollars in her purse. Since Les dumped her and ran off with all their money, leaving her nothing but the house, the Hummer, and a half interest in Swift Investigations, she'd had to keep close track of all her pennies.

"Not much of anyplace to keep valuables, is there?"

"These men mostly don't have valuables, Gigi," Nutt pointed out. "What they value, they keep with them. Kungfu had a backpack, as I recall, a red one. I'm sure his camera's in there."

"Camera?"

"That boy was always taking pictures." Nutt smiled. "He had a digital camera, a nice one, he said was a present for his sixteenth birthday."

"Where was he from?"

"China, I think."

Gigi was startled, having expected him to say California or New York or even Denver. "Is he an illegal?"

"Undoubtedly," Nutt said, amused by her shock. "He didn't share his story with me, but his English was sketchy, and I got the feeling he wasn't in the country legally. It's not unusual, you know."

"I know." Certainly she knew there were plenty of illegals in El Paso County, but she'd thought most of them were Mexicans like the domestic staff and yard workers employed in her

Broadmoor neighborhood. She thought about Angelica, the maid who'd cleaned for her BLL (Before Les Left), and her insistence on being paid in cash. Maybe she had aided and abetted an illegal alien. "How did he end up here, then?" she asked Nutt. "Are you allowed to take in illegals?" She bent to replace the book in Kungfu's milk crate.

"Our charter is a liberal one," he said proudly, putting a hand to her elbow to usher her out of the room. "We don't ask questions. Sometimes a social worker will refer a teen here, but more often they just show up on the doorstep. Word of mouth on the street, I guess. As long as they're drug free and adhere to our rules, we take them in if we have room."

They descended the stairs to the entry hall. "How do you fund this place?" Gigi asked.

"Donations," Nutt said. "Jill, our director of development, spends all her time writing grants, planning fund-raisers, and hobnobbing with all the agencies and people most likely to open their wallets. It keeps us afloat, barely."

"It's a great cause," Gigi said. She pulled a ten-dollar bill out of her purse and handed it to him, wishing it could be more. "I'd like to help."

"How kind." He smiled again.

Gigi felt herself flush. This was not a good moment for a hot flash.

"Is there a Mr. Goldman?"

"Les? He's not . . . I mean, we're not . . . I'm divorced." Gigi fanned herself and wished she could take off her jacket, but it would look odd since she was on the verge of leaving.

"Me, too," Nutt said. "Look, would you like to have dinner sometime?"

Gigi hardly registered that he was asking her for a date. Every inch of flesh on her body prickled with heat. She was going to explode if she couldn't cool down. Gasping, she reached for the door and yanked it open. A refreshing blast straight from the Arctic blew in. Nutt stared at her as she stepped through the door and turned her face into the wind like a dog at a car window, arms held away from her body. "I'm late . . . late for another appointment," she said over her shoulder. An appointment made a less humiliating excuse for her headlong departure than "I'm a menopausal wreck being tortured by hormones run amok." She tripped stepping off the stoop but caught herself before she fell.

"Are you okay?" Nutt's voice held equal parts concern and confusion. He took a step toward her but stopped when she held up a hand.

"Fine. Thank you . . . most helpful . . . yes." She could feel herself turning even redder, if possible, this time from embarrassment.

"Yes?"

"Dinner."

She'd walk to Tattoo4U, Gigi decided, although the hot flash was starting to subside. Exercising more was one of her New Year's resolutions—along with lose thirty pounds—and a brisk two-block walk would be a good start. It would also give her time to plan her strategy. She had the photo of Kungfu Father Dan had given Charlie; it wasn't much to work with. Mature trees stretched their bare branches overhead, and their roots buckled the sidewalk, making walking hazardous. She passed a Laundromat, a small liquor store, and a convenience store with advertisements in Spanish and some Oriental language before sighting Tattoo4U.

She'd never been in a tattoo parlor, but the small storefront across the street seemed innocuous. Lighted letters spelled out TAT OO4U over the windows. She waited for the light, then crossed, a twinge of apprehension tweaking her. The shop had painted-over windows so she couldn't see inside. Taking a deep breath, she pushed open the door. A bell jingled. Inside, Gigi spotted a counter with a cash register, walls full of photos and drawings of tattoo designs, a young couple arguing in the back, and a middle-aged woman studying a selection of butterfly designs to the right of the door. A large bald man with a long gingery beard was applying a tattoo, Gigi assumed, to the inside of a young man's forearm. He sat in a chair with his arm stretched across a table, watching closely as the tattooer—tattooist?—worked a foot pedal and maneuvered the needle contraption that looked like some of the power tools Les used to buy at Home Depot. Gigi shuddered and looked away, not wanting to see how the needle punctured the skin, or whatever it did.

Without looking up, the man said, "Be right with you, doll." His accent sounded Australian.

"No hurry," Gigi said faintly.

"What do you think of this one?" the woman to her right asked, holding up a picture of a green butterfly about one inch square. She was shorter than Gigi with badly permed mouse-brown hair. Hazel eyes framed with stubby lashes regarded Gigi expectantly.

"Pardon me?" Gigi asked, not sure the woman was talking to her.

"Or do you like this one better?" The woman held up another butterfly, this one in yellow and black with a swallowtail.

Was this woman, who must certainly be her age or older, really going to get a tattoo? Gigi goggled at her. "Is it . . . are you . . . where . . . ?"

"Right here," the woman said, slapping her right butt cheek. She chortled at Gigi's expression. "It's my sixtieth birthday tomorrow, and I decided that it was time for a new me. I got my hair done"—she fluffed the mousy curls—"and now I'm getting a butterfly on my derriere."

Gigi hoped the tattoo turned out better than the hair.

"You only live once, you know. That's what I told Burt. He's all for it." She nodded decisively. "What are you getting?"

"Me?" Gigi took a step back. "I'm not—" She stopped, wondering if she might get more information from the shop owner if she were a potential customer. "That is, I'm thinking about it. I'm not sure what . . ." She dropped her voice to a whisper. "Can't you get hepatitis or something from tattoos?"

"Only if the needles aren't sterile," she said, "but they use a new needle for every customer here. Isn't that right, Graham?"

"Right, doll," the bald man said, still not looking up. Gigi was pretty sure he had no idea what the woman had said.

The arguing couple pushed past Gigi to get to the door.

"If you really loved me, you'd get it," the girl said, tucking her hands into the kangaroo pouch of her sweatshirt and bumping the door open with her shoulder.

"But 'Christina Elizabeth' is too long," the boy said, trying to reason with her. "It would go all the way around my—"

The door closed behind them, leaving Gigi to imagine where the tattoo was supposed to go.

"The green one," the woman beside Gigi announced. "I've made my decision, Graham," she called to the man still hunched over the man's forearm. "I'm going with the green butterfly."

"Great, doll." The machine stopped whirring, and he looked up, sizing up Gigi and her companion. "Now? I'm about done here." He carefully applied a square Band-Aid to the customer's arm, but not before Gigi noticed how red and puffy the skin was. She looked away.

"Leave the bandage on for twenty-four hours, mate, and then use the Tattoo Goo three times a day. You know the drill." He slipped a tube of ointment into a small brown paper bag and handed it to the young man.

"Right, Graham. Thanks, dude." The newly tattooed man left, holding his right arm at a funny angle.

Gigi waited while the other woman talked to Graham and agreed to come back at nine the next morning to have her green butterfly applied. "Happy birthday," Gigi said as the woman left.

"So, what were you thinking about, doll?" Graham asked Gigi as the door closed. "You look like a daffodil, or maybe a ladybug." He rose and got a binder from the counter. Flipping pages, he turned it for Gigi to see a photo of a ladybug tattoo on a smooth, cellulite-free thigh. It *was* kind of cute.

Aghast at the thought, Gigi said, "I'm not sure yet. I'm not even sure I want a tattoo, but a friend of mine recommended this place."

Looking as if he didn't particularly care whether Gigi got a tattoo or not, Graham replaced the binder and said, "Yeah? Who?"

"His name is Kungfu," Gigi said, pulling the photo out of her purse. She unfolded it and spread it on the counter. "Him." She pointed.

"I don't remember anyone like him," Graham said after a brief glance. His response was too quick, Gigi thought. He combed his fingers through his wiry beard, gaze straying back to the photo. "What did he get?"

"Get?"

"The tat?"

"Oh," Gigi said. "Um, he never showed me."

Graham shrugged lumpy shoulders as a phone rang in the back room. "Gotta get the phone," he said, already turning his back to Gigi. "Whyn't you come back when you make a decision, doll, 'kay?" He lumbered into the back room, closing the door behind him.

Gigi refolded the photo and tucked it into her purse, convinced Graham was lying—but why? It was clear the photo meant something to the man, but Gigi recognized a brick wall when she came up against one. *Maybe I need to stake the place out,* she thought with anticipation. She could use some of the new PI gadgets she'd found online and hadn't had a chance to try out yet. Charlie thought they were a waste of money, but Gigi just knew the technology would boost their bottom line. She was only slightly dismayed when she remembered this was a pro bono case. Well, the stakeout would be a good trial for the gadgets, anyway. She tried to keep up her cover story by glancing at a few designs on the way out but barely slowed down as she headed for the door.

11

I offered to treat Kendall to a late breakfast at Denny's and listened to her dish on the way about the international skating community with its rivalries, judging controversies, love affairs, and endorsement deals.

"When does anyone find time to skate?" I asked, fascinated despite myself. We settled into a booth. The smells of coffee and syrup wafted around us, along with the sounds of clattering silverware and a baby crying. "It sounds like *The Young and the Restless* on ice."

"Except it's *real*," she said, prepared to be pissed off if I was dissing her sport. She ordered an egg white omelet and dry toast from the hovering waitress and correctly interpreted my raised eyebrows. "I can't afford to gain an ounce and have my costumes not fit. They're expensive."

"What's it cost to become a skater?" I only ordered a Pepsi, earning a look from the server that either meant she was worried about her tip or she disapproved of cold caffeine for breakfast.

"You mean an Olympic-caliber skater? Including coaching fees, ice time, travel, skates, costumes, and everything?"

I nodded.

"About a hundred thousand a year."

I spewed Pepsi across the table. "Dollars?"

"Uh-huh." She ticked items off on her fingers. "An hour of ice time alone is over a hundred bucks, and the top skaters train up to six hours a day. There's also PT—physical therapy—a sports psychologist, massages, ballet classes, the choreographer . . . I could go on."

"Is that what your mom pays for you to skate?" I was suddenly looking at Gigi's money troubles in a whole new light.

"Not half that," Kendall said. "I don't go to a lot of competitions, and we can't afford that many lessons." She pouted. "If only my mom—"

I forestalled the whining. "How good are you?"

"I was nineteenth at the national championships last year. Junior," she explained.

I looked at the slim girl opposite me with new respect. "That sounds pretty good to me, to be nineteenth in the country."

"It's not good enough," she said. "Not good enough for the BSC—Broadmoor Skating Club—or United States Figure Skating to contribute to my training. And I'm not getting any younger." She gathered up her purse and let her napkin fall to the floor. "Are we going or what?" She stalked toward the door.

I took my time finishing my Pepsi, paying the bill, and visiting the restroom. Kendall was waiting for me on the sidewalk when I emerged, the tip of her pert nose red, her hands tucked into the sleeves of her teal hoodie because she'd refused to wear a jacket when Gigi prompted her. Why are teenagers allergic to outerwear? I frequently saw high schoolers waiting for

84

the bus near my house wearing nothing but T-shirts, jeans, and flip-flops in subfreezing temperatures.

"Ready?" I asked pleasantly, unlocking the Outback's door.

She plunked onto the seat without answering and stared pointedly out the passenger window as I started the car and pulled out of the parking lot. "Where are we going?" she asked after a moment, still not looking at me.

"I'm going to see Dara Peterson. I tried to call her, but she's not answering her phone. I can drop you by the office."

"No!" Her head whipped around. "I mean, I'd like to go with you. I could help."

I hesitated, not wanting to be saddled with a disaffected adolescent.

"Please?"

―――――

I had time to regret my moment of weakness on the ride to Dara Peterson's house. To hear Kendall talk, Dara was a conniving bitch whose last name should be Machiavelli and who couldn't skate as well as a pug. Given Dara and Dmitri's international achievements, I discounted most of what she told me, wondering if she was jealous of a girl only five years older who had accomplished so much more. How sad, I thought, to feel that you were a has-been, or worse, a never-was, before your Sweet Sixteen was even on the horizon.

Dara lived with her parents in a house across from Ute Valley Park. It was a medium-sized two-story home, virtually indistinguishable from hundreds of others in the neighborhood. A woman wearing a brown wool suit opened the door when I rang. She had wiry strands of gray in her brown hair and looked harassed.

"Yes?" Her voice was not welcoming. Yips sounded from

behind her, and a golden retriever puppy skidded into the hall. "No, Honey," she said, restraining the pup, who was eager to greet us.

I introduced myself and explained I was looking for Dara. Kendall dropped to her knees to fondle the puppy and let it lick her face. It was all paws and tongue.

"Dara spent the night at LeAnn's," her mother said with an exasperated sigh. "They were going straight to the rink this morning."

I didn't tell Mrs. Peterson that it was unlikely Dara had gotten anywhere near the rink. She clearly hadn't heard about the attack on Bobrova. "What's LeAnn's last name?" I asked.

"Merculies." She supplied a phone number. "Look, I've got to get back to work. I came home over lunch to let Honey out. Why did we get a puppy?"

She didn't seem to expect an answer, scooping the wriggling ball of yellow fuzz into her arms. Yelps and whines issued from what I guessed was the kitchen as Mrs. Peterson crated the puppy. She reappeared, trying to pick long yellow hairs off her suit. "If she's not at LeAnn's, you might try Maggie Moo's," she offered, joining us on the porch and locking the door. "When you catch up to her, tell her I expect her to walk Honey before dinner."

"Will do." It occurred to me that the Petersons probably knew Dmitri pretty well since he'd been their daughter's partner for seven years or so. Despite the woman's obvious haste, I stopped her with a question. "Did Dara tell you that Dmitri Fane is missing, Mrs. Peterson?"

She gave me a measuring look out of clear hazel eyes. Faint crow's feet branched from the corners, and I guessed she was in her midforties. "Sometimes I rue the day we met that man," she said.

I raised my brows. "Why?"

She hesitated, glancing at Kendall, who was kicking pebbles from the rock border and watching them roll down the driveway. "Don't I know you?" she asked. "From the Ice Hall. Kelsey, isn't it?"

"Kendall Goldman," the girl said, looking surprised and pleased at being recognized.

"You did pretty well at Junior Nationals last year, didn't you?" Mrs. Peterson asked. "Look, I forgot to give Honey her treat, would you mind?" She unlocked the door again. "They're in a box on the pantry floor. Just one or two."

Having disposed of Kendall in an efficient way I admired, Mrs. Peterson turned back to me. "Dmitri Fane is a fabulous skater, very athletic, but very lyrical, too, and he takes good care of Dara on the ice. She's a household name with endorsement opportunities—"

She sounded like her daughter was Tiger Woods.

"—largely because of Dmitri. Off the ice, he's irresponsible. He gave her her first drink when she was fifteen. Fifteen! She was so hungover the next day I had to keep her home from school. Then he talked her into a tattoo last year—even paid for it. He lives in the fast lane. He drinks more than is good for him, and he hangs with a rough crowd."

"Other skaters?"

"No." She shook her head. "I don't know where he knows them from. They don't usually come around the Ice Hall, but one of them was there last week. They had an argument. I was there to pick up Dara—her car was in the shop—and I bumped into them in the hall. Dmitri's friend was yelling and so red in the face I thought he was going to have a stroke. He was saying something about cards, but he shut up fast when he saw me."

Cards . . . maybe Dmitri gambled. It seemed in keeping with Mrs. Peterson's description of his lifestyle.

A car whooshed past, and her eyes followed it as it disappeared around a corner. I shivered as a gust of wind goosed a plastic bag into a shrub.

"Who was he?"

She shrugged. "We didn't do introductions."

"What did he look like?"

"Older . . . my age, at least. Kind of tough. Dark hair and eyes, medium height, carrying a bit of weight around his middle. He had a splint on his nose like it'd been broken. Why?"

"I'm trying to track down Dmitri's friends, see if anyone's heard from him or knows where he might be. Dara seems really worried about him."

Mrs. Peterson's lips curved in a small smile. "She's my daughter and I love her, but she does have drama queen tendencies. He'll turn up. He might be a bit of a flake, but he's passionate about skating. Look, I've really got to get back to work," she said as Kendall appeared at the door. Jingling her keys, she trotted down the sidewalk to the brown LeSabre parked at the curb.

"I wish we had a dog," Kendall said, back in pout mode.

"You do," I reminded her. "Nolan?" Nolan was Gigi's shih tzu, a fierce little mop of a dog not best suited for surveillance work. He'd been instrumental in landing Gigi in the ER with a broken arm a few months back.

"I mean a real dog, like a golden retriever or a Lab," Kendall said.

I sympathized with her but didn't want to say so. "You've got dog hair on your sweatshirt," I pointed out instead.

I called LeAnn Merculies from the Petersons' front porch as Kendall picked long yellow hairs off her clothes, only to be told Dara had not spent the night at her apartment and hadn't been expected. "Did you hear about Coach Bobrova?" LeAnn asked after suggesting I look for Dara at Maggie Moo's. "Isn't it the awfullest?"

"The awfullest," I agreed before dialing the ice cream shop.

Kendall looked a question at me when I hung up. "She's not there," I said, "and her boss is pissed off that she didn't show for her shift."

Kendall wrinkled her brow. "Do you mean our client is missing?"

I overlooked the "our." "Apparently so."

12

Since I didn't know where Mrs. Peterson worked and I didn't have her cell phone number, I wrote a note asking her to call and tucked it between the storm door and the jamb. I didn't want to worry Dara's parents, but bad things were happening to people close to Dmitri, and I thought they should get the police involved sooner rather than later if Dara hadn't turned up by the end of the day.

"What do we do now?" Kendall asked, tugging at the waistband of jeans cut lower than J.Lo's necklines. "Or is the case over because we don't have a client to pay us anymore?"

She had the business instincts of an ambulance-chasing lawyer or a land-raping developer. Those genes must've come from her dad. "Dara's retainer covers a couple more days of work, so I'll keep plugging." I wasn't sure what I'd do after that if Dara was still missing. Maybe her folks would want to hire Swift Investigations.

"So, what's the next step? I think we should search Dmitri's apartment."

"Why?" My tone was damping.

"For clues," she said with her "duh" voice.

No way was I letting the hormonal teenager anywhere near Dmitri's belongings. "We talk to more people who knew Dmitri well," I said. "Skaters. Somebody has to know something." I hoped. "We also find the cabin near Estes Park that may or may not have belonged to Dmitri or Bobrova."

We got in the car, and I backed down the drive. As we merged onto I-25, I dialed Gigi at the office and told her what I knew about the cabin, suggesting she check property records in the names Fane and Bobrova. I listened as she told me about her interviews at Dellert House and the tattoo parlor. "Sure, a stakeout, um-hm, whatever," I told her, distracted by Kendall huffing hot breath onto the car's window and drawing Hello Kitty faces in the condensation. "Stop that! No, not you," I said to Gigi as Kendall sulkily erased the window with her sleeve. "Give me a call when you get something."

I cut the connection and asked Kendall where we were likely to find Dmitri's skating friends, given that the rink was closed. "Angel and Trevor have costume fittings today," she said after a moment's thought. "They're doing a new long program, to the *Firebird Suite*—they've put in side-by-side triple axels and another lift—and Estelle is doing their costumes."

She breathed the word "Estelle" with equal parts envy and awe. Who knew costumes needed designing and weren't bought off the rack in a special section at Target? "Where's her store?"

"She doesn't have a store in Colorado Springs," Kendall said. "She's from Paris. You must have heard of Estelle? She did the wedding dress for Sienna Miller's friend, the one who married Paris Hilton's ex-boyfriend?"

I shook my head, and she rolled her eyes at my ignorance. "Tell me where we can find this Angel and Trevor," I said.

Kendall pulled out a slim pink cell phone and conducted a

brief and cryptic conversation with a friend on the other end. "At Estelle's room at the Broadmoor," she said, flipping the phone closed with an air of satisfaction. "Four oh two."

"Does Estelle design your costumes?" I asked.

"I wish." She relapsed into sulkiness. "My mom's too cheap."

"You could use the money you've made working for us over Christmas break," I suggested.

"Oh, please. That hardly pays for my cell phone."

I was plenty tired of her gimme-gimme-gimme attitude, and I'd have dropped her back at the office except I thought her knowing Angel and Trevor might come in handy.

—~~~—

The Broadmoor is a gracious five-star resort on the southwest side of Colorado Springs. It features golf courses that become points of controversy whenever our semidesert city adopts water rationing because its green lushness sucks up water the way an alcoholic swills martinis. It also has a couple of four- or five-star restaurants and a spa that (Gigi says) is as relaxing as the Garden of Eden. I assume she's talking pre serpent and apple stealing. The Broadmoor and its amenities don't figure into my budget, and cases don't usually bring me this way, so I looked around at the marble and antiques and solicitous staff with covert curiosity tinged with awe. Kendall sailed through the lobby as if it were no more special than a Holiday Inn Express. Considering that the Goldmans had probably wined and dined at the Broadmoor's Charles Court or Penrose Room several times a month before Les left, the hotel probably wasn't worth a second look to her.

She led us directly to the elevators and punched a button before I got on. The doors closed with barely a hiss of sound, and we glided upward. "Let me ask the questions," I cautioned

Kendall as we trod down the carpeted hallway to Estelle's room. A young man with the cowed mien of an assistant's assistant or indentured servant appeared in the doorway as we approached 402. His arms full of spandex, chiffon, and sequins in a rainbow of colors, he didn't close the door as he scurried to the next room. Through the gaping door we heard a gravelly voice with a French accent say, "You have put on weight." I couldn't tell whether the speaker was male or female, but the tone was accusatory. "At least two pounds."

"Poor Angel," Kendall whispered. Her expression belied her sympathy; her delight in hearing the other skater chewed out was apparent.

It was a male voice, though, insouciant and confident, that answered. "Muscle, baby, all muscle. I've been doing some extra weight training. You think it's easy to hold a hundred and five pounds—"

"A hundred and one!" a girl's voice chimed in.

"—over my head with one arm?"

I knocked lightly and went in when there was no response. An open door is an invitation, right? A small foyer opened into a large sitting area with a closed door—the bedroom, I presumed—to the right. A small round platform was set up in the middle of the room, and a young man stood on it, posing like a bodybuilder in a flame-red costume so tight it displayed his muscles in sufficient detail for a drawing in an anatomy text. A girl in a matching costume with a sequined bodice and a short skirt trimmed with feathers glared at the young man, while another assistant—this one female but wearing the same scared-rabbit expression as the young man who'd left the room—pinned up her hem. Trevor and Angel, I presumed.

"What's a costume like that cost?" I whispered to Kendall, finding myself fascinated by the details of this new world.

"Two thou," she whispered back.

Good God. As far as I could tell, that came out to about a buck a sequin. I was pretty sure my entire wardrobe wasn't worth two thousand dollars.

A woman tall enough to play for the Nuggets stood with her arms crossed over a turquoise angora sweater that hung to below her butt. Heavy black hair cropped in bangs straight across her forehead and falling to just above her shoulders framed a bony face devoid of makeup except for eyes fringed by fake lashes. "You call this muscle?" She leaned forward as she spoke and pinched Trevor's waist between her thumb and forefinger.

"Solid muscle, baby." He grinned, apparently not minding the pinch or the accusation. "Read it and weep."

"Pah!" The woman turned away and spotted Kendall and me. "Who are you?" Her tone was brusque but not hostile.

"Charlotte Swift." I pulled out a card and handed it over. "I'm looking for—"

"Kendall! What are you doing here?" The girl in red focused on Kendall, a pucker between her brows. "Don't tell me Estelle's doing your costume?"

"Hi, Angel," Kendall said, twisting her ponytail. "Hi, Trevor."

"Yo, Kenny, 'sup? Whaddaya think of my Firebird threads?" He did a 360 and finished with his biceps flexed at shoulder height. He looked like he belonged on a surfboard, not an ice rink, with streaky blond hair, toothpaste-ad teeth, and dimples.

"You're done, Trevor," Estelle said in a tone that made me wonder if she'd been a middle school teacher before taking up design. She accented Trevor's name on the last syllable—Trev-OR—giving it a Gallic lilt. "Change."

He gave her a mock salute, stepped off the dais, and disappeared into the bedroom.

"You were saying?" Estelle turned back to me. Full on, she looked older than she had in profile, maybe in her early fifties, with almost colorless lips and pale eyes framed by those absurd lashes.

"I was really hoping to talk to Angel and Trevor," I said. "About Dmitri Fane. He's missing, and I've been hired to find him."

"Good riddance, if you ask me." Trevor stood in the doorway, his smile gone, clad now in jeans and a striped rugby shirt. I could see the red costume on the bedroom floor behind him.

"Don't start with that again!" Angel said, putting her fists on her hips. "I can't stand to hear about how he stole Dara away from you one more time. You'd think he'd done a Tonya Harding on your legs, or something, but, no, all he did was pair up with Dara Peterson. So what if they've won a medal or two? This is our year, Trev—don't lose your focus."

Trevor scowled at her. "That championship should've been mine. If Dmitri hadn't—"

"When did you last see him?" I interrupted. "What kind of mood was he in?"

"Why should I help you find him?" Trevor asked, all trace of surfer boy vanished behind slitted eyes. "I hope the bastard stays gone." Slinging a gym bag over his shoulder, he stalked out of the room.

"Trevor, wait!" Kendall scooted out the door after him before I could stop her. I hoped she had a plan for getting home, because I wasn't going to traipse around the multi-acre hotel looking for her.

I exchanged a speaking glance with Estelle.

"He doesn't mean anything by it," Angel said in a soft voice. The fire seemed to have drained out of her with Trevor's departure, and her shoulders slumped.

"I'll finish this." Estelle dismissed the assistant with a curt nod and knelt to put pins in the skirt. "Turn."

Angel pivoted obediently.

"Have you talked to Dmitri lately?" I asked, speaking to the girl's back.

"Friday. At practice. I thought he seemed worried."

I had to strain to hear her words. "Really? About what?"

"I don't know. I don't know him that well. I mean, it's not like Trev and I pal around with him and Dara." She sounded wistful but resigned. "Just he talks to me sometimes. I think he's lonely."

That was a new insight. No one had described Dmitri as lonely. Now that I thought of it, though, no one had given me the name of a best friend, either, or even the names of people he hung out with. Fiona, at the catering company, seemed like the closest thing he had to a friend; at least, she had described him as her best friend. It didn't necessarily go both ways, though.

"If you had to guess, what was he worried about? Something to do with skating? His catering job? Family? A legal or financial problem?"

"It wouldn't be skating," Angel said, her voice wry. "Dmitri doesn't worry about skating. He assumes he'll win." In response to Estelle's pressure on her leg, she turned again until she faced me. "And he doesn't have much family, just his mom. She was out here for a visit a couple of months ago, and she seemed fine then. You know his dad died last November?"

I nodded.

"He was really broken up about that. I found him crying

one day—I think we were the last ones to leave the rink—and he told me a lot about his dad."

"It was a car accident, right?" I tried to remember what Dara had told me.

"Yeah. It was icy. Mr. Fane slid off the road and crashed into a tree. Died instantly, from what I heard. Dmitri was obsessed with it for a while, convinced there was another car involved, but he hasn't talked about it recently. I told my mom—she's a psychologist—and she said that it wasn't unusual for people in Dmitri's situation to want to blame someone else, to look for a scapegoat. She said it was probably hard for him to accept that his dad's carelessness may have caused the accident, or to come to terms with . . . with the randomness of it all."

That made some sense. It takes a certain amount of maturity to accept that life is not all about you personally, to accept that bad things—disease, accidents, home invasions—happen to good people, as some popular book put it. Even though he was twenty-six, I didn't have the impression that Dmitri was maxing out the maturity scale; quite the opposite, in fact.

"Do you know where he might have gone? I'm interested in any ideas, no matter how far out they might seem." I was at the grasping-at-straws stage of the investigation, and I hated it. I couldn't seem to grab hold of Dmitri, get a feel for who he was, untangle his relationships.

"*Fini,*" Estelle said. She picked up stray pins from the carpet and straightened to her full height. Without a word, she crossed the room and exited through the hall door.

Angel stepped off the platform. "Let me think about it while I change." She ducked into the bedroom, leaving the door cracked. "Y'know," she called, "I forgot. I saw Dmitri Saturday. He was coming out of the Whole Foods, the one by the DSW?"

I knew the store she meant. It was on the east side of

Academy, a couple of blocks down from Swift Investigations. "What did he say?"

"I didn't talk to him. I was going into the DSW, and I saw him come out of the Whole Foods pushing a cart of groceries. I waved, but he didn't see me. He was talking with a guy. Arguing, maybe."

"Who?"

She pulled the bedroom door wide and strolled into the living room wearing jeans and a sweater. A chopstick skewered her light brown hair into a messy knot at the back of her head. "I dunno. Not a skater. He was older and a bit overweight. He had brownish hair, I think. I really didn't pay much attention. Is it important?"

"Maybe." I thought about what she'd told me. Based on my brief reconnoiter of Dmitri's apartment, he hadn't stashed a cartful of food there. Did that suggest that he'd been stocking up for a trip, maybe a trip to the mountain cabin? Was the man she'd seen him with the same man Mrs. Peterson had seen? Could he be a boyfriend? A sugar daddy? I had no clue. It'd be nice to know what they were arguing about.

"I've got to go," Angel said with an apologetic grimace. "Trev and I are talking to a new coach."

"You trained with Bobrova?"

"Yeah, like Dara and Dmitri."

"That must have been cozy." I thought of Trevor's anger toward Dmitri. How awkward for Dara. Then again, she might have liked having two men fight over her . . . some women get off on that. If I caught up with her, I'd ask her.

"Bobrova thought the competition between us made all of us train harder, especially Dmitri and Trev," the girl said. "It's okay most of the time. Only, every now and then things get tense, you know? Trev—" She bit back whatever she was going to say. "Have you heard how she is?"

She was back to Bobrova, and I realized I hadn't called the hospital or Montgomery to see how the coach was. Maybe she was conscious and could talk about the assault. Maybe she'd like to talk to me, the woman who had saved her life. I'm not above capitalizing on gratitude when the opportunity arises. I'd swing by the hospital as soon as I was done here. "No."

"I've really got to go," Angel said, inching toward the door. "I hope you find Dmitri." She slipped through the door, passing Estelle, who returned carrying an armload of costumes.

I had started to follow Angel, murmuring apologies for having interrupted the fitting, when the tall woman said, "That one didn't fall far from the tree."

I wrinkled my brow. "Angel?"

Estelle shook her head so the ends of her dyed black hair whisked against her shoulders. "Dmitri. I'm sorry; I couldn't help overhearing."

"No, it's okay. So you knew his dad?"

"I knew both Stuart and Irena. I designed their costumes when I was first starting out. It is fair to say they gave me my start. They were already established—world champions—when I showed them my designs."

I watched as she draped the costumes individually over the curved back of the sofa, her large hands surprisingly graceful as she smoothed and tucked the fabrics. If she was in her fifties as I guessed, she was certainly old enough to have worked with Dmitri's parents. "What were they like?"

She turned, appraising me from irises so pale I couldn't tell if they were blue or gray. "Stuart Fane was a lovely man," she said finally. "A gentleman in the true sense of the word: gentle. An exquisite skater."

"Dmitri takes after him?" I asked doubtfully.

"*Non,*" she said scornfully. "*Absolument, non.* Well, only in that he, too, is a once-in-a-generation skater. Of course you know Stuart was not his biological father?"

I remembered Dara saying Fane had adopted Dmitri when he married the boy's mother. "But you said acorn . . . tree?"

"Dmitri takes after his *maman,*" Estelle said. "Agnes!"

The female assistant appeared, hovering in the doorway. "Yes, Estelle?"

"Nicole's costume." She pointed to an emerald chiffon number with rhinestones spattered across the bodice. "It needs more stones along the neckline."

The assistant nodded her head. "I see what you mean. I'll take care of it." In a blink, she snatched the costume up and disappeared again.

"That one will go far," Estelle said with an approving nod. "Pierre . . ." She rolled her eyes, the fringe of fake lashes giving her an almost comical air. "He is my sister's son."

Nodding with understanding—nepotism sucked—I prodded, "Dmitri?"

"So like Irena," she murmured. "That woman had focus—I'll give her that. Focus on her skating and focus on Dmitri. She hadn't wanted a baby, she told me—afraid it would derail her skating career—but by the time I met them, she adored that boy. She taught him to skate, scared away bullies, challenged coaches who said he wasn't good enough."

"Doesn't sound so bad to me," I said, thinking of my own absentee parents. "What about Stuart?"

"Ah, Stuart loved him, too," she said, her expression softening. "His death was a tragedy." She turned away to fuss with the costumes, but not before I caught the gleam of wetness in her eyes. She'd loved Stuart Fane, I realized, and been jealous of Dmitri's mother. She must have been plain and awkward as a young woman, not yet confident in her height and style, while Irena Fane, as a pair skater, was probably petite and lovely. I felt inexplicably sorry for the young Estelle.

"Do you have any idea where Dmitri might be?" I asked when she remained silent.

"None at all," she said, her tone brusque now, as if to make up for her brief display of emotion, "but he'll turn up in time for Nationals. Skating is everything to him." She paused as if reconsidering. "And winning. Skating and winning."

13

Kendall was waiting by the car when I got back to it, jiggling from foot to foot with suppressed excitement. For the first time, she reminded me of her mother. "Guess what Trevor said," she ordered as we belted ourselves in.

"He confessed to kidnapping Dmitri and promised to take you to the dungeon where he's holding him prisoner."

"No, he—"

"He has proof Dmitri is a terrorist who's going to bring the world to its knees by detonating a bioweapon at the next big skating event."

She crossed her arms over her chest and sat back with a huff. "Fine, don't take me seriously."

A twinge of remorse zapped me. I looked at her stony profile. "I'm sorry, Kendall. I was kidding. Anything you got from Trevor would be useful. Heaven knows I haven't dug up anything yet."

Mollified, she slewed in her seat to face me. "Well, you know he was really pissed when he left Estelle's room. I caught up with him in the elevator and, well, I let him think I'm on his side."

"His side?"

"Yeah, you know, on the Dara thing. I told him how rotten it was that Dmitri had stolen Dara away from him. Like, it was totally unfair. Boys like it when you take their side." She nodded sagely.

I bit back a smile and prompted, "And he said . . . ?"

"He said he knew for a fact that Dmitri was splitting up with Dara." She sat back with a satisfied air, knowing she'd surprised me.

"Really? Did he say why? Or how he knew this?"

"No." She looked disgruntled. "I asked him, but he closed his mouth tight like he was sorry he'd said anything. When the elevator got to the lobby, he took off."

I mulled over this piece of information, making the turn from Circle Drive onto the I-25 ramp. "So, would that mean Trevor thinks he can get back together with Dara?"

"He couldn't do that. Not before the Olympics, anyway. You qualify as a pair—it's not like you can swap partners whenever you want. Besides, there's no way they could learn new routines, or . . ." She shook her head rapidly, unable to verbalize the complexities. "There's no way."

I believed her. "I think I need to talk to Mr. Trevor Anthony."

"So I helped?" She looked at me eagerly, a blond Yorkie waiting for a treat.

"You did. Good job." I smiled at her.

"Does that mean I get a raise?"

My laughter put her back in moody teenager mode, and her silence lasted until we arrived back at the office. As we pulled into the unusually crowded lot, her eyes got big. "What's that about?"

My gaze followed her pointing finger to a small crowd—maybe fifteen people—carrying signs and marching up and down the sidewalk in front of Domenica's. Parking in my usual spot, I got out slowly, trying to read the pickets without betraying interest. God knows I didn't want to attract the attention of a marcher who might want to convert me to her cause. Most of the marchers were female, although there were a couple of men, both of whom had been AARP eligible for at least three decades.

The sign nearest me said KEEP SMUT OUT in stenciled red letters.

"What smut?" Kendall asked, betraying more curiosity than distaste.

I tried to shush her, but her voice had carried to the marchers, and a thin woman with a sign reading WHEN PORN/ WAS BORN/WE ALL MOURN strode to us. A parka hood rimmed with fake fur framed a bony face with strong black brows and a nose like a ski slope. Righteous indignation (or maybe the freezing wind) stained her cheeks red. She carried a clipboard in her other hand and sixty years of dissatisfaction in her face.

"Very poetic," I said, nodding at the sign, hoping to distract her.

"Isn't it?" A pleased look lightened her face. "I think poetry is so much more powerful than prose."

"Absolutely," I said. More powerful still if the verb tenses matched. I was no English major, but "Was born/We all mourn" bugged me. "I've always liked 'Nothing sucks like an Electrolux,'" I offered. "The vacuum, remember? Very powerful."

Poetry Woman looked offended.

Maybe "sucks" was an unfortunate turn of phrase in this context. I tried to edge Kendall toward the office door.

She didn't take the hint. "What smut?" she asked again.

Poetry Woman slid her eyes toward Domenica's. "In there," she said in a hushed voice. "That store sells—" She broke off as if suddenly assessing Kendall's age. "Well, it sells products that aren't suitable for a child your age to even know about." She primmed her mouth into a tight purse.

"Like vibrators and stuff? Cool."

The woman gaped at Kendall, then bent her flinty gaze on me. I could see she was debating calling Child Protective Services to accuse me of corrupting a minor.

A news van pulled into the lot, generating a twitter of excitement among the protesters. Kendall's eyes lit up as a handsome reporter from the local CBS affiliate climbed out of the van. She smoothed her hair and reached for the lip gloss in her pocket. I did not think Gigi would appreciate seeing her daughter discuss the merits of a sex toys store on the nightly news. "Inside," I ordered her.

"But—"

"It's time to study your catechism."

"Huh?"

"Kids," I said with a "what can you do?" smile at the picketer as Kendall stuck her lower lip out and reluctantly trudged the four steps to Swift Investigations. I heaved a sigh of relief as she disappeared inside, grabbed the leaflet Poetry Woman thrust at me, and ducked into the office before the reporter got within recording distance.

Once inside, I balled up the page and tossed it toward the trash can.

"Did you hear about Domenica's?" Gigi asked, with a sideways look at her daughter.

Kendall had settled at her card table and was busy painting her fingernails cotton candy pink.

"Hard not to." I jerked my head toward the demonstrators outside. They were chanting something now, probably for the benefit of the news crew. Thankfully, the words were muffled. "Have you been over to check out her stock? Maybe she's having an after-Christmas sale."

"Charlie!" Gigi stared at me, then giggled when she saw my grin.

"I don't know why they're kicking up such a fuss about a few dildos," Kendall said nonchalantly. "It's not like you can't buy them, like, all over the Web." She blew on her wet nails.

"What do you know about—? Where did you hear—?" Gigi goggled at her daughter, clearly agitated. "We are canceling our Internet—we can't afford it anyway."

I'd never heard Gigi sound stern. I didn't know she was capable of "stern." I suppressed the urge to yell, "Go, Gigi!"

"Mo-om!" Kendall shot to her feet, face a picture of outrage.

"Maybe Kendall should take the rest of the day off," I suggested. "We're not going to get any customers through here with all that going on outside. This might be a good time for me to head up to Estes Park if you found Dmitri's cabin."

"It's Yuliya Bobrova's cabin," Gigi said, crossing to Kendall and trying to hug her. "I'm sorry, sugah."

For what? Trying to protect her daughter from Internet smut?

Kendall held up her hands to fend off the hug. "Now look what you've done—my nails are smudged." She flounced to her table.

So much for acting parental. Still, Gigi'd actually been angry with Kendall for 6.2 seconds—a record in my brief experience with the Goldmans.

"Why don't you call your brother? He can pick you up." Gigi returned to her desk and sorted through a stack of papers. "The title's in her name. Here's the address. She's owned it since 1990. There's no phone listing."

I glanced at my watch: one thirty. I was suddenly eager to get away. The morning's discovery of Bobrova—was it really almost nine hours ago?—and the day's interviews, not to mention my injuries from yesterday, had worn me out. I wanted time alone to think and sort through the bits and pieces of the Fane puzzle without interruption. The two-and-a-half-hour drive to Estes Park was just the ticket. If I left now, I'd arrive before dark.

I told Gigi my plan. "Oh, and I'll stop by Memorial and see if I can talk to Bobrova on my way out of town," I added, hoping the woman was conscious. The sight of Gigi taking notes as I talked jogged my memory. "Didn't you say you're staking out a tattoo parlor? Something to do with that kid Dan wants to find?"

She nodded. "I'm sure the man that works there—Graham— recognized Kungfu's photo. In fact," she leaned closer and dropped her voice, "it wouldn't surprise me if there was skull-duggery going on at Tattoo4U."

"Really? Skullduggery?" I'd never heard the word used in conversation and wondered if she'd picked it up from one of the PI magazines she devoured. "Well, it wouldn't be the first time there's been a little back-room drug dealing at a tattoo parlor. Try not to blow the place up."

Gigi looked hurt. "That only happened once. Besides, I won't be going into the place; I'm going to try out some of the new long-range surveillance equipment. The parabolic microphone should work great, and maybe I'll take the NVGs"—she used the acronym self-consciously—"in case I'm there after dark."

"Don't get caught." I thought her chances of getting a lead on Kungfu were nil, but if it gave her joy to try out the spy gadgets she'd insisted Swift Investigations purchase, I wasn't going to stop her. After all, how much trouble could she get into with a microphone and some night-vision goggles?

--*mm*--

Memorial Hospital on the north side of Colorado Springs is a modern-looking building of stone and curves and glass. When I arrived after packing an overnight bag at home and leaving a note on Dan's door, the parking lot was mostly empty. At almost three o'clock on a Friday afternoon, the doctors had left for their ski condos in Aspen and Steamboat. Visitors were taking a break before sitting with their sick loved ones for a couple of hours in the evening. I hurried across the windswept parking lot and into the lobby. With its open plan, cozy seating areas, and Pikes Peak views, it looked more like the lobby of an upscale hotel than a hospital. Yuliya Bobrova was still alive, the woman staffing the information desk told me, but in ICU. She wouldn't update me on Bobrova's condition beyond "not dead." Following the signs, I elevatored up to the ICU and bumped into Montgomery as I got off. Literally.

He grabbed my shoulders to steady me, and the warmth of his hands tingled clear down to my toes. He smiled down at me. "I've fantasized about you running into my arms, Charlie," he said, "but I didn't think it would be in a hospital."

"I don't want to hear about your fantasies," I lied.

"You're right. So much more satisfying to act them out, don't you think?" The glint in his eyes made me catch my breath. My pulse thrummed in my fingertips.

Vaguely aware that I should move away from him, I found

myself trapped by his gaze. He had such warm brown eyes. Caring, seductive. I licked my lips, and his eyes darkened. For a moment, I thought he was going to pull me into the nearest empty room, but the elevator dinged open behind me and a clutch of red-hatted women got off, holding bouquets of balloons and cookies.

"Is this maternity?" one woman asked, peering around. "We're looking for Marjorie's grandbaby."

I took a couple of steps away from Montgomery and worked on slowing my heartbeat as he directed the women to the correct floor.

"Bobrova's still unconscious," he said, returning to my side. He nodded to a room where a still figure lay surrounded by machines with tiny lights blinking green, yellow, or red. A nurse hovered over her, squeezing the bag hanging from an IV pole. "The docs aren't sure if she'll make it. Skull fracture, hematoma, shock, a couple cracked vertebrae, surgery to relieve pressure on the brain, and I don't remember what else. Even if she lives they're not sure what she'll remember. Hell, she may not remember her name or what an ice skate is."

I took in the sadness of that in silence. How much memory did you have to lose before you weren't you anymore? Would I still be me if I forgot the parents who serially abandoned me with various relatives so they could missionary around the globe? What about if I forgot my first kiss with what's-his-name, or my air force commissioning ceremony, or the thrill of skiing Mary Jane with the rising sun rinsing the snow with pink? I shook my head to dislodge the melancholia. "Bummer. I guess that means she wasn't any help with ID'ing her attacker."

"Nope."

"Have you got any leads?"

Without answering, he cocked his head and studied me. "We got a call from Sally Peterson. Says her daughter Dara's missing. Know anything about it?"

"Not really." I filled him in on my conversations with Dara and my own unease when I couldn't reach her that morning. "It hasn't even been twenty-four hours—why are you on it?"

"Given the circumstances, Captain Kean decided to issue a BOLO. He's concerned there's a connection between the attack on Bobrova and Peterson's disappearance."

Something in his voice alerted me. "You think Dara's a suspect?" I moderated my volume when a nurse behind a semicircular desk shot us a "shut up already" look. "Why would she try to kill her coach?"

"Too many laps? Coach Grimsler used to make us run laps when—"

"This is ice-skating, not football."

"Boy, your sense of humor really suffers when you get up early. How'd you make it in the air force? Isn't their motto 'We do more before nine than most people do all day'?" One side of his mouth slanted up.

"That's the army, and quit trying to change the subject. If you think Dara attacked Bobrova, do you think she had anything to do with Fane's disappearance?"

Montgomery sobered. "Maybe." He drew the word out, and I could see him considering it. "I don't know why she'd've hired you, though, if she offed him or made him disappear."

"She's a nineteen-year-old kid," I said, exasperated. "Quit talking like she's some Mafia kingpin who can have people 'offed' or 'disappeared.'"

"I'm not saying she's guilty of anything," Montgomery said, "but I'd like to have a conversation with her." His expression grew serious. "Besides, if she's not the perp, she might be in danger. You will have her call me if you run across her." He made it a statement.

"I'll let her know you'd like to chat," I said, determined to wring every ounce of information from Dara Peterson before passing on Montgomery's message, "and you'll let me know if anything changes with Bobrova, right?" I snugged my purse under my arm and turned to go. Trying to talk with the injured woman was clearly pointless, even if I'd been allowed into her room.

"Where are you off to?" He beat me to the elevator and held the door for me when it dinged open.

"The mountains." As the doors shushed closed, I felt a tingle at being alone with Montgomery in such a small space. He stood close enough for our arms to brush, and the fine hairs on my forearms stood up at the brief contact.

"Skiing?"

He half-turned as he spoke, and I found myself pressed into the corner of the elevator, a stainless steel rail digging into my back at waist height. I looked up, and my explanation died on my lips at the expression in his eyes. I gripped the rail with both hands to keep from flinging my arms around his neck.

"I could go with you," he said in a low voice, bending so his lips almost touched my ear. "Skiing, a soak in the hot tub, a glass of brandy in front of a crackling fire . . . sounds like fun." His lips grazed my ear, then whispered across my cheek to the corner of my mouth.

My mind ran with the scene he sketched, adding a sheepskin rug and subtracting unnecessary distractions like clothes. My whole body buzzed and I felt light-headed. My lips parted. If I turned my head slightly . . .

The elevator thudded to a halt, and Montgomery put a quick body's width between us as the doors opened to admit two orderlies wheeling a gurney.

"We'll have you down to X-ray in a jiff, sir," the black orderly said, tucking a blanket more securely around the old man on the gurney. Age spots speckled the man's rubbery scalp, and a nose like an ax blade dominated his thin face. Sharp eyes shifted from me to Montgomery, and he sniffed deeply, nostrils flaring. Apparently, he picked up the scent of pheromones and desire, because he cackled and shook a bony finger at me. "Not in an elevator, you shouldn't," he said. "In my day, ladies didn't—"

To my fury, I felt myself blushing. I darted out of the elevator as the doors began to close, tossing a quick "Later" over my shoulder to Montgomery. Listening to the old man's litany of what ladies didn't do back in his day wasn't on my agenda. Besides, I'd bet they did, although maybe not with him—and I wasn't going to with Montgomery, I told myself, taking the stairs two at a time. He was younger than I was. He lived for the adrenaline rush of danger, like my fighter pilot husband had. He was hotter than an erupting volcano, my undisciplined side pointed out. Yeah, well, I didn't want to get burned.

Pushing through the lobby doors, I welcomed the cold that knifed through me. By the time I reached my Subaru, I'd compelled my mind to shove my id back into its cave and concentrate on the case.

14

I reached the outskirts of Estes Park three hours later, as dusk edged into night and snow began to fall. I'd hit rush hour in Denver and been enmeshed in traffic heading west for a weekend's skiing. Lucky bums. Now, tired and stiff, I wanted a room, a good meal, and a single-malt Scotch, not necessarily in that order. My cogitations about the case on the drive up had left me with a slight headache and no answers. I had a handful of facts but couldn't line them up with supportable conclusions. Fact one: Dmitri Fane was missing, either willingly or un. Fact two: Someone had attempted to kill Yuliya Bobrova, Dmitri's coach. Fact three: Dara Peterson, Dmitri's pair partner, had also dropped out of sight. Fact four: The Olympic trials started next week, and if Peterson and Fane didn't compete, Trevor Anthony and his partner were likely to win trips to the Olympics. The only common denominator I could see was Dmitri Fane, but I was darned if I could pinpoint a motive for his disappearance.

If Trevor Anthony (or anyone else) wanted to stop Dmitri skating, he (or she) could accomplish that by getting rid of Dmitri. There was no need for the attack on Bobrova or Dara's disappearance. If Dmitri was into something hinky— say, dealing drugs—and disappeared himself, why come back to beat up Bobrova? How did Dara's disappearance fit into that scenario? Gaagh. I hit the steering wheel. I wasn't going to think about it any more tonight. Motel. Food. Scotch.

I turned into the parking lot of the first motel I came to, across Route 36 from Lake Estes, and secured a room by the ice and vending machines. Pausing in the room only long enough to dump my overnight bag and brush my teeth, I sallied forth in search of sustenance. Unlike the ski resorts, Estes Park is more of a summer town than a winter town, with its main attraction being Rocky Mountain National Park a couple of miles north. Consequently, the sidewalks weren't crowded as I hiked a few blocks from my motel to find a restaurant. I enjoyed an elk steak and a Glenmorangie in a restaurant decorated in the rustic lodge mode favored in the mountains: exposed log walls, upholstery patterned with deer or bears, a taxidermied moose head reproaching diners with its glassy eyes, and a roaring fire. I enjoyed a second Scotch by the fire, tipped my server generously, and headed back to the motel to find a note tacked to my door. The gist of it was "No hot water until midday Saturday." I glanced down the hall to see similar notes on all the doors. Damn. A freezing cold shower had about as much appeal as rolling naked in the snow.

An idea hit. Why not check out Bobrova's cabin now and hit the road for home? The traffic would be lighter heading south, and I could be basking in my hot tub by eleven thirty or midnight. The Glenmorangie made the idea seem like a good one, and I quickly retrieved my bag and checked out. Memorizing my MapQuested directions to the cabin by the dome light in my car, I hit the road again, turning south on Route 7. Almost immediately, I slipped the Subaru into low gear as the road headed uphill at a steep angle, slicked by the still-falling snow. Lights glowed from houses clustered on my left, while a dark area on the right was probably a meadow. My headlights skittered off red eyes on the shoulder, and I hit my brakes, fishtailing slightly, as six elk sauntered across the road in front of me, unfazed by my presence. My heart beat faster at the near miss— no one wins in a car-elk collision—and I pressed the gas gently as the last elk's white butt bounded out of sight.

I passed mile marker seven and the dude ranch that were my landmarks and looked for the driveway that should lead to the cabin. I missed it the first time and flipped a U-ey, cursing the snow that was making it tough to read the house numbers nailed to trees. I found the number on my second pass and urged the Subaru into the slight gap between the trees that appeared to be a driveway. The grade was steep and the road unpaved. The car lurched over a small boulder and nosed into a shallow ditch to the left of the driveway, wheels spinning uselessly. Damn, damn, double damn. I threw it into reverse, and the car rocked back onto the driveway. Thank God. I might have to walk to the cabin from here, but at least I wasn't stuck for the night. Grabbing a flashlight from my glove box and my ski parka from the backseat, I abandoned the Subaru and headed uphill on foot.

The cone of light from my flashlight showed only a short length of driveway. When I scanned it to either side, it glanced off the trunks of lodgepole pines and scrub oaks that merged into an impenetrable wall of darkness a few feet off the driveway. I shivered and slipped my arms into my parka, zipping it to my chin. I trudged uphill. A tenth of a mile later, my feet were cold, the hems of my jeans heavy with snow, and I was contemplating suing the hot-waterless motel for breach of contract resulting in RSD . . . really stupid decision-making. Just then, a glimmer of light on my right told me I'd arrived. I studied the clearing. I could make out the bulk of the cabin as a darker rectangle against the snowy background of trees. A faint light seeped from beneath a door and illuminated a step. A stair with a boot print captured in the inch of snow coating it, I discovered as I crept closer. Someone had been here since it started snowing. Someone with boots several sizes larger than mine. I held my breath and listened. I heard nothing from inside. Should I aim for surprise and burst through the door unannounced (assuming it was unlocked), or try the socially acceptable route?

I knocked. "Dmitri?" My voice sounded small, deadened by snow and wilderness and darkness. "Hello?"

Nothing. I tried the knob. It turned. Avoiding the boot print, I stepped across the threshold and found myself in a window-less laundry room crowded with a washer, dryer, utility sink, and small rowboat propped against the wall. The light came from a Nemo night-light plugged into a socket six inches above the floor. Something smelled off, maybe mildewy clothes left in the washer. I left the door open to air out the space. Cautiously, I inched into the room, my boots skidding on tired linoleum. My hip clanged into the dryer. Shit! I stilled, but heard no response from inside. Impatient now, and sensing nothing but emptiness, I pushed open the interior door, groping for a light switch along the wall. I flicked it. Nothing.

I swept the beam of the flashlight in front of me. For a moment, I thought someone had left the windows open and snow had drifted into the room. A second glance, however, showed me that the drifts were stuffing from inside the sofa and easy chairs. Someone had searched this room much more thoroughly—and viciously—than Dmitri's apartment. I scuffed forward through the debris of confettied paper from an overturned shredder—a strange item for a mountain retreat—and feathers from eviscerated pillows. Glass shards from a shattered TV and computer monitor glinted when the light flashed over them. The beam glanced off an old rotary phone, an antler chandelier, a Coors can lodged against a space heater, and the stainless steel of appliances in the kitchen, a continuation of the living room/dining room delineated by parquet flooring rather than the great room's low-pile carpet. My steps slowed as I neared the kitchen and saw a dark, asymmetric puddle staining the floor. I trained the flashlight on it and bent over to confirm my suspicions. I sniffed. Blood. A lot of blood. Not totally hardened, by the look of it, so fairly recent blood. Maybe Dmitri—or whoever had been staying here—had shot himself an elk and dressed it on the kitchen floor, but somehow I didn't think so. I backed up a step, reaching for my cell phone to dial 911.

The same smell from the laundry room was much stronger in here, and I finally identified it as my finger paused over the nine on my cell phone: gas. I needed to get out. Breathing shallowly now, my head beginning to thump, I sprinted toward the laundry room, tripping over a bolster by the couch. I skidded several feet on my knees, regained my feet, and reached the laundry room as a phone began to ring behind me. Two more steps— *Whump!* The force of the cabin exploding lifted me from the threshold and slammed me into a drift at the base of a tree. My head thudded against the trunk and I blacked out.

15

Gigi Goldman shifted from one cheek to the other in the driver's seat of the Hummer, trying not to rock the parabolic microphone she had aimed at the window of Tattoo4U. Who knew your rear end could fall asleep? After two hours of sitting in the small lot across the street from the shop, with the temperature steadily dropping, her whole body felt as tight as Joan Rivers's face. She hadn't been able to figure out how to hook the recorder up to the microphone, so she was having to take notes on the conversations from inside the shop, most of which had to do, not surprisingly, with the choosing and application of tattoos.

There hadn't been a lot of activity in or around the shop. Pedestrian traffic had been light, with the bulk of it ducking into the liquor store two doors down from Tattoo4U and emerging minutes later with brown bags or a six-pack. One old bum, drunk maybe, stayed slumped beside the liquor store door, the bottle in his hand traveling to his mouth at regular intervals. He wore a shapeless coat and wiped his mouth with the scarf wound around his neck. The convenience store with the Asian signs had seen steady traffic, too, and Gigi was wondering if she could dash over there to use the bathroom when a slim male figure emerged from the door of Tattoo4U. Gigi updated her notes.

Next to "White male, 20s, black Megadeth sweatshirt, arr 4:13pm," she wrote "Dep 5:02pm." Nothing of interest had transpired during his time in the shop, and Gigi looked at her sparse notes with despair. She wasn't one step closer to finding Kungfu than when she arrived. It had taken her close to half an hour and two changes of location to figure out how to set up and aim the mike to pick up the conversations inside the shop, and it worked a treat, but no one was saying anything worth listening to. She didn't care if the man who'd left got the barbed wire tattooed around his left bicep or his right.

A movement at the door caught her eye. It was Graham, flipping over a CLOSED sign. He didn't emerge, so Gigi supposed he must exit by a back door. Should she follow him? She reached for the ignition as the sound of a door opening skritched over the microphone. Must be the back door, Gigi realized, since the front entrance remained deserted.

"You! I was expecting—" The voice was Graham's, tenser and more clipped than Gigi had heard him earlier, his Australian accent pronounced.

"He's not happy." The newcomer had a flat, almost monotone voice that was unsettling in its blandness, Gigi thought. Sinister. She reached for the notebook.

"Look, mate, I promise—"

"Not good enough. The kid—"

Gigi's brows drew together. Kid? Were they talking about Kungfu? She leaned forward, as if being closer to the dashboard would help her hear better. She missed a few words as papers rustled.

"—fix him," the stranger was saying. Then, "You do good work. When?"

A thudding sound drowned Graham's response.

Sweat beaded in the valley between Gigi's breasts as she struggled to take down the conversation word for word. It didn't sound like they were talking about tattoos. Could she be listening to a drug deal, as Charlie had suspected?

A movement to Gigi's left caught her eye. The bum near the liquor store had pushed to his feet, leaving his bottle behind. Moving with swift strides that suggested he was neither drunk nor old, he slipped into the dark gap between Tattoo4U and the dry-cleaning store. Gigi could barely make him out in the darkness, but he seemed to have climbed onto something— a Dumpster?—and to be peering into the small window on the side of Tattoo4U. He didn't look remotely drunk. As she watched, he pried at the bottom of the window frame with his fingertips.

Suddenly, Gigi remembered the camera. She reached for it on the passenger seat, bumping the parabolic microphone, which shivered, then fell into the passenger side footwell with a clanking sound that did not bode well for its continued operation. Gigi let out an "Oh!" of frustration, then concentrated on getting a picture of the strange man spying on the men in Tattoo4U. Trying to adjust for the darkness, Gigi snapped several shots before noticing that the slim figure had stiffened. She lowered the camera and watched as he jumped off the Dumpster and ran flat out, past the rear of the shop, disappearing from view as a wedge of light poured from the back of Tattoo4U and Graham's voice shouted, "Hey!"

Her fingers trembling, unable to make sense of what she'd witnessed but sensing real menace, Gigi decided to abandon her surveillance post. Starting the Hummer, she backed out of the slot. She paused at the entrance to the tiny lot, then started to turn right, almost striking a bicycler who appeared from nowhere, traveling south on the sidewalk. Gigi stamped on the brakes as the rider wrenched the bicycle's front wheel aside and stopped inches from the Hummer's door panel. She tumbled out, saying, "I'm so sorry. Are you okay? I'm so sorry," as she hastened around the back of the vehicle to check on the biker.

"No harm done," the man was saying, swiveling the handlebars right and left as if to check their responsiveness. The bike was an old-fashioned one with fat wheels, no gears, and a wire basket clamped to the front. "I should watch where I'm going."

"I'm so sorry," Gigi said again, heaving a huge sigh of relief that the man was unhurt and, apparently, unlitigious. He looked up and smiled at her. Recognition was instantaneous.

"Roger!"

"Gigi." Roger Nutt's smile widened. "I didn't expect to see you again so soon. What are you doing down here?"

"Uh . . . I'm . . . I had to—"

"Look, I picked up a few things at the Albertson's." He gestured to the bag in the bike's basket. "Let me run them home and then what say we have that dinner we were talking about? Do you like Greek? Jake and Telly's is just down the street."

"That sounds lovely," Gigi said, returning his smile. "I'll meet you there."

"Great. Give me twenty minutes." He straddled his bike again and pedaled off with a cheery wave.

Heaving a huge sigh of relief, Gigi clambered back into the Hummer and checked both ways three times before pulling into traffic. She'd discuss what she'd overheard with Charlie in the morning. An unaccustomed bubble expanded her chest, and she realized it was anticipation. She was looking forward to dinner with Roger Nutt. He was an attractive man—she especially liked how the corners of his mouth disappeared into his beard when he smiled—and the dolmades at Jake and Telly's were to die for. She sped up, wanting to reach the restaurant in time to powder her nose and fix her lipstick before Roger arrived.

16

I didn't know how long I'd been out when I awoke, but I was soaked to the skin from the waist down—my parka had protected my torso—and shivering uncontrollably, despite the blazing fire creating a Bosch-esque hell of dancing flames and shadows in the clearing. I dragged myself to a sitting position. My head hurt abominably, and I figured I was probably concussed. I sat for a moment, my back propped against the tree, and watched the cabin burn. No way was anything salvageable. A wave of nausea washed over me, maybe triggered by the strobelike effect of the reds and oranges and yellows of the flames gyrating on the blinding white snow, and I threw up. Done heaving, I scrubbed my mouth with clean snow. Yep, definitely a concussion.

A loblolly pine behind the cabin burst into flame with a loud pop of sap exploding. I needed to get help before the forest started to burn and left Bambi and Thumper homeless. Geez, I was losing it. I glanced around, looking for my cell phone, but it was hopeless. For all I knew it was a blob of shapeless plastic in the inferno. Using the tree for balance, I climbed slowly to my feet and stumbled back to the driveway by the fire's light. Putting one foot in front of the other with great care, I headed downhill to my car. Without my flashlight, I veered off the path more than once, getting slapped with needles from low-hanging pine branches before finding my way back to the driveway.

After ten soggy, cold, miserable minutes, I reached my car. The moon chose that moment to peep from behind a cloud, and I stared in dismay. The car that I had left in the middle of the driveway was now lodged in the ditch along the left side of the drive. It lay on the driver's side. The passenger side was a mangled mess of metal, and the headlights and windshield were busted. Something big and fast coming downhill from the cabin had plowed right through it. If there'd been more light, I would have seen the tire tracks and been forewarned. As it was, I had to fight to keep back tears. Someone or a couple of someones had parked a vehicle behind the cabin where it wouldn't be seen. They'd ransacked the cabin. Someone had been injured or killed, as the blood in the kitchen testified. Ransacker or ransackee? Dmitri? No way to know. They'd turned on the gas and waited for it to fill the cabin. Had they seen me arrive? Had they deliberately ignited the gas in an attempt to kill me? Or would I have been collateral damage?

These cheery thoughts sloshed in my brain as I trudged downhill toward Route 7, hoping to flag down a passing motorist. I heard a siren before I reached the road and closed my eyes with relief. Flashing red lights preceded a fire truck's turn into the driveway. A neighbor must have spotted the fire's glow and summoned help. Hallelujah. I edged off the driveway to avoid being mowed down and waved at the startled firefighters.

An ER doc had confirmed my diagnosis and given me painkillers for the concussion. I'd drunk three Pepsis and gone over my story with an Estes Park police detective multiple times when the round clock on the interview room wall ticked over to midnight and Montgomery walked in. I'd given Detective Radik his name at the beginning of our interview, knowing he'd be interested in Bobrova's cabin being blown to smithereens the same day someone put her in the hospital. I didn't know he'd be interested enough to make the drive up here, but I was damned glad to see him, especially as the ER doc had strictly forbidden me to drive for twenty-four hours. Even if I'd wanted to disobey, I had no drivable vehicle. My Subaru would be towed to a repair shop in the morning, and I suspected my insurance adjuster would pronounce it DOA.

Montgomery introduced himself to Detective Radik, who assessed him from under straight dark brows. He apparently passed muster, because her gray eyes seemed a lot warmer than they had when she was grilling me about my presence in the cabin and the blood I'd "allegedly" seen. I couldn't blame her much; his Clive Owen good looks heated up a lot of women.

"Thanks for the call, Detective," Montgomery said as they shook hands.

"Gretchen," she said. "Coffee?"

"Thanks." He smiled at her, and I realized she was above-average cute in trouser-cut jeans that showed off her well-toned butt and a melon-colored blazer that contrasted nicely with her chestnut hair. Hmph.

They discussed the fire, the findings of Radik's team so far (tire tracks and my story), and the preliminary report from the fire investigator (gas go boom—duh). They agreed in a too friendly way to pool their information, although Radik didn't have much to offer from my point of view. Her officers would canvass the neighbors tomorrow, she said, and see what they knew about the cabin's recent inhabitants. Montgomery thanked her warmly. Very warmly. You'd think we were at a caramel factory with all the warm goo coating everything. It was making me nauseous. Or maybe that was the concussion.

He turned to me, and his smile faded. "Why the hell didn't you tell me you were coming up here to toss a house belonging to Bobrova? I've got more than half a mind to charge you with obstruction."

So much for sympathy. I glared at him, my head pounding and sparkles of light wheeling at the edges of my vision. "Go ahead. I'd like to see you make it stick. I followed up a lead on my missing person case that has nothing to do with your investigation." I didn't believe that, but I was damned if I knew what the link was. "I checked out the cabin, and it blew up. That's not my fault!"

"I can hold her on a breaking and entering charge," Gretchen Radik offered helpfully.

"Tempting," Montgomery said.

"Maybe I saw the blood through the window and went in to see if someone was injured and needed help," I said. "I was being a Good Samaritan." I held the cold Pepsi can against my temple.

"That's not what you said earlier," Radik said, her eyes narrowing.

"I have a concussion. I'm confused. Is today Monday?" My stare dared her.

"Ramos, you got cuffs?" she asked the patrol officer standing by the door. She never took her eyes off me as the officer handed over his cuffs. "You have the right to—"

Oops. She was calling my bluff. I hate it when that happens.

Montgomery heaved a put-upon sigh. "I'll get her out of your hair, Gretchen," he said. He pulled my chair out and helped me stand. I fought the urge to upchuck on his shoes. Something was wrong with my vision, because I saw two of him when I looked up. My eyeballs throbbed.

"You sure?" Radik said. "I wouldn't even mind doing the booking paperwork for this one. She's got a mouth on her."

"Tell me about it."

Assessing my condition, Montgomery put his arm around my waist and steered me toward the door. His touch was gentler than his words, and I let my head fall against his shoulder as we reached the hall, unable to keep sparring.

"Can you make it to the car?" Without waiting for an answer, he scooped me up in his arms and carried me down the hall and out the door.

The cold air revived me slightly. I could feel his heart thudding against my rib cage. *KA-thump, KA-thump.* It clashed with the *boom-boom-boom* rhythm in my head. " 'Snice," I slurred. "Like the groom carrying the bride over the threshold. Tradition. Brad didn't carry me. He said it was sexist and he didn't want to throw out his back. King Kong carried Fay Wray Jessica Lange. Up the Empire State Building. I don't see it." I didn't see anything except swirling lights.

The rumble of Montgomery's laughter vibrated through me, and I thought I felt him press a kiss against my hair as he slid me into the passenger seat of his Jeep Commander.

17

My head was substantially better when I awoke Saturday morning. I remembered little of the drive back to Colorado Springs, except for Montgomery waking me at intervals to ask who was president and how many fingers he was holding up. I guess I answered right, because he brought me home instead of to the hospital. I hadn't really asked him to carry me over the threshold, had I? The memory refused to gel. He'd removed my shoes before tucking me into my bed, but that was all, I realized thankfully. I still wore the smoky-smelling, vomit-spattered jeans and top I'd had on the day before. Yuck. Now I needed to wash my sheets, too. First things first: a shower.

After a shower long enough to lower the reservoir an inch, I dressed in my ratty air force sweats and stripped the bed. With an armful of laundry, I headed for the washer. A trailing bit of sheet knocked scraps of paper off my dresser as I passed, and they fluttered to the ground. After setting the washer on the mega-hot-kill-bacteria cycle, I returned to my bedroom and stooped to retrieve the slips. Credit card receipts. I stared at them for a moment, puzzled, then remembered they'd come from Dmitri's condo. One was from the Men's Wearhouse and one from a Sunglass Hut. The curious thing was that neither belonged to Dmitri. The first was signed by a Lawrence Grossinger and the second by Darren Johnson. I frowned. Why would Dmitri have credit card receipts belonging to two other men in his pocket? Something about the signatures caught my eye. The loops coming off the *o*'s in Grossinger and Johnson looked similar. I held the slips side by side and compared them. What I wouldn't give for a sample of Dmitri's handwriting.

The ringing phone broke my concentration. "Yeah?"

"Ms. Swift? This is Sally Peterson. Dara's mother? We met yesterday." The way the *r*'s slanted looked the same, too. . . . Was it possible Mr. Olympic Skater was into credit card theft?

"I remember, Mrs. Peterson. What can I do for you?" I moved into the kitchen, wanting to study the receipts in a brighter light. Her next words made me drop the receipts on the counter.

"Dara called. She's in danger."

We met at a Starbucks near the University of Colorado's Colorado Springs campus, where Sally Peterson worked as a communications instructor. She refused to let me come to her home for fear it was being watched. I parked my Enterprise-delivered rental car and ground my teeth at the thought of car shopping. Hopefully, I'd hear from my insurance agent today and could set about replacing my poor Subaru. As I strode toward the door, attired in black jeans and a green flannel shirt, sun cut through the thin atmosphere, melting yesterday's snow with a steady *drip-drip* off the eaves. I got splashed as I went in. The familiar smells of coffee and steamed milk pervaded the space. Patrons ignored each other, absorbed in newspapers or laptop screens. Sally Peterson sat in a corner by the window, hands tight around a stainless steel travel mug, face sallow with fear or lack of sleep. Her wiry hair, light brown flecked with gray, was pulled back in an unbecoming ponytail. She jumped as I settled into the chair across from her and pulled a Pepsi from my purse.

"Sorry. Ever since Dara called I've been . . . well . . ."

"What did Dara say?" I asked, sensing that polite chitchat was not going to set this worried mother at ease. I took a long swallow of Pepsi.

"She called from a pay phone. She wouldn't say where she was. She just wanted me to know she's all right." Tears leaked from her eyes, and she wiped them with a napkin. "Sorry. She said Dmitri called her and said she had to disappear, that she was in danger. Damn him!" Her voice shook.

"Dmitri? Did she say where he was calling from or what kind of danger she was supposedly in?"

Sally Peterson shook her head. "No. She only stayed on the line for about twenty seconds. She was worried someone would trace the call." She looked around wildly, eyes lingering on the twenty-something barista making lattes as if suspecting he was a CIA agent, and on an octopus-shaped rattle hanging from a stroller as if it might be a recording device. "Can they even do that?"

It depended on who "they" were. "Mrs. Peterson—"

"Sally. Please call me Sally." Her fingers shredded a napkin as her gaze settled anxiously on my face.

"Okay. Have you any idea—any at all—of what Dmitri might be mixed up in? You mentioned overhearing something about cards . . . was he a gambler? Could he owe somebody money?" A hell of a lot of money, I thought, to result in Dmitri's friends being threatened. A grim thought wiggled into my con-cussed and sludgier-than-normal brain: Had anyone talked to

Dmitri's mother recently? I made a mental note to call her in Detroit.

"I don't know. Let me think." She pressed her fingers to her temples. "I remember he spent a whole night gambling in the Bellagio once when he and Dara did an exhibition in Vegas, about two years ago. He came straight from the casino to the airport, reeking of cigarette smoke." Her nose wrinkled. "He bragged about 'cleaning up' and showed us a new Rolex he'd bought with his winnings." Sally shrugged, clearly not impressed. "He gave Dara a gold chain with a charm in the shape of a figure skater. She never skates without it now. He won," she reiterated, "and I've never heard him talk about going to Vegas for the weekend or anything like that."

The occasional big win keeps the obsessed gambler coming back to lose more. And the real addict didn't need to go to Vegas: he or she could place bets on anything from dog races to football games to the outcome of Olympic skating events from the comfort of home via phone or Internet. Too bad Dmitri's computer was missing. I made a note to ask Montgomery to check Fane's phone records. Maybe there'd be calls to or from a known bookie.

"Dara wanted me to tell you to stop looking for Dmitri," Sally interrupted my thoughts.

"I'm fired?" Shit. I hate to abandon cases once I've sunk my teeth into them, although clients do occasionally change their minds about wanting someone found. Plus, I *really* hate giving back unearned retainer money.

"Dara's firing you, yes." Sally leaned forward, her hazel eyes intent. I caught a glimpse of the stage mama who must have encouraged her daughter—if not browbeaten her—to achieve international skating success. "But I want to hire you."

Hm, potential ethical dilemma, known in professional

circles as "conflict of interest." Still, if Dara had fired me, working for her mother shouldn't be a problem. "To find Dara?"

"No, to find Dmitri. It seems to me his situation is the root of the problem. If Dara's not safe at home, I want her to stay wherever she is until this thing with Dmitri gets settled." Sally's expression and tone were resolute. "I don't want her to end up like Yuliya Bobrova."

Who could blame her? She wrote me a check on the spot, and I promised to give her an update soon. "If—when—I find Fane, what do you want me to do?" Dara had wanted me to restore the status quo, bring Fane back so they could skate their way to Olympic glory. I figured Sally Peterson would want me to make sure he stayed far away from her daughter.

Her eyes hardened. "Make his problems go away so he can come back and skate. If he needs to pay someone off, let me know, I have a mutual fund I can tap into. I've invested—Dara's invested—fifteen years of sweat and tears and money to get to the Olympics. I'm not letting go of that dream because a spoiled young man can't keep his eye on the prize. This is what Dara's worked for all her life. I've—she's—given up everything for a chance at Olympic gold."

Dara. Uh-huh.

"Nationals start Tuesday." Sally Peterson rose to her feet, telling me I'd better deliver Dmitri by the deadline.

I nodded, keeping my expression carefully nonjudgmental. Mother love comes in many guises, I thought, assuring Sally Peterson I'd have news for her soon.

Since I was already out and about, I decided to drop into the office and update my Fane file with the information from Estes Park and Sally Peterson. The usual Saturday morning gotta-go-out-and-buy-stuff traffic clogged Academy Boulevard, and I turned into the office parking lot with a sigh of relief. The lot was almost full again, but no demonstrators marched on the sidewalk, thank goodness. As I watched, a pair of giggling women emerged from Domenica's clutching shopping bags with the store's name in gold script. I caught a glimpse of several other shoppers inside the store before the door closed. I grinned. It seemed the demonstrators' plan had misfired; instead of sounding a death knell for Domenica's, the publicity they'd generated had boosted business.

I was debating whether or not to scope out the shop's merchandise—out of neighborly curiosity, of course—when Gigi burst out of our office door. She wore a tunic-length white turtleneck over velour leggings stretched to the max. An orange quilted down vest topped the ensemble, making her look like the Poppin' Fresh Doughboy in a life preserver.

"Charlie! I thought I saw you drive up. Guess what?"

Before I could make a disparaging comment about grade-school guessing games, she continued, "I found Kungfu!"

"Really?" Realizing that the incredulity in my voice might be interpreted as casting doubt on her investigative abilities, I cleared my throat and tried again. "Really."

"Yes, really," she squeaked. "Come see." She beckoned with one hand and popped back through the door.

What, she had him stashed in the office? I followed her in and, not immediately spotting a homeless Asian teen, helped myself to a Pepsi from the fridge. "It looks like he's invisible," I said. "No wonder Dan thought he was missing."

"He's not here, silly," Gigi said, not one whit disconcerted by my sarcasm. "He's here." She pointed to her computer monitor with a chubby forefinger tipped by a ruby-painted nail.

I crossed the room and peered over her shoulder. A photo

filled the screen. A vaguely humanoid figure stood on something that could have been a van, a Dumpster, or a restaurant-sized refrigerator turned on its side. "You're kidding."

"That's not the good one." Gigi clicked the mouse, and a better-focused photo sprang up.

I could make out the man's features in this one and positively identify the object he was standing on as a green Dumpster. He seemed to be emulating Peeping Tom.

"Look." Gigi held the photo Dan had given us up close to the monitor and clicked a few keys. The face on the screen grew larger and clearer, and damned if it didn't look a bit like Kungfu.

"Where'd you take these?" I asked, my eyes flitting from the group photo to the face on the monitor. The eyes were right, the slant of the brows was similar, the ears stuck out at the same angle . . .

"At Tattoo4U last evening," Gigi said, beaming. "He was pretending to be a homeless drunk—he completely had me fooled. I'll have to remember that trick when I do surveillance again—"

My mind boggled at the thought of Gigi swilling gin from a bottle swaddled in a paper bag. She'd probably substitute Evian. And which of her designer duds was best suited to an undercover op as a homeless person? The Juicy Couture sweats? The Burberry trench coat? The manicured nails, salon highlights, and expensive teeth might also make it hard to pass herself off as a street person.

"—because no one notices a bum. Anyway, he was spying on Graham and his visitor—"

"Graham?"

"The tattoo artist. They must have seen him or something,

because all of a sudden he took off like a rabbit chased by a tick hound."

Sometimes Gigi's southern roots peeped out and made me wonder about her life before marrying Les Goldman. "Have you called Dan?" I asked.

"Not yet," she said.

"Why don't you print a copy of that, and I'll see if he agrees it's Kungfu," I said. "If so, it looks like there's a bit more to Kungfu dropping out of sight than just a runaway moving on. Why would he be interested in the tattoo parlor? It's not like there'd be anything worth stealing in there—the equipment would be hard to cart off and harder to fence." I was thinking aloud, but Gigi answered.

"Listen to what I heard." She read back the conversation from the tattoo shop, mangling Graham's Australian accent.

"Sounds like a business deal gone bad," I said. "Question is: What kind of business?" I finished my Pepsi and clanked the can into the trash as Kendall emerged from the bathroom and took her seat at the card table, her lower lip pouted out far enough for a pigeon to land on.

"You should recycle," Gigi said reprovingly. "We could advertise ourselves as a 'green' business if—"

"Why don't you call Dan." I interrupted the familiar lecture. "You're the one who made the discovery. You should tell him."

"Really?" Her cheeks flushed with gratification. "Okay."

She carried on a short conversation with Dan while I updated the Fane file. I needed to touch base with Montgomery . . . maybe his new best bud, Detective Radik, had passed along something useful from Estes Park. Besides, I owed him a real thank-you for bringing me home last night.

"He's coming over," Gigi announced as she hung up.

On the words, the door opened and a woman entered, looking around curiously. At least seventy, she had white hair, wore a lavender twinset and long gray skirt, and carried a small pink shopping bag with a bow tied around the handles. "Your sign says 'Swift Investigations.' Are you private investigators?" Her voice vibrated with interest.

"Yes," Gigi and I said together. I figured her for a missing pet case—we got three or four calls a month from people wanting us to find their lost Muffy or Rover—and rehearsed how I would decline the case without seeming unsympathetic.

"That is fascinating." She advanced into the office, eyeing Bernie the Bison interestedly.

"Can we help you?" I asked.

"Oh, no! I just came over to say hello and introduce myself. I'm Domenica. From next door?"

I stared at her. This was the proprietor of the sex toys shop? She looked more like a librarian or an aging Betty Crocker. "Nice to meet you, Domenica. I'm Charlie Swift, and this is Gigi Goldman."

The woman lowered her voice to a whisper. "Oh, call me Carol. My parents didn't christen me Domenica—I'm really Carol Maureen Tweedy—but Domenica sounds so much more . . . exotic, don't you think?"

"Absolutely." Gigi bobbed her head in agreement.

"You sell dildos?" This, of course, from an incredulous Kendall, who had risen from her chair and advanced toward the newcomer.

The woman positively twinkled at her. "Among other things." She held the shopping bag out in Gigi's direction. "Here. This is for you. One for each of you." She included me in her smile. "A little something from the shop, just to be neighborly."

"How kind of you!" Gigi exclaimed, eyeing the bag uncertainly. "I was telling Charlie yesterday that I was going to bake cookies and bring them over." Before she could take the bag, Kendall swooped down on it.

I watched with unholy amusement as Kendall untied the bow. Gigi's voice betrayed her uneasiness as she said, "Kendall, I don't think—"

When Kendall pulled a small bottle from the bag, Gigi and I let out a collective sigh of relief and disappointment. I'd been expecting a leather or metal-spiked garment of some kind, and I could tell Gigi had been afraid the bag would contain something that needed batteries. "What's that, sugah?" Gigi asked.

"'Sinsual Massage Oil in Musky Coconut,'" the girl read. She unscrewed the cap and sniffed. "Mmm." She rubbed some along her arm. "Silky."

Within seconds, the scent drifted to me, and I stifled a cough. It smelled like a herd of yaks stewed in Hawaiian Tropic. Kendall was welcome to it.

"It's one of our most popular items," Carol said, looking gratified. "Well, I've got to get back. Customers, you know! So lovely to meet you."

"You, too," we chorused as she exited.

Stowing the massage oil in her purse and handing me the gift bag with an identical bottle in it, Kendall made to follow her. "Gotta go, Mom. Dexter'll be here in a sec." She grabbed her jacket, flipped her blond hair over her shoulder, and left without waiting for a response. The scent lingered after she'd gone. I gave the bag I held to Gigi with a magnanimous "You can have this since Kendall took yours. Where's she off to?"

"The Ice Hall reopened," Gigi said. "She's practicing. She's worried about a couple of elements in her short program and wants to nail them down before Nationals."

"You mean she's competing at Nationals? Like Dara and Dmitri?"

"Of course." Gigi looked puzzled by my surprise.

Despite knowing the girl was a competitive figure skater, I hadn't put two and two together. Blame it on the concussion. "When do Nationals start?" I asked.

"Tuesday afternoon for the junior ladies short program. If she makes the cut, she'll do the free skate Saturday morning. I'll be taking some time off to watch," she said. "Just a few hours."

"I think I can manage," I said drily. I filled Gigi in on my conversation with Sally Peterson.

"That poor girl," she said when I finished. "We've got to find her."

I shook my head. "Nope. Our job is still to find Fane. Only we're working for Sally now, instead of Dara. Besides, the police are looking for Dara." I didn't tell her Montgomery considered the girl a suspect in the Bobrova incident. "That reminds me . . ."

Flipping through the Fane file, I found the number I wanted and called Detroit. No answer at Fane's mother's house. Why was I not surprised? I hoped Irena Fane was safely hidden away, like Dara, and not bleeding to death on an ice rink, à la Bobrova. Maybe Montgomery could have the local Detroit cops do a health and welfare check on her. I left a message.

I was about to phone him when Dan Allgood walked through the door. He wore a red plaid lumberjack's shirt tucked into jeans showing white at the knees. He paused on the threshold, completely blocking the doorway with his bulk, and let his gaze travel around the office. "Nice buffalo," he said with a smile, nodding at Bernie.

"Bison," Gigi and I corrected simultaneously.

His smile grew wider. "You must be Gigi," he said, shaking her hand.

"Georgia Goldman," she confirmed, seeming a bit flustered by his size. "G. G. Get it?"

"So you've found Kungfu already? You're a fast worker."

I observed his interaction with Gigi with a slight smile on my face. He was such a nice man. It had taken him less than half a second to suss out Gigi's insecurity and bolster her confidence. Maybe I should be more like that? Nah.

Gigi opened the Kungfu photo on her monitor, and he studied it.

"It sure looks like Kungfu," he said. "What's he up to?"

Gigi filled him in on her surveillance from the night before.

Dan looked thoughtful. His eyes met mine. "I knew there was something different about him." he said. "He had a sense of purpose that was unusual, but damned if I know what he's after."

"Money? Drugs?" I named the obvious.

He shook his head. "There's more to it than that."

I cocked a skeptical eyebrow. "Would he talk to you, do you think? If you have the time, you might hang out down there, make yourself accessible. Or put the word out that you'd like to talk to him, help him."

Dan nodded slowly. "That might be the best course of action. I'll spend some time down there this afternoon. Let's keep this between us for now. If Kungfu's up to something, I don't want to spook him into splitting for good. And if someone's after him . . ."

Gigi squirmed in her chair. "I already mentioned it to someone," she confessed. "I didn't think it would hurt. I—"

"Who?" Dan asked, his voice carefully nonaccusatory.

"Roger. Roger Nutt. From Dellert House? We were having dinner and—"

"You had a date?" I heard the yelp in my voice and moderated it. "I mean, that's great."

"He's really nice." She blushed. "We went to Jake and Telly's. Anyway, since Kungfu was staying at Dellert House, I thought . . . I didn't tell Roger about staking out Tattoo4U, or anything, or about Kungfu spying on the place. I said I'd seen him in the area and wondered whether he was back at Dellert House." She repetitively squished one of the down-filled squares on her vest like a kid popping cells on bubble wrap.

"It's fine, Gigi," Dan reassured her. "Roger does good work with those boys. What did he say?"

"He seemed surprised. He said he hadn't seen him."

"No harm, no foul," I said.

Dan said he was going to stroll through Old Colorado City, keeping an eye out for Kungfu or suspicious-looking drunks on the street. Gigi had summonses to deliver and I was wondering if another chat with Boyce Edgerton might yield anything when my phone rang.

"Miss Swift?"

Garbled noises in the background made it hard to hear the woman's light soprano voice. "Yes?"

"This is Irena Fane. You called me."

Dmitri's mother. "Yes, thank you for calling back. It's about Dmitri. He—"

"I am at the airport," the woman interrupted, "about to board a plane for Colorado Springs. Pick me up there and we can talk." She gave me her flight information and hung up.

I stared at the phone for a moment, then looked at my watch. I had three hours before Irena Fane's plane would arrive.

Enough time to interview Boyce Edgerton again and maybe scare him into giving up some details about Dmitri's activities or other friends by playing up the cabin explosion. Maybe he could even tell me what was in the cabin that someone was so desperate to obliterate.

18

At Boyce's apartment, I held the door for a woman backing a double stroller down the stairs, the twins inside crowing little laughs with every plunk down a step. "Thanks," she said wearily. I imagined she did and said everything wearily with twins under two.

"Sure." I took the stairs two at a time, not pausing to admire the old house's woodwork and fittings this time around. I'd played good cop—well, good PI—last time I'd interviewed Boyce. This time, I was prepared to unleash my inner bad cop. Seven years with the air force's Office of Special Investigations had taught me a little something about interrogation.

It would have been dramatic and satisfying, but also counterproductive and possibly injury inducing, to kick in Edgerton's door. Kicking in doors is not as easy as they make it look in the movies. Trust me. I'd once spent a couple of weeks with a cane after kicking in a door to a child pornographer's lair. It was enough to make me as grumpy as Dr. House. I contented myself with knocking.

The door inched open. Well, it did after I tried the knob.

Unlocked. Colorado Springs is a safer city than most, but leaving your door unlocked was plain stupid. Asking for trouble. Hesitating on the threshold, I poked at the door with a stiff forefinger, and it swung inward six inches. "Edgerton?" I called. "Boyce?" No answer.

"I don't think he's home."

The voice came from below, startling me. I turned and looked over the stair railing to see a woman in her seventies or early eighties peering up at me from the floor below. Wearing a turquoise velour sweatsuit with red Converse high-tops, she had improbably blond hair and glittered with enough costume jewelry to outfit the whole cast of one of those *Housewives* reality shows. The door to her apartment was open and emitted a tempting scent of warm cinnamon buns.

"We were supposed to meet." I put on a miffed voice. "Do you know where he's gone?"

She furrowed her brow and craned her head back a bit more to get a better look at me. "You and Boyce had a date? Well, I'll be. Are you one of those cougars I read about in all the ladies' magazines?"

Ouch. I might be ten years older than Boyce, but it shouldn't have been so apparent to a septuagenarian looking at me upside down. "Business," I said shortly.

"Oh, business." She nodded like that made sense. "Excuse me. I've got to get my buns out of the oven." She hustled into her apartment with a shuffling step that spoke of arthritic knees.

Hurrying now, not wanting Boyce's neighbor to find me still here when she finished with her baking, I eased the door wider, debating whether or not to go in and see if Edgerton was conked out in bed or just plain avoiding me. Cool air drifted from the apartment, a welcome change from the overheated stuffiness of my last visit. Something streaked past me, furry little body brushing my ankle, and I jumped straight up, twisting my foot when I landed. I swore. The slender ferret looked over her shoulder at me from three steps down, chittering.

Damn. I couldn't let the stupid weasel escape; she'd probably freeze to death in this weather. I didn't know where ferrets were from originally, but I didn't figure this one would fare well on the streets of Colorado Springs in January. "Here, ferret girl," I called softly. What was her name? Sadie. "Here, Sadie. Come back like a good ferret." She slunk down another step, beady eyes trained warily on me.

A treat. I needed to bribe her with food. I searched my pockets but came up empty. Maybe there was ferret kibble in Edgerton's kitchen. "Wait," I commanded Sadie and stepped into the apartment. Were ferrets plant eaters or meat eaters? If I couldn't find ferret chow, should I try a bit of cheese or a slice of apple, assuming Edgerton had either? My Aunt Pam and Uncle Dennis's schnauzer-beagle mix had loved peanut butter. That dog would break off chasing a cat if you offered him Jif on a spoon. Maybe I'd try—

I stepped into the kitchen and all thought of ferret bribes left me. Boyce Edgerton lay faceup on the floor, eyes open, congealed pool of blood gluing his body to the linoleum. I didn't need to check his pulse to know he was dead. The waxy look of his skin and the film over his staring eyes told me he was gone. I glanced around, needing to focus on something other than those dead eyes. The mountain of Budweiser and Mountain Dew empties in the recycling bin had toppled, sending an avalanche of aluminum cans across the small kitchen floor. Orange goo puddled near the sink, and it took me a moment to recognize it as dishwashing liquid from the bottle knocked off the edge. The smell of hot dogs permeated the small room, and I craned my neck to see three fleshy pink franks floating in the saucepan on the stove. Apparently, Edgerton had been making dinner—surely not breakfast?—when his murderer surprised him. Had the murderer turned off the burner when he left, not wanting the whole house to go up in flames? Thoughtful of him.

Knowing better than to disturb a crime scene, I backed carefully away from the kitchenette, careful not to touch anything as I returned to the landing. Descending to the second floor, I lowered myself to a stair and called the police on my cell phone to report finding the body. As I waited there for the cops to show up, shivering slightly, Sadie crept up to me and laid her tiny pointed snout on my thigh. I stroked her gingerly, then with more confidence. "Sorry, girl," I murmured. "Looks like you're an orphan."

The patrol officer who arrived first took one brief look and called for a homicide detective. Montgomery showed up within minutes, looking grim. "Stay," he told me in much the same voice I'd used with the ferret, before donning booties and gloves to check out the crime scene. By this time, the downstairs neighbor had emerged, quivering with excitement, and invited me into her apartment for a cinnamon bun. Telling a uniformed officer where Montgomery could find me, I joined the woman, who introduced herself as Claudine Massey, in her cozy apartment. Sadie trailed behind us and responded favorably to Claudine's offer of a bit of iced cinnamon bun. She was a cake-ivore, I realized, not a carnivore or an herbivore. Satisfied with her morsel, she scrambled onto one of the cushioned chairs in Claudine's kitchen and curled up in it, very much at home. I accepted a warm bun and a glass of milk from Claudine, who joined me at the table with her own plate.

"Oh, my yes," Claudine said when I mentioned how comfy Sadie looked. "She comes and visits me most days when Boyce goes to work. She and I are old friends, aren't we, dear?" She stroked the ferret's head. "Boyce is dead, I take it?" A faint tremor sounded in her voice.

"Yes," I said gently. "Were you friends?"

She nodded, fat tears rolling down her crumpled cheeks. "He used to take out my trash for me—I have trouble on the stairs—and I babysat Sadie for him. If he wasn't working, we watched *Survivor* together. He used to talk about trying out for the show. I know he'd have won."

I couldn't picture the pale, soft Edgerton making it one week on a deserted island with a bunch of attention-starved fitness freaks, eating grasshoppers and coconuts, but I didn't say so.

"Was it a heart attack?" Claudine asked. "I told him and told him that he couldn't live on hot dogs and Mountain Dew, that he needed to get some exercise. Why, I walk three miles a day, rain or shine, unless it's really icy."

"Really?" I was impressed.

"You look like you stay fit, too," she said approvingly.

"Thanks." I found myself ridiculously pleased by the compliment. "When was the last time you saw Boyce?" I asked.

She pondered, mushing a crumb of cinnamon bun with her fork. "Last night? About seven?" She nodded to herself. "Yes, that was it. I had finished watching *Jeopardy!*—the categories were impossible last night—when I heard him come up the stairs. I popped out to say hello, and we chatted for a couple of minutes."

"About . . . ?"

"Nothing much. He mentioned he was working a party the next night—tonight. He was in catering, you know, and did the most marvelous desserts. Sometimes he brought a little something home for me, one of those mini cheesecakes, or a slice of lemon meringue pie. Leftovers, he said. He knew about my sweet tooth." She put three fingers to her mouth.

"Did he have any visitors last night or today that you noticed?"

She didn't bridle at the implication that she was nosy; indeed, she seemed to take pride in it. "I try to keep on top of what happens around here. There are a couple of college kids on the ground floor, and they're so careless about leaving the front door unlocked—and there are babies in the house to worry about! Poor McKenzie is coping with those twins all on her own while her husband is deployed. I try to help out where I can, but—"

"Boyce's visitors?"

"Oh, yes. I heard someone up there this morning, but I don't know who it was. I was kneading the dough for my buns, and I didn't want to open the door with my hands all floury. Maybe it was that whiny Vanessa. Although she usually wears heels that make a pock-pock sound, and I didn't hear them. It's hard not to hear footsteps upstairs." She paused, and we both listened to the thud of cop shoes reverberating through the ceiling.

"I see what you mean. What time was that?" Maybe Boyce did eat hot dogs for breakfast.

"Oh, very early. A bit past six thirty, maybe?" She paused, an arrested look on her wizened face. "You know, I don't remember hearing the front door close or hearing Boyce's visitor climb the stairs. I must have been in the shower." She nodded to herself. "Yes, that must be it."

"Besides Vanessa, who visited Boyce?"

Claudine pursed her nearly colorless lips. "Well, that friend who worked with him at the catering company, that skater. I've seen him on TV. Very handsome. And another young man I think Boyce knew from high school."

"Did you—" A knock on the door cut me off.

Claudine shuffled to the door—it must take her half a day to walk her three miles—and opened it to reveal Montgomery, sternly handsome in his black leather jacket and slacks. He flashed his badge, introduced himself, and dislodged me with a meaningful jerk of his head. "I'll be by to chat with you in a little while, Mrs. Massey," he said with the smile that never failed to set women fluttering. Except me. I'm not the fluttering type.

"Any time, Detective," she said.

"Is Sadie okay here?" I asked, joining Montgomery at the door.

"Sadie?" His brows snapped together.

"Boyce's ferret," Claudine and I chorused. As if responding to her name, the slinky creature put her tiny front paws on the table and peered at Montgomery over its edge.

"She can stay with me," Claudine said. "It's not like she has anywhere else to go now, and she's comfortable here."

—⁓⁓—

"Okay, Charlie," Montgomery said when he had walked me down to the first floor and a room off the entryway that the cops had apparently commandeered. It was chilly—probably because the front door had been propped open by the coroner's team—and severely formal, with two uncomfortable-looking gray sofas, an occasional table or two, and a fireplace that looked like it hadn't held a cheery blaze since trolley cars trundled down the streets of Colorado Springs. A buck glared at me from over the mantel, his fur a bit mangy and one antler cracked at the tip. A fedora hung whimsically from the other antler, giving the old guy a rakish look. "Tell me what you were doing here, why you broke into Edgerton's apartment, and anything else you know—or think you know—about Edgerton's death."

I gave it to him straight, not about to hedge my answers in a murder case. "I came to see Edgerton, hoping he could tell me something more about the cabin that blew up or about Dmitri's associates, and I didn't break into Edgerton's place— the door was unlocked, and I went in to find some ferret kibble."

"Ferret kibble?" Montgomery's eyebrow soared the way it does when he doubts my veracity. Which is fairly often.

"Ferret kibble," I said virtuously. "Sadie got out, and I needed something to bribe her with. I never entered the kitchen and didn't touch anything; it was clear Edgerton was beyond help. I called 911 immediately."

"You're a freakin' model citizen," he said. The corners of his mouth softened. "So, now that we've established that you only entered the apartment out of the purest motives for animal welfare, tell me what you think happened."

"Someone shot Edgerton," I said promptly.

Montgomery heaved a sigh.

I relented. "Probably sometime early this morning. Claudine says she heard someone up there while she was baking, probably around six thirty, but she didn't hear anyone come up the stairs."

"Whoever it was came up the fire escape and left the same way," Montgomery said. "The window was forced."

"Pretty risky at that hour," I observed.

"Still dark at this time of year. The house backs to an

alley—not much traffic." Montgomery shrugged. "Still, I'll admit it was ballsy."

"Why didn't Claudine hear the shot?" I wondered

"Suppressor, maybe, or she left her hearing aids out."

"Not an item your average Joe has on hand."

"Not that hard to obtain, either. The Internet . . ."

I dipped my chin to acknowledge that the World Wide Web had made it much easier for criminals—and PIs—to obtain useful equipment and gadgets.

"What else did you discover?"

Montgomery hesitated.

"C'mon," I urged him.

"A stash in the toilet tank. Enough to get him prison time as a dealer."

"The hard stuff?"

"Marijuana, some coke."

I figured that put Boyce in the frame as the girl's supplier at the party Friday night. "What are you thinking—a falling-out between stoner and supplier?"

"Maybe." Montgomery's expression didn't give much away, but I got the feeling he knew more than he was saying.

"I don't like it," I said, having given it some thought. It was too pat. Following on the heels of Dmitri's disappearance and the cabin blowing up, Edgerton's murder gave me the heebie-jeebies. If he and a junkie had a falling-out, why didn't the junkie take the drugs after he murdered Edgerton? Something could have spooked him, I supposed, made him run off without finding the stash.

"You're not required to like it," Montgomery said with a laugh. He shot his cuff to look at his watch. "As much as I enjoy interrogating you, I've got other witnesses to interview. I know you'll keep me posted on anything you turn up that might have the smallest relevance to my case." He said it warningly.

"Of course." I widened my eyes in a "can you doubt it?" way.

He snorted, chucked me under the chin, and trotted back upstairs, presumably to visit Claudine. I slipped out the door, avoided a reporter looking for witnesses to misquote, and jogged to my car. If I sped like a demon, got lucky with the lights, and didn't get pulled over, I might just make it to the airport on time to collect Irena Fane.

19

Slowing to a crawl in the lane outside the arrivals doors at the Colorado Springs Municipal Airport, I considered the people standing by their luggage, scoping out approaching cars. Not the army major in uniform, not the college girl texting like mad, not the zoned-out businesswoman tapping her pump-shod foot. I gave myself a mental slap for not having arranged a way of recognizing Dmitri's mother. A woman standing at the far end of the pickup area looked possible: She was petite like a former pair skater, and studying the passing cars like she was waiting for someone, but she looked too young. Nonetheless, I cruised up to her and lowered the window. She gave me a nervous look and clutched her purse to her chest. "Mrs. Fane?"

Drawing in a deep breath, she nodded. Wearing a red knit hat with a rolled brim pulled to her brows, she had mink brown hair lightly flecked with silver that fell to her shoulders in a casual tumble. It was the hair and her slim build that had fooled me into thinking she was too young to be a twenty-seven-year-old's mom; up close, deep grooves bracketed her mouth, and her neck showed the first faint signs of crepeyness. Wary dark eyes assessed me as she took a tentative step toward me.

"I'm Charlotte Swift. Call me Charlie. Hop in."

She reached for the door with a leather-gloved hand and slid onto the seat. "Thank you for coming."

"Don't you have any luggage?" I asked, scanning the sidewalk for a suitcase or duffel bag.

"No. I didn't take the time." A faint Russian accent lent a charming lilt to her voice. "I have necessities in here." She patted her purse, a messenger-style bag that might hold a toothbrush, a bikini—not much use in Colorado in January—and a change of undies but not much else.

I put the car in gear, swerved around a taxi, and headed for the airport exit.

Irena stayed quiet the couple of minutes it took me to get clear of the terminal traffic. "Where is my Dmitri?" she asked as we passed the rust-colored metal statues of a mounted brave near a bison. A real pronghorn grazed nearby.

"I was hoping you might have some ideas about that," I said. "What prompted you to come to Colorado Springs?"

She looked at me as if I were an idiot. "My sister has been brutally attacked and my son is missing and you can ask me that?"

"So, Yuliya Bobrova is your sister?" Boyce Edgerton had been right; Bobrova was Dmitri's aunt.

"Yes. She is the oldest and I am the youngest of eight. We were not close, but when I came to America with Stuart, she was very supportive. She was still in Michigan then, and she helped me adjust."

"Do you want to go by the hospital?" I asked.

She shook her head. "No. Dmitri's."

"I don't know if we'll be able to get in," I said.

In answer, she pulled a key from her pocket. The brassy color glinted in the sunlight pouring through the car windows. She turned her head to look out the side window at the stores and businesses lining Powers Boulevard and I debated whether or not to tell her about Boyce. I decided to keep his murder to myself for the time being. She was already worried about her son—hearing that his friend had been shot might goose her into hysterics.

Pulling into the still-empty parking lot at Westhaven, I had barely stopped the car when Irena jumped out and ran to the front door of Dmitri's unit. She slid the key home with a trembling hand and pushed into the foyer, calling, "Dmitri!"

I was half a step behind her and almost gasped as I entered. The disarray that had greeted me the other day was gone; in fact, everything was gone. The sofa, the TV, the DVDs, the red pillow—gone. I turned in a circle while Irena dashed up the stairs. Who had cleaned the place out? And why? I wandered into the kitchen and opened a couple of drawers at random. Empty. Not even an old takeout menu or a paper clip wedged into a drawer seam.

"He's not here," Irena called from the top of the stairs.

"The condo didn't look like this when I was here Thursday," I told her, returning to the empty living room.

Irena plodded down the stairs, one weary step at a time. "I am so worried." She sat on the next-to-last step and dropped her face into her hands, elbows propped on her knees.

I joined her. "Do you want to go somewhere else to talk? A Starbucks or a restaurant?" She shook her head, not looking up, and I gave in, sliding my back down the entryway wall until my butt hit the cold wood floor. "What do you think is going on with Dmitri?" I asked.

She looked up after a moment, dug the heels of her hands

into her eyes, and then met my gaze. "He called me this morning."

"He did? Then he's alive!"

She nodded. "He told me I might be in danger, told me to leave my house and spend a couple of nights in a hotel or with a friend."

Instead of which, she'd come straight to Colorado Springs, leaping from the sinking boat into the crocodile-infested river, I suspected.

She read my expression. "He is my only son. Of course I am going to try to help him."

"Did he say why you were in danger?"

"No. He said he had some business to sort out and then everything would get back to normal."

Somehow, I didn't think we were talking about skating business. Even the most cutthroat, Tonya Harding–esque competitor would draw the line at threatening a skater's mother, I felt sure. "You're his mom," I said, "and you probably know him better than anyone."

"I do," she said fiercely.

"So what's he mixed up in?"

She bristled. "What makes you think he's 'mixed up' in anything?"

I just looked at her. After a moment, she squirmed, then pulled off the knit cap and ran her fingers through her hair. I stayed silent. Finally, she burst out, "You have to understand that ice-skating is a very expensive sport."

"I know."

"Training and competing at the level Dmitri does can cost a hundred thousand dollars a year."

I was going to ask about sponsors, but I didn't want to derail her, so I said, "That must be hard."

She jerked her head down hard once. "Yes. So you cannot blame Dmitri for taking advantage when opportunity presented itself."

"What kind of opportunity?" From the way her eyes slid away from mine, I knew we weren't talking about a mutual fund.

"As a caterer with the run of people's kitchens, he found that sometimes he had access to . . . to certain documents. So many people, especially well-off couples, seem to have those built-in desks in their kitchens, and they leave papers there— bills, investment statements, and the like."

"So Dmitri helped himself to customers' financial data and then—what? Stole their identities?"

"No!" Her slender brows drew together, cutting a deep groove over her nose. "If he came across credit card data, he would . . . borrow it."

Hah! Just as I'd guessed when I'd studied the receipts from Dmitri's pockets. I love being right. I considered Irena.

Her affront when I accused Dmitri of identity theft seemed disingenuous; credit card fraud—excuse me, "borrowing"— was equally low, not to mention equally felonious. I bit back my sarcasm and said, "So how does that lead to you being in danger?"

She bit her lower lip, showing small, crooked teeth with a gray cast. Communist dental health at its finest. "I don't know," she said.

She was lying. I eyed her averted profile as she gazed out the window to the parking lot. Time to bring out the big guns. "A friend of Dmitri's was killed today," I said.

She gasped and slewed around to face me. "What? Not Dara?"

Shaking my head, I said, "No. A man he worked with, Boyce Edgerton."

"Boyce?"

"You knew him?"

"Dmitri mentioned him once or twice, I think. You said . . . 'killed'?"

"Shot. Now, don't you think you should tell me what you know, before someone else—maybe Dmitri—ends up like Boyce?"

Agitated, she rose from the step and paced the empty living room. At the far end, near the kitchen, she whirled to face me. "He got caught."

"Who?"

"Dmitri."

"Recently?"

She shook her head rapidly. "No. Months ago."

"So why don't the cops have a record of it? Why isn't he in jail?"

"The man who caught him didn't turn him in. He made him a deal."

Her story smelled worse than a fish market in a heat wave. "Really? Dmitri agreed to 'go forth and sin no more' and the man turned him loose?" I wished I had phrased it differently; my religious upbringing pops up at odd moments.

"Not exactly."

Slamming my hand on the floor so hard it stung my palm, I pushed to my feet. Irena looked startled. "The time for pussy-footing around this is past, Irena," I said, striding toward her. "A man's been killed. Your sister's in the hospital. It's clear your son is no Boy Scout, that he's mixed up in something criminal. So spit it out!"

Backing up a step, her eyes fixed on me as if she thought I was going to beat the truth out of her, she held up her hands placatingly. "The man made a deal with Dmitri. He knew who Dmitri was, knew he skated internationally. He suggested that he could let Dmitri walk away if Dmitri would agree to occasionally carry small packages for him on his trips."

"So Dmitri became a drug smuggler?" I asked incredulously.

"No, it wasn't drugs," Irena said. "The man swore it would never be drugs. Dmitri wouldn't do that."

Right. Like it's smart to take the word of a man who blackmails you. I arched my eyebrows skeptically but only said, "Who is this man?"

"I don't know."

At my disbelieving look, she said, "I don't! Dmitri said it was safer for me not to know."

That sounded barely plausible, so I let it drop. "So Dmitri started couriering something—not drugs—and all of a sudden this archvillain—let's call him Mr. X—decides to start offing Dmitri's friends and relatives?" I shook my head. "I think you're leaving out a few pieces of the story, Irena."

Glaring at me, cheeks flushed a becoming red, Irena spat, "It's none of your business. I should never have called you back, but you sounded . . . I thought maybe you could help Dmitri. Just forget it!"

She stalked toward the door, brushing past me roughly enough to knock me a little off balance. She jerked the door open, her gaze on a cell phone she pulled from her jacket pocket.

She wouldn't get far without a car. "Where are you—"

A bullet zinged past Irena Fane and buried itself in the staircase.

20

Irena Fane shrieked and dropped the phone. Diving at the door, I slammed it shut and locked it in a single motion. I scooped up the cell phone and dialed 911 as glass exploded from the front window, fanning out in a deadly burst of sparkling shards. That was going to cost Fane his security deposit. I felt stinging cuts open up on my face and arms. Luckily, my eyes seemed unaffected. I blinked rapidly as Irena screamed again and put her hands over her ears. I grabbed her hand. "C'mon."

We pounded up the stairs as another bullet thunked into the wall where the television had stood. When I'd searched the condo a couple of days ago I'd been happy to see that the place was largely deserted during business hours. Now, I wished for a coffee klatch of at-home neighbors to tackle the unknown shooter and/or summon the police. The 911 operator was still squawking from the phone in my hand, and I shouted the address at her as Irena and I ran, adding, "Shots fired!"

Irena and I dashed through the door of Dmitri's bedroom—also denuded of furnishings—and slammed it behind us. I turned the lock in the knob. Of one accord, we ran to the window as the sound of splintering wood drifted from downstairs. The shooter was kicking down the door. It might take him a couple of minutes to breach the front door, but the flimsy bedroom door would give him no trouble at all.

"It's too far," Irena gasped, looking down at the inhospitable mix of landscape rock and old snow a long way below us.

"Up," I said. "We have to go up."

An eave overhung the window, sticking out far enough to make for an awkward grab.

"I can't," Irena said, leaning out the window and twisting at the waist to survey the roofline.

"I'll hold you," I said, thrusting the cell phone into my pocket.

Another gunshot rang out, and I thought our determined attacker must have given up on the whole kick-the-door-in idea and resorted to shooting out the lock. The sound propelled Irena onto the windowsill. I held her feet as she scooched out backward until her weight rested on her thighs and she could reach up and grab hold of the eave. With one hand gripping the edge, she swung her other forearm up and over. I slowly eased her legs out the window as she pulled herself up until her whole torso disappeared from view. Luckily, she had a decent amount of upper body strength, either from her skating days or because she trained with weights. She got one knee over the lip of the roof and quickly pulled her legs up and out of sight. I heard her footsteps above me as I settled myself on the sill.

I knew immediately that this was going to be next to impossible without someone to brace me. Reaching for the eave with one hand, I felt myself slipping backward and quickly grabbed the sill again. *Bang!* The front door slammed into the wall, making the whole condo shudder. Footsteps thudded on the stairs, and I knew the shooter would be on me in a second.

Quickly standing, I repositioned myself on my stomach with my legs hanging out the window. Slithering backward, scraping my stomach and arms against the sill, I lowered myself until I was hanging by my fingertips, my body pressed against the splintery siding of the condo. Police sirens sounded surprisingly close by.

I was losing sensation in my fingers, and my arms trembled with the strain of holding my weight. I looked back over my shoulder at the inhospitable terrain below. Should I drop or hope the shooter overlooked me? It wasn't *that* far down, not like leaping off the Golden Gate Bridge or the Empire State Building. I mean, a serious suicide wouldn't pick this as her jumping-off point. I had about decided to risk a broken leg by letting go when I heard a foot slam into the bedroom door, which popped open, whacking the wall and probably leaving a hole.

A patrol car squealed around the corner into the parking lot, running Code Three with its lights flashing and siren blaring. The footsteps headed for the window halted, then reversed, and relief sagged through me. "Help!" I yelled as those anonymous footsteps bounded down the stairs. I struggled to pull myself up, but I didn't have enough strength left in my arms to manage it. My shoulders screamed. Damn.

"Drop your weapon," an authoritative voice commanded.

Relief whistled through me. The police had caught the shooter.

"And come down from there," the cop added.

What? I looked over my shoulder again, feeling my fingers beginning to slip. A lone uniformed cop stood almost directly below me, gun held steady in two hands, pointed at me. "You have got to be kidding me," I yelled. "I don't have a weapon, the guy ran out the front, and if you don't move right now, I might fall on you." With my luck, they'd charge me with assaulting a police officer. "Help me!"

Another cop came running up, assessed the situation, and disappeared around the front of the condo. In a minute, strong hands grasped my wrists and he hauled me up and in. "Thank you," I gasped. Leaning against the wall, I tried to flex my cramped fingers. No go.

"What happened here?" the cop asked. A burly twenty-something with a lumpy nose, he maintained a calm expression as I filled him in. His name tag said GRADNEY, and he took notes with tiny, precise capital letters.

"The roof!" I exclaimed, halfway through my recitation. "Irena is up on the roof." I wondered why she hadn't called out once she saw the patrol cars arrive. Glancing out the window, I saw there were now four police cars in the parking lot. Officer Gradney radioed a compatriot, and in a surprisingly short time a man in painter's overalls topped with a University of Colorado sweatshirt pulled up in a pickup and unloaded an extension ladder.

Gradney and I hurried down the stairs and out the open door in time to see a cop descending the ladder, shaking her head.

"Nothing up there but a pissed-off squirrel," she reported.

Several sets of suspicious cop eyes swiveled to me. "She was up there," I insisted. "Irena Fane, mother of Dmitri Fane, the man who rents this condo."

"Not anymore he doesn't," the man in the sweatshirt piped up. I pegged him as the condo's maintenance supervisor. "He moved out yesterday. Saw the U-Haul truck."

"Did you actually see Dmitri?" I asked before the cops could get a word in. I had trouble believing Dmitri Fane, on the run from God-knows-who, had casually rented a U-Haul, packed up his belongings, and trundled off to . . . where?

"Wouldn't know him if I did," the man said simply. "Can I go now? I've got a toilet to unplug in 12C."

Officer Gradney waved him away with a word of thanks and turned back to me. "Let's go over your story again. You say you picked up this woman at the airport, came here for a chat about her missing son, and someone opened fire on you?" His tone was still polite, his demeanor calm, but his eyes were narrowed and watchful.

"On her," I said, suddenly remembering that it was Irena who had opened the door and drawn the first bullet. I wondered whether she was the shooter's target or if he was aiming for anyone at the condo. "Can we walk around the building while we talk?" I asked Gradney.

"I don't see why not. You want to see if there's someplace she could've come down?"

"Exactly," I said, pleased with his quickness. Montgomery might have some competition in the detective ranks before long.

On the far side of the block of four units, a leafless oak tree extended limbs to within a foot of the roofline. "There," I said triumphantly. "I'll bet she climbed down the tree."

Gradney shook his head doubtfully, examining the tree. "That limb's not too sturdy looking," he objected. "It wouldn't hold her."

"Irena's about as big around as my pinkie," I said, convinced the woman could have done it. What I wanted to know was *why* she had escaped from the roof and then run off. Maybe she'd gotten down before the police arrived and gone to get help? I looked around. No sign of her or any cavalry she might have summoned. No, I knew Mrs. Fane had followed in her son's nimble footsteps and done a runner. Maybe because being shot at scared her—not entirely unreasonable—or maybe for some other reason.

―—

I dragged myself back to the office once my frozen, cramped fingers thawed sufficiently to allow me to drive. Gigi was back from her outing in Old Colorado City, and Kendall was nowhere to be seen. Still at the Ice Hall, maybe. I made a mental note to ask her what the scuttlebutt among the skaters was about Dmitri's disappearance. Gigi had tugged down the zipper on her quilted vest and was fanning herself with a back issue of a PI magazine. A red flush mottled her face.

"Are you okay?" I asked, headed for the fridge and a Diet Pepsi.

"Hot flash," she moaned, fanning harder.

I hoped scientists invented a cure for menopause before I got there. "No sign of Kungfu, I take it?"

She shook her head. "No. I'm going to stake out the tattoo parlor tonight. Do you want to come?"

The hint of pleading in her voice made me grind my teeth. No, I did not want to come. I wanted to go home, cut out the vanity countertop from the length of plywood I'd bought two weeks ago, and then laze in my hot tub. We were only looking for Kungfu as a favor to Dan, and he was my buddy, not Gigi's. "Oh, all right," I said ungraciously.

She beamed. "Thanks, Charlie. I have a good feeling about this."

―—

At nine o'clock that night we sat scrunched down in the front seats of my rental car, facing Tattoo4U from a block away on the cross street. I'd vetoed taking Gigi's Hummer since Kungfu might have spotted it last night. The temps hovered in the midthirties, but I refused to let Gigi keep the engine running, knowing the exhaust streaming from the tailpipe would draw attention to us. I'd worn dark layers of warm clothing, plus gloves and a knit cap pulled low on my forehead. Gigi had on a violet parka with a fur-trimmed hood and lace-up suede boots, also fur trimmed, that made her look like a plump blond Eskimo. She hadn't worn gloves, so she sat on her hands in the passenger seat.

"Do you think he'll show up again?" she asked, practically pressing her nose up against the window glass.

"No idea," I yawned. We'd been here an hour already and had watched a man Gigi identified as Graham lock up the store and walk west. Most of the lights on the block were out, including the streetlights, which the city had turned off to save on electricity costs. I don't know how many streetlights remained lit, but it seemed like only one in every eight or ten. Darkness pooled around Tattoo4U, and none of the diminishing trickle of passersby, all of them headed to or from the liquor store, showed any interest in the business.

"Irena Fane must be worried sick about Dmitri," Gigi said out of nowhere. "I know how I'd feel if Dexter up and disappeared."

Relieved is how she ought to feel. Dexter was an arrogant, selfish ass who made Kendall look like Child of the Year. "She's got reason to worry," I said, arching my back against the stiffness of long immobility. "She knows he was involved with credit card fraud and who knows what other criminal activities. People he was close to are getting beaten and shot, and someone took potshots at us in his condo. That adds up to a lot worth worrying about, in my book."

"I don't know how you keep kids from ruining their lives by doing stupid things," Gigi sighed. "There are so many traps out there for kids these days—drugs, pregnancy, body piercings that get infected—"

Ow and ick.

"—cyberbullying, eating disorders, misfits spraying automatic weapons around school cafeterias. I've tried to help them understand . . ." She trailed off as if thinking about all the things a parent needed to cover with teens exhausted her.

"At least you're there for your kids," I said, thinking about my missionary parents, who serially abandoned me, first with my grandparents and then with my Aunt Pam and Uncle Dennis. "You're trying. They're probably absorbing more from your talks than you realize."

"That might be the nicest thing you've ever said to me, Charlie," she said. Her amazed and gratified tone made me feel slightly guilty. "Do you really think the kids listen to me?"

No, but it sounded good. My experience with teens, limited though it was, suggested they installed a V-chip equivalent that filtered out all parent noises. "It's not like Dmitri is a teenager," I pointed out. "The man's twenty-six. It's not his mommy's job to keep him out of trouble anymore." A flicker near the tattoo parlor caught my eye. Was it tree limbs swayed by the chilly breeze? I leaned forward to peer out the windshield. No, there was definitely something moving on the east side of the building. It might be nothing more than a stray cat, but . . .

"Come on," I told Gigi, opening the door. My hand went to the H&K 9 mm snuggled in its holster at the small of my back. I didn't expect to need it, but after coming under fire today, I liked the security blanket feeling of having it with me.

"Did you see something?" she asked, pulling her hands out from under her and reaching for the door handle.

"Don't slam the—"

Wham. Gigi turned with a guilty wince as the door slammed closed, alerting everyone in a three-block radius to our presence.

"I'll follow him around back. You wait in the front in case he makes a run for it."

"Got it," Gigi said, trotting at my side as I strode quickly toward the tattoo parlor. We passed a couple arguing about beer brands by the liquor store, and I slipped into the narrow gap between the tattoo parlor and its neighbor. Shards of broken glass glinted underfoot, and clumps of brittle weeds trapped newspaper pages, plastic bags, and other debris it was too dark to identify. I paused for a moment, halfway back, and listened. I heard nothing at first except the ambient evening noises, but as I tuned those out I picked up a funny scraping sound coming from the rear of the building. Stepping carefully to avoid crunching down on a discarded beer can or something equally noisy, I made my way to the back of the tattoo parlor and peered around the corner.

I could barely make out a hunched shadow, darker than the surrounding night, scraping at Tattoo4U's back door. It took me a moment to realize he was trying to pick the lock, a shiny padlock. A muffled "Shit" drifted to me, and I surmised he hadn't had much training in basic breaking and entering. I sidled silently around the corner, hoping to get close enough to tackle Kungfu before he noticed I was there. I rated my chances as pretty good because he hadn't once looked up from the doorknob since I'd arrived. I didn't want to have to draw my gun, not even as a threat, because bad things happen when guns come into play.

I had cut the distance between us to barely fifteen feet when he suddenly looked up, alerted by some tiny noise I'd made, or clued in by a subliminal sense of danger. The pale oval of his face turned toward me and he sprang to his feet, dropping whatever instrument he'd been using to pick the door. It clattered to the ground.

"Kungfu, wait!" I called as he whirled and began to run. I lunged at him, catching the tail of his jacket as he reached the corner. I tugged, breaking his stride, and flung myself forward just far enough to get my arms around his thighs and bring him to the ground.

"Charlie! Are you okay?" Gigi called out. I could hear her crunching over dried leaves and broken bottles as she hurried toward us.

Kungfu heard her, too, and struggled to his feet, kicking at my hands, which had slid down to his ankle and gripped it tightly. The youth was slipperier than a greased eel. He tried hopping away on his unencumbered foot, but my weight attached to his ankle slowed his progress considerably. He'd hop, dragging me about six inches, then pause to catch his breath. Hop, drag, pause.

"Father Dan wants to talk—" I gasped in between his hops.

The pause this time was longer. "Father Dan?" he asked, looking down at me where I played limpet.

Suddenly, Gigi appeared in front of us, violet parka visible even in the low light, bent knee, straight-arm stance like something out of a cop show's credits. What was she holding? I knew she didn't have a gun because I'd locked hers away "for safekeeping" and only took it out when we went to the shooting range for practice.

"Don't worry, Charlie," she yelled. "I've got him."

"Don't—" I started, "don't" being my default word of choice

when dealing with Gigi, but before another sound could leave my lips, pain jolted through me, making every muscle spasm. My hands clenched reflexively around Kungfu's ankle, and everything grayed out as he toppled.

21

I'm not sure I was completely unconscious, but I might as well have been. Grogginess and pain immobilized me for several minutes. The ability to think and analyze my surroundings slowly returned, and I realized I was lying on the gravelly ground behind Tattoo4U, with Gigi kneeling beside me, chafing my wrists as if I were the fainting heroine in some period romance. I tried to bat her away, but my hand flopped spasmodically.

"Oh, Charlie, thank goodness you're alive," she said, fear and relief pitching her voice higher.

I became aware of a heavy weight on my legs and tried to heave it off without success. I lifted my head and peered toward my feet. There seemed to be a body sprawled across my legs. Kungfu.

"What—?"

"I didn't know it would shock you, too," Gigi said. She put her face inches from mine, apparently trying to examine my eyes. "Do you have a headache? I hope you didn't get another concussion when you fell. How many fingers am I holding up?"

Since the fingers in question were a half inch in front of my nose, I couldn't focus on them. "Did you tase me?" I asked.

"No, oh no!" she gasped, rocking back on her heels. "I tased Kungfu, to stop him from getting away."

I rolled my eyes. "Since I was holding on to Kungfu at the time, you tased me, too," I said. "Don't you know anything about electricity and conductivity?"

My tone brought tears to her eyes. "I'm so sorry," she whispered. "Did it hurt?"

"Try sticking your finger in an electrical outlet and then ask me if it hurt," I bit out, shoving myself up on one elbow. At least my muscle function was coming back. So was Kungfu's; he rolled off my legs and lay staring up at the sky.

"Damn, that smarts," he said in impeccable, accentless English. "Shit!"

Even in my befuddled state, it occurred to me that he sounded like the product of the American public school system, not a scared immigrant from mainland China.

"Give me the Taser," I said to Gigi, holding out my hand. "Where did you get it?"

"The Internet," she said, handing over the weapon.

I stuck it in my pocket and clambered to my feet, brushing aside Gigi's helping hand. I reached down to grab Kungfu by the upper arm. "Come on, Kungfu, or whatever your name is. Probably something like Bill or Jason."

He got to his feet willingly enough, slapping gravel bits and dirt off his jeans. Standing, he was about three inches taller than me. The muscles in his arm tensed under my hand. "Did you say something about Father Dan?" he asked.

"Yes," I said, cheered that he didn't seem inclined to make a run for it. I wasn't up to chasing him after my near electrocution. "He's worried about you. He asked me to find you."

"Why you?" Kungfu asked, walking beside me as I headed for the street. Gigi trailed us, leaning forward to hear the conversation.

"I'm a PI." I stuck out my hand. "Charlie Swift." We had reached the street by now, and the light from the liquor store windows showed me a slim young man with black hair, smooth almond skin, and an Asian cast to his eyes.

Kungfu shook my hand with a firm grip. "Aaron Wong."

"I'm a PI, too," Gigi piped up. "Gigi Goldman."

Aaron and I turned and glared at her, united in our memory of the painful tasing. She dropped back a step, muttering, "Sorree! It was an accident. Well, not an accident, exactly, because I meant to shoot you—Kungfu, that is, not Charlie—but a misunderstanding. The directions didn't say—"

"How about we go see Father Dan?" I suggested.

Aaron cast a disgruntled look over his shoulder at the tattoo parlor and then at a middle-aged man emerging from the liquor store with a case of Corona. "Might as well," he agreed. "There's nothing more I can do here tonight."

Aaron and I pulled up in front of the rectory half an hour later, having dropped Gigi back at the office, where she'd left her Hummer. She wanted to get home and talk to Kendall before the girl went to bed. "Not that she'll be in bed before midnight," she sighed, "but she is only fourteen, and I don't like to leave her alone too long, especially after dark. I don't know what Dexter had planned for tonight, so . . ." She got out of the car slowly and beeped open the Hummer's locks. Her shoulders slumped as she crossed the parking lot.

"It was the right thing to do," I called to her after a brief internal struggle. "Tasing Kungfu." He made a disgusted sound from the backseat, but I ignored him. "For all you knew, he might have been armed, might have been going to shoot me."

"Thanks, Charlie," she said, climbing into the Hummer with a little more of her usual bounce.

I'd phoned to let Dan know we were coming, and he opened the door immediately when I knocked. "Charlie!" Dan said, his large frame filling the doorway. "What happened?"

"I look that bad, huh?"

"Not bad," Dan said, smiling, "but like you could use a Scotch."

"When can't I?" I crossed the foyer and headed to the kitchen, where I knew Dan kept his booze.

Aaron hung back as if unsure of his welcome but stepped into the entryway when Dan said, "It wasn't my plan to heat the great outdoors." They joined me in the kitchen, Aaron rubbing his hands together.

"Anyone else for Scotch?" I asked, raising the bottle I'd found in the cabinet over the stove. I eyed Aaron, who looked sixteen but held himself with the confidence of someone older. "I'm betting you're legal."

"Twenty-four," he admitted. "I'll take a beer, if you've got one."

Without comment, Dan pulled two beers from the fridge and opened them, handing one to Aaron and keeping the other for himself. "Let's sit," Dan said, leading us to the den at the back of the rectory, where a corner stove glowed with warmth and scuffed leather chairs beckoned invitingly. I flopped into the nearest one, sitting in it sideways with my knees over the squashy arm. Aaron stood with his skinny rear facing the stove's heat, and Dan headed for the chair opposite mine; it sighed a great poof of air as his weight settled in. Our reflections hovered palely in the dark, uncurtained sliding glass door that looked out to the backyard and my house beyond it.

"So, let's have it, Aaron," Dan said, setting his bottle on the scarred coffee table with a click. "You're obviously not a runaway like I thought. Where are you from and what are you doing here?"

"And why were you trying to break into Tattoo4U?" I asked.

Aaron edged his thumbnail under the bottle label and peeled up the corner. "I'm from California," he said finally. "West Hills, in L.A. I'm a reporter."

"Hello!" That made me sit up straighter. "Are you working on a story?"

He shook his head, dislodging silky bangs that fell into his eyes. He pushed them back impatiently. "No. I wish. I'm looking for my brother." His dark eyes flicked from me to Dan. Apparently reassured by what he read in our faces, he continued, "It's a long story."

"There's more beer where that came from," Dan said, nodding at the bottle in Aaron's hand.

Aaron flashed a quick smile but then sobered. "It all started when my brother enlisted in the army last year. He was only eighteen and had just graduated from high school. He wasn't much of a student—more because he's a little spacey than because he's not smart—and he didn't apply to any colleges. He worked at a grocery store for a month or so, but then, out of the blue, he visited the recruiting office with one of his buddies and signed on. I actually thought it might be good for him— give him a little discipline, you know, and money for college later—but it freaked our mother out. She was sure he'd get killed in Afghanistan."

Dan nodded. "With Fort Carson down the road, I counsel

a lot of army spouses and parents when the units deploy. Living with uncertainty about a loved one's well-being can be hard, too."

Aaron looked grateful for Dan's understanding. "Yeah, well, Mom got Nate all worked up about it, and he decided he didn't want to do it, but he'd already signed the contract. I talked to him, got him settled down a bit, and he went off to basic training feeling pretty good about the decision, I thought. Then one of the guys in his unit or platoon or whatever you call it, committed suicide, and Nate totally lost it, insisted he had to come home immediately. Well, of course the army didn't let him, so he just left."

Aaron looked from me to Dan again, searching our faces for—what? Judgment? Understanding? I'd spent several years in a military uniform and had little sympathy for troops who took the paycheck but didn't pull their weight. Still, it sounded like Aaron's brother wasn't cut out for life as a soldier. I raised my brows as an invitation for him to continue.

"I didn't see him," Aaron said. Flecks of soggy paper sifted to the carpet as he continued to work at the beer label with his thumbnail. "He got home and told Mom he was AWOL, that he'd be sent to prison if the MPs caught up with him. She gave him the money she had on hand, and he told her he was going to head for Canada."

"So what are you doing here?" I asked. I drained the last sip of Scotch from my glass and contemplated getting more. I was too comfortable in the chair to bother moving.

"He hitchhiked here," Aaron said, tension invading his voice. "I guess he was working his way gradually north when he could get a ride. He called Mom from Dellert House and told her he had a line on a fake ID. He said next time she heard from him he'd be in Canada. We never heard from him again,"

Aaron said quietly. "That was a month ago. When she finally told me what was going on, I took vacation time and headed up here, thinking I could get a lead on him."

"I can see why you didn't involve the police, but why bother with the illegal immigrant routine?" Dan asked. From the set of his jaw I knew he was annoyed that Aaron had lied to him, and that he'd bought into Aaron's tale.

"I thought I might learn more if I seemed to be in Nate's situation," Aaron said. "Someone who needed an ID, someone who might be in a bit of trouble with the law."

"So did you?" I asked.

He nodded, narrowing his eyes. "Yeah. Someone left me a note in my stuff at Dellert's. It said that if I was interested in a new identity, I should visit Tattoo4U. So I did. I hung out there some and talked to the guys who seemed to be regulars, but when I hinted around about needing some ID, I got nothing."

"Maybe someone wasn't buying your illegal alien act," Dan suggested.

"Or maybe they didn't think you could pay the going rate," I said. "Do you still have the note?"

He shook his head. "No. I tucked it back in my book, where I found it, but it was gone the next time I looked for it."

"Someone's being cagey," Dan said, sliding a look at me.

"Slick," I agreed. "No exposure. No trail."

"Did anyone remember your brother?" Dan asked.

Aaron looked a little sheepish. "I couldn't really ask about him, not when I was pretending I hardly spoke English. How would I explain knowing Nate? Besides, most of the guys there seem to be in and out in a matter of days. I doubt there's anyone there now who was around a month ago when Nate came through. Maybe he scored some ID and moved on to Canada and we'll hear from him when he gets settled."

He didn't sound convinced.

"Have you been in touch with your mother since you got here?" Dan asked.

Aaron nodded. "Yeah, she hasn't heard from Nate."

We were silent, pondering the possibilities. They didn't seem good from my vantage point. I found it hard to believe that an apparent mama's boy like Nate would suddenly stop communicating with his mother for no reason. I couldn't think of a good reason; most of them were bad.

"Why were you trying to break into the tattoo parlor?" I asked Aaron.

"I got a feeling that place wasn't on the up-and-up," he said. "Call it reporter's instincts."

"What's your beat? Crime?"

"Sports." He shrugged and gave me a tired smile. "Hanging around that place, pretending to be undecided about getting a tattoo—I overheard parts of some conversations that didn't sound right. They've got a room in the back that's always locked, too. Graham—the owner—used a key to open it a couple of times. What's that all about in a tattoo shop? What are they hiding? One-of-a-kind tattoo designs?" He made a *prrp* sound that dismissed the idea that tattoo designs were worth guarding.

"What did you hear when you tried to break in Friday night?"

Aaron's head jerked up. "You were there? You saw me?"

"Gigi saw you," I said. "She took your picture."

"She's dangerous."

Dan cocked an eyebrow, inviting explanation, and Aaron told him about Gigi tasing us.

"Both of you?" Dan asked, a smile playing around his lips as he studied me. "I'll bet that hurt." He chuckled.

I gave him the finger.

Edging away from the stove, Aaron set his beer bottle beside Dan's on the coffee table.

"Let's find you a spare toothbrush and get you to bed," Dan said, noticing his guest's weariness.

"I can stay here?" Aaron looked surprised and relieved.

"Sure. You can help the custodian with some chores around the church in the morning."

"That's great," Aaron said. "I got fired from my newspaper when I didn't go back last week, and my credit card's getting declined now, so I really don't have anywhere to sleep. Ironic, huh? I showed up at Dellert House pretending I was homeless, and now I really am, until I get back to California anyway."

I pondered the sacrifices he was making to find his brother while Dan ushered him out of the den and down a hallway I presumed led to the bedrooms. He'd given up his job and put his life at risk to find the Nate-the-Deserter. I wondered if Nate, assuming we found him, would appreciate what his brother had done for him, or resent it.

Dan returned a few minutes later and grasped my hand to pull me out of the soft chair. I was tired and achy and supposed I should blame the tasing. Dan kept a grip on my hand once I was up. His large, callused thumb traced circles absently on the back of my wrist, sending shivers of warmth up my arm.

"You okay?" he asked.

"You ask that a lot," I said with a small smile.

"I wonder it a lot," he said, looking down into my face.

I squeezed his hand and released it. "I'm fine," I said. "Or as fine as someone gets to be after being electrocuted."

"You didn't make Gigi feel bad about it, did you?"

I stared at him in disbelief. "No, I told her I like being

zapped with a kajillion volts of electricity and asked for another round. Jesus, Dan!"

He backed away a step, his face closing down. "You're tough on her sometimes. She tries hard."

"Whoop-de-doo." Was I really such a bitch that Dan felt he had to protect Gigi from me? I'd told her she'd done the right thing, for Pete's sake. "I'm tired," I said shortly. "I'll see you tomorrow."

Dan stepped aside silently, and I walked past him to the front door. "Thanks for finding Aaron," he said as I yanked the door wide.

The frigid air bit my face. "Sure," I said. "It's what I do."

22

My house seemed cold and empty after the warmth of Dan's. I flicked on the kitchen light, my eyes going immediately to the length of plywood leaning against the wall. I'd already removed the old counter, a mustard-colored Formica, and I found the half-finished look of my kitchen depressing. Usually, I found it exciting, enjoying the process of transforming an old, dingy room to something vital and fresh. Tonight, though, maybe because I was tired, it weighed on me, an unfinished task. Pulling the OJ from the fridge, I glugged some straight from the carton, noting by the microwave's digital clock that it was only ten o'clock. It felt later.

I restored the OJ to the fridge and was debating whether I wanted to soak in the hot tub or just tumble into bed when a vibration against my thigh, accompanied by a slight buzzing, made me jump. Sliding my hand into my pocket, I pulled out Irena Fane's cell phone. I hadn't given it a thought since calling 911 on it earlier. I mentally smacked my forehead for overlooking it as the phone vibrated again. I pushed SEND, lifting the phone to my ear.

A man's voice, tense with anxiety, said, "Mom! Where've you been? I was worried when I didn't hear from you. Mom?"

"It's Charlie Swift, Dmitri," I said when he paused. "Don't hang up. Someone shot at your mom and me today."

An indecisive silence drifted down the line, but he didn't cut the connection. "We need to meet," I said. "I can help you." Probably.

"Who are you? Where's my mom?"

"I'm a private investigator. I've been looking for you. I don't know where your mom is. We were talking at your condo when someone opened fire on us; your mom escaped, and I haven't seen her since."

Suspicion crept into his voice. "Why do you have her phone?"

I explained. "Let's meet. Maybe I can help you figure a way out of this. Your mom told me about the credit cards."

"Shit."

I tried to make out the background noise coming over the phone and finally decided it was traffic. That didn't help me pinpoint Dmitri's location. "Your mom's in danger," I said when he'd let thirty seconds elapse without responding.

"Do you do any bodyguard work?" he asked finally.

"Sometimes." I'd done it once and decided never again. Most people who wanted bodyguards, according to a friend of mine in the personal security business, either grossly exaggerated their importance or were so nasty that they inspired people to want to shoot them. Who needed the aggravation? Still, if saying I did bodyguard work convinced Dmitri to meet with me, I was all for it.

"Okay."

He paused again, and I could hear what sounded like a roar in the background. It came again, a lion or tiger announcing dinnertime or wooing a nearby female. Maybe Dmitri was near the Cheyenne Mountain Zoo. The zoo wasn't too far from the Ice Hall.

"Meet me at the Garden of the Gods visitor center at eleven."

"I'll be there."

The prospect of finally catching up with Dmitri swept away my exhaustion, and a couple of ibuprofen pills took care of my aches. I was back in the rental, headed toward the rendezvous point, in fifteen minutes. The Garden of the Gods is one of the city's big tourist attractions, an expanse of rock formations set on the city's west side. During the day, the formations were a sandy red. Set against the backdrop of Colorado's pure blue sky, they made beautiful postcards. Rock climbers tested their skills against the formations, occasionally tumbling to their deaths. Hiking trails wound through the thirteen-hundred-acre park and were a favorite with joggers in the early morning. At night, however, even with a half-moon shining, the park was a featureless collection of gray and grayer lumps casting inky shadows.

I eased into the visitor center parking lot, across the road from the park proper, and coasted to a stop. No other cars loitered in the lot, and the visitor center was deserted and dark. I'd had enough of sitting in cars for one night, so I switched off the ignition and climbed out, marching in place to stay warm. Moments later, a car's headlights panned the lot and a car pulled in. Dmitri's silver Mustang. He parked a healthy distance away, leaving his headlights on and pointed toward me. I walked outside the light cones, not liking the spotlit feeling. My H&K was still reassuringly heavy at the small of my back. When I was twenty feet away, Dmitri called, "Charlie Swift?"

"That's me," I said, stopping near the passenger window, which was rolled down to let heated air and the throbbing bass of an Aerosmith tune escape. I bent to peer in but could get only a vague idea of Dmitri's appearance in the backwash from the headlights. I got an impression of dark hair, pale skin, and a strong profile.

"Hop in." The locks clunked open.

"You get out," I countered. I had no intention of getting into his car and ending up God-knows-where.

"But it's cold," he said.

The man was an ice-skater, for heaven's sake. He and cold should be on first-name terms. "Deal with it."

Grumbling, he got out, ostentatiously rubbing his hands together. The headlights showed a lean, athletic figure clad in jeans and a dark hoodie. A broad expanse of brow and high cheekbones made his face arresting, and I could see why Kendall found him appealing.

"I still haven't heard from my mom," he said.

"Have you tried the hospital?" I asked drily.

"The hospital?"

"Where your aunt is on life support?"

His lips thinned. "I didn't want that to happen. I'd visit her if I didn't figure they'd be watching for me."

"Who's 'they'?"

Dmitri leaned against the hood of the car, between the head-lights, and crossed his arms over his chest. A *yip-yip-yip* sounded from Garden of the Gods, and I figured a hungry coyote was hunting. "You said you do bodyguard work," he said, not an-swering my question.

"Sometimes, but I don't think you need a bodyguard. You need to go to the police, tell them what you know."

He gave a crack of unmirthful laughter. "I'm not looking for a bodyguard for me; I want you to watch out for my mom."

I shook my head. "No can do."

"You just said you do bodyguarding!"

"I've been hired to find you, Dmitri."

"Find my mom and take care of her. I can pay you."

"I'll keep an eye out for her. The best thing you can do for your mom is talk to the police. From what she says, you're into something criminal, something way over your head. You need to suck it up on the credit card fraud and tell the police what you know about the men who beat your aunt and killed Boyce."

He stiffened. "Boyce is dead? How? When?"

He could've been faking his astonishment, but I didn't think so. "Shot. Early this morning."

"Oh, God. Boyce didn't know anything about anything. Why'd they kill him?"

He sounded like he was talking to himself, but I answered. "To put pressure on you, maybe. What've you got that 'they' want?"

"I'm going to level with you," he said in an earnest voice that told me he was about to lay a whopper on me.

"Great."

"I was using the catering gigs to lift people's credit card data. To make things a little easier, what with all the skating fees and everything."

Why is it crooks always think they deserve for things to be "easier"? "You didn't get a family discount from Bobrova?"

"Have you met her?"

At my nod, he said, "Then you know the answer to that. Coach Bobrova is my mom's oldest sister. She and Mom were never close, mostly, I guess, because she was so much older. When she offered to take me on and paired me with Dara, Mom thought it was an olive branch of sorts. I think she knew I was going to make it big and she wanted in on that."

His off-putting hubris didn't mean he wasn't right. "Why hide the relationship?"

"Would you want to introduce her as your aunt?" Without waiting for an answer, he added, "She didn't want anyone thinking she played favorites, so we didn't play up the relationship. Some of the old-time skaters, from when she and my mom and dad were still skating, they remember."

"Did she know you were hiding out in her cabin?"

He jerked forward, losing contact with the Mustang's hood. "How did you—?"

"Boyce told me about the cabin. I was there when it blew up. Know anything about that?"

"They almost got me." Remembered fear made his voice shake. "I stuck one of them with a knife." His face seemed a little paler.

That explained the blood on the cabin floor. "What happened then?"

"I ran. I got lost in the woods and almost froze to death. I saw the glow from the fire, but I didn't know what it was until I found my way into Estes Park the next morning and read about it."

Dmitri had probably been within half a mile when I got to the cabin. If only I'd arrived an hour earlier! Maybe Boyce would still be alive. "So, you stole credit card data and got caught. The guy that caught you made you a deal, and you started couriering for him and—"

"Mom's got a big mouth," Dmitri muttered. "I suppose she told you the rest of it?"

"Enough," I said, trying to make it sound like I knew more than I did.

"I didn't tell her everything," he said, and I felt rather than saw his sidelong glance at me. "I wanted to keep her safe."

Yeah, that was working great. I wondered how safe she felt fleeing from a gunman spraying bullets around like Glade air freshener. "Of course," I said.

He shifted against the car's hood, and I figured his butt was getting as cold as mine was against the frigid metal. "I took a couple of the packages and delivered them as instructed," he said. "One in the Czech Republic and the other in Japan. They were small, didn't tick and didn't smell. I was worried that TSA would stop me, but they went right through the scanner, no problem. Then, on a trip to France, I got curious and I opened one of the packets. I'd studied the way the other two were wrapped, and I came prepared with the same kind of tape and everything."

He sounded proud of himself, and I fed his ego, wanting to keep him talking. "Clever," I said admiringly. "What was it?"

"IDs. A passport, driver's license, an ATM card, even a library card. I didn't know what to think. I'd expected drugs or diamonds, something like that."

"What did you do?"

"Wrapped it back up and delivered it like I was supposed to. I guess I felt a little better about the whole thing. I mean, I'd've felt bad if I'd found out I was passing along drugs."

"It's important to feel good about your illegal activities," I said. What a toad.

"Hey! I didn't think there was anything so bad about it, not until . . ."

"Until what?" I pulled my leather jacket tighter and stamped my feet to get some feeling back in them. Something scrabbled at the edge of the parking lot.

"Well, I took to opening the packets every now and then, just curious, you know. A few weeks back, I recognized the photo on the driver's license. It was a guy who'd been on the news, a man convicted of raping and killing a twelve-year-old girl in Oklahoma." Revulsion sounded in his voice, and I was glad to know that he found some crimes distasteful. "I realized then that I couldn't do it anymore—couldn't help make it possible for pervs like that to get away." Scuffing at pebbles with his boot, he sent them skittering across the lot. "Anyway, my mom probably told you what I did next."

"Um."

"So you know I'm working with the feds."

Hell, no, I didn't know that! "Working with the feds can be frustrating," I said, feeling my way.

"You got that right. When I first went to them with what I had, they were like, 'Yeah, man, let's go get 'em.' They said this bust could make some people's careers."

I was furiously trying to figure out which agency he was working with. FBI, probably. How could I finesse more information out of him without revealing that I had no clue what he was talking about? If he realized his mother hadn't blabbed all the details , he might clam up on me.

"Now they want me to turn over my proof, but it's the only insurance I've got. It's not like I can go into witness relocation or anything. How could I skate then?"

"It's probably not easy to skate if you're dead, either," I pointed out.

"I'm not going to be dead," Dmitri said with breezy confidence. "I'm too smart for them."

It would be way easy to dislike this guy. "I'm sure Bobrova and Boyce are impressed."

Sulky silence descended. A glint of red appeared at the far edge of the headlights. Two eyes stared at us.

"Get out of here!" Dmitri bent suddenly, and my hand went to my gun. He scooped up a rock from the asphalt and flung it at the coyote, which loped away. "Go on!" He scrabbled on the ground for another handful of stones and flung them uselessly into the dark.

I let my hand drop to my side and raised my brows. Portrait of a man on the edge. I shifted, momentarily stepping into the headlights' glare. Dmitri straightened, letting pebbles dribble between his fingers. His eyes widened as he stared at me.

"Hey, you were in my condo! In my bathroom! I only saw you from the back, but— You—" He pulled a gun from the hoodie's kangaroo pocket.

"You knocked me out!" I said, stilling at the sight of the weapon in what I was pretty sure were untrained hands. I didn't want to add a bullet to my body's tally of abuse for the day. "Easy with that."

"I came back for this." He waved the gun in a way that reminded me of Gigi—not reassuring. "I heard you sneak in, so I hid in the shower."

"I was looking for you," I said. "Dara hired me—"

"Ha! You're with them." Keeping the gun trained on me, he backed around the car to the driver's door. "You tell them that if something happens to me, they are so fucked."

"Tell who?" I asked as the door thunked closed and the engine turned over.

For answer, Dmitri revved the engine and headed straight for me. I leaped sideways, and the car's nose grazed my thigh. As I sprawled on the asphalt, the Mustang gathered speed and zoomed out the exit, fishtailing as it turned left onto Thirtieth Street. The brake lights flared for a moment and then receded into the distance, disappearing altogether as the car swung around a curve. I pushed slowly to my feet and plodded to my car, rubbing my thigh. I'd found Dmitri as I'd been hired to do, but I wasn't ready to chalk it up in the "win" column. I hadn't convinced him to talk to the police, and I still didn't know why "they" were beating up and killing Dmitri's family and friends. Further, I didn't get the feeling that he was ready to return to skating practice and Olympic competition, which was why Dara had hired me to find him in the first place.

I sighed and lowered myself gingerly into the seat, counting up the various ways people had inflicted harm on my poor body today: guns, Tasers, cars. I guessed I should feel grateful I hadn't been knifed or poisoned. Feeling stiff and distinctly ungrateful, I put the car in gear and headed for home.

23

I awoke Sunday morning feeling like I'd gone three rounds in a ring with Chuck Norris, Jean-Claude Van Damme, and a troop of wild chimpanzees. When was the last time Norris made a movie? I used to love *Walker, Texas Ranger*. Good guys win, bad guys lose, with a little martial arts and romance thrown in for good measure. At any rate, it was all I could do to swallow a handful of ibuprofen, grab a Pepsi from the fridge, and sit in the hot tub until my muscles loosened up enough to allow me to dress. There was no movement at Dan's house as I drove past, and I winced at the memory of the coldness between us when I left last night.

With Boyce Edgerton's murder investigation less than twenty-four hours old, I knew Montgomery would be working on a Sunday, so I pointed the car toward downtown and police headquarters. Undercover operations and the witness protection program were way out of my league—it was time to fill in Detective Connor Montgomery and see what he could chisel out of his contacts.

"Did we have a breakfast *date*?" Montgomery asked, landing hard on the last word, when he responded to the desk sergeant's notification that I was in the waiting area. He looked good in a yellow dress shirt tucked into gray suit pants with his badge looped over his belt. "I must've forgotten to put our *date* on my calendar."

"This is impromptu," I said, trying to ignore the broad grin from the desk sergeant and the curious looks from other people in the waiting room, "and it's not a date. It's friends having breakfast."

He slanted a wicked grin my way. "Friends with bene—"

"Do you want a free meal or not?" I headed for the door.

Catching up with me, he draped an arm over my shoulders. "So, where are we going—and what bit of information do you want in return?"

"The Olive Branch," I said, naming a downtown Colorado Springs institution. "And what makes you think I'm after any information? Can't I take a friend to breakfast without an ulterior motive?"

He laughed as if I'd suggested something outrageous— Lady Gaga doing a photo shoot wearing a Brooks Brothers suit, for example—and held the door for me.

When we were settled into a cozy booth with eggs, pancakes, coffee, and Pepsi in front of us, I told him about my meetings with Irena Fane and Dmitri.

"I saw the report on the shots fired at the condo," Montgomery said, crunching into a piece of toast. "I was meaning to call you about that today. What's your read on what happened?"

"Someone was watching the condo," I said promptly, having already sifted through the possibilities, "probably hoping

Dmitri would show. I don't see how anyone could have followed us from the airport—no one knew I was picking up Irena—so the only alternative is the shooter was already in place."

"And he opened fire because . . . ?"

I shrugged. "He was bored? He was trying to scare us? I suppose he could have been trying to kill Irena as a warning to Dmitri—" A stray piece of information tumbled into place and I set down my fork. "Dmitri's father, Stuart Fane, was killed in a car accident last November—I'm not sure of the exact date. What if—"

"It wasn't an accident?" Montgomery nodded consideringly. "I'll check it out."

I made a mental note to follow up with a friend in the insurance biz. "Can you also find out which agency Dmitri might be working with?"

"Might be? You don't believe him?"

"I don't *not* believe him; I'd just like a little independent confirmation."

"Trust but verify."

"Exactly. It seems strange that the feds would let their target—whoever he is—mow down their source's family and friends."

"Anything to make the case and earn that promotion," Montgomery said cynically.

"He tried to run me down, you know," I said, "so you can put out an APB on his car now. Assault with a deadly weapon." I described the Mustang and gave him its license plate.

"Tried to run you down?" Montgomery's face darkened. "Are you hurt?"

"A bruise on my thigh." I didn't mention that it was the size of a dinner plate and throbbed like the dickens. "All in all, it hurt less than getting tased."

"Fane tased you, too?" Real anger sounded in his voice, and it made me feel good to know he was concerned.

Shaking my head, I said, "Gigi." I told him about our stake-out but didn't feel compelled to correct his assumption that Kungfu was a run-of-the-mill runaway case. I'd clue him in later, if need be.

"Gigi should come with a warning label," he said. "Are you going to finish those pancakes?"

When I shook my head, he pulled the plate toward him with his fork and tucked into them. A family of tourists behind us debated the relative merits of visiting the Cave of the Winds or the Pioneer Museum that day, and a clutch of Colorado College students on our left moaned about a professor's grading policies. I sipped my Pepsi and watched with a half-smile as Montgomery inhaled the pancakes.

He looked up and caught me watching him. "What?"

"Nothing." I shook my head, embarrassed that I found the sight of a handsome man shoveling syrup-soaked pancakes into his mouth strangely appealing. I refused to admit that it was *this* handsome man, and not any generic pancake wolfer, that set my pulses thrumming. It was homey, even though we were at a restaurant. Somehow intimate, too, since they were my pancakes. Geez, I was losing it.

"Anything new on Bobrova?" I asked. "Is she conscious?"

Montgomery shook his head. "No, but she's doing better, according to the docs; they're more optimistic. Our background check on her has turned up something interesting, though."

"What?" I watched impatiently as he swabbed up syrup with the last bite of pancake.

"Seems her family has quite the history in Russia."

"Heirs to the throne history? Members of Stalin death squads history?"

"More like the latter. They controlled a crime empire in the 1970s and '80s."

I did some quick math. "That's about when Bobrova came to the States."

"Nineteen eighty-two. Their influence has diminished apparently in recent years—the old guard dying off and the younger generation wanting to go straight, maybe—but they were into everything from extortion and protection rackets to prostitution and murder-for-hire in the good old days."

I chewed at my lower lip, trying to absorb the implications. Could Bobrova's beating be connected to her family's criminal activities? It didn't seem likely. It would be a long way—in time and miles—for someone to come to get payback for some crime her family committed. "Do you think it plays into the attack?"

"Hard to see how," Montgomery admitted. "On the other hand, we're looking more closely into her finances and travels, to see if there's any evidence that she's carrying on the family tradition."

"And?" Despite her irascible manner, I had trouble seeing Yuliya Bobrova as boss of a Colorado Springs outpost of the Russian Mafiya.

"Nothing so far."

I reached for the check and slid my credit card onto the tray. "Those of us not taking the taxpayer's dime have to get to work," I said.

His hand closed on my wrist. "Let's have a real date," he said, his brown eyes fixed on mine. "Not a you're-paying-me-back date or a friends-doing-lunch date, but a real date."

My breath caught in my throat. "Okay," I heard myself saying while my brain reminded me that Montgomery was an adrenaline junkie like Brad, my fighter pilot ex, and that he was four or five years younger than I was, and that I hadn't had anything resembling a "relationship" in going on for three years, and—

"Don't look so panicked," Montgomery said, flicking my nose with his finger. "It'll be fun." He scraped back his chair, looking inordinately pleased with himself. "I'm working this weekend, so let's make it Wednesday. Seven o'clock. Dinner and a movie. Or maybe CC's got a home hockey game. I'll make the arrangements." He grinned down at me as we left the restaurant. "This is where you say, 'I'm looking forward to it, Connor. Can't wait!'"

"Don't forget to check on Fane's new undercover career," I said, not wanting to admit that I *was* looking forward to going out with him. My undisciplined mind zoomed right past the meal and hockey to what happened when he dropped me back at my house. Absolutely nothing, I told myself sternly. Nada. Well, maybe one teeny, tiny kiss on the doorstep.

As if he'd read my mind, he leaned down and brushed my lips with his. He tasted like coffee and syrup. "Something to think about until Wednesday," he said before turning and striding off toward police headquarters.

Damn the man. I scowled as I headed back to the rental. Once inside, warmed by the greenhouse effect of the sun streaming through the windows, I dialed my friend Jeanine, now a vice president with a major insurance company. She'd come a long way since we met as second lieutenants in the air force. I consciously tried not to compare my puny income with her mansion-buying-, cruise-vacationing-, art-collecting-sized paycheck; it would be too depressing. Even if her company hadn't covered Stuart Fane, she could find out who did and what their investigation revealed.

"It's Sunday," she protested, when I told her what I needed.

"You're at work," I pointed out.

"Yeah, well, I need my head examined. I'll see what I can dig up." With a put-upon sigh, she hung up.

It was forty-five minutes later and I had a sack of Gala apples, a bag of frozen blueberries, and a twelve-pack of Pepsi in my shopping basket at King Soopers when Jeanine called back. "That was fast," I greeted her.

"Yeah, well, it wasn't that hard. He was with State Farm. Their report showed no sign of intoxication or involvement by another vehicle. Icy road conditions, a moment of inattention—maybe he swerved to avoid a dog—and pow! Dead on impact. State Farm paid the claim."

"Any witnesses?"

Keyboard clicking told me she was scanning a document on her computer. "No. A homeowner heard the crash, though, and called the police. Ambulance and Detroit PD were on scene within ten minutes."

Detroit. For some reason, I'd assumed the accident happened here, even though I knew the Fanes lived in Michigan.

"So, nothing unusual? Nothing that aroused suspicion?"

"Nada," Jeanine said, a trace of impatience in her voice. "They don't get much more cut-and-dried than this."

I thanked her, told her I owed her, and hung up, ready to accept Stuart Fane's death as an accident that had nothing to do with the current rash of explosions, shootings, and deaths that all coincided with Dmitri Fane's disappearance.

24

"I've got good news and bad news," I announced to Gigi and Kendall when I arrived at the office. They stared at me expectantly; well, Gigi stared at me while Kendall finished applying her eighteenth layer of mascara. "I found Dmitri Fane."

"That's great, Charlie," Gigi enthused.

Kendall's mouth parted with anticipation, and her eyes brightened. Frankly, I didn't know how she could hold the lids open with all that mascara gooped on her lashes. The wildebeest-coconut smell wafted off her, and I stifled a rude comment. Too bad Domenica-Carol hadn't given her an unscented appliance of some kind.

"Then I lost him again," I said before Kendall could comment. "He pulled a gun on me, ran me down, and took off."

"Oh, Charlie!" Gigi said, concern on her face.

"What did you do to him?" Kendall asked.

"Silly me," I said caustically. "I offered to help him make his case with the police so people would stop shooting at his family members."

"Well, of *course* if you tried to get him arrested," Kendall said in a voice that indicated she thought he was justified in driving over me.

"I didn't—" I cut myself off. I was not going to explain myself to a fourteen-year-old. "What did you hear at practice yesterday?" I asked. "Are the skaters speculating about Dara and Dmitri?"

"Well, duh," Kendall said. "Trevor and Angel are skating around like they've already got the national championship sewn up, and Trevor's saying that Dmitri took off because he couldn't handle the pressure. As if!"

"What else?"

"Well, they're taking up a collection for flowers for Coach Bobrova. I said we'd put in ten dollars, Mom," she told Gigi.

Gigi merely nodded, but I ground my teeth, knowing money was tight for them. "That's it?"

"Pretty much," she said.

I sipped my Pepsi, thinking about what I needed to do today. Another visit with Sally Peterson was in order, to check on Dara's well-being—I was more worried about her since Irena and I had been shot at—and report on finding Dmitri. Sally Peterson was paying me, after all. I also wanted to swing by the hospital and check on Bobrova for myself, even though Montgomery had said she wasn't conscious yet. Maybe she woke up overnight. Another run at the catering company might also yield some clues; it hadn't escaped my attention that both Dmitri and Boyce had worked for Czarina Catering and both, it seemed, were crooks: Fane stole credit cards, and Edgerton dispensed illegal chemical substances. Maybe that was more than coincidence.

Gigi was filling me in with her tasks for the day—a couple of employee background checks for Brian Yukawa, owner of

Buff Burgers, site of Gigi's first undercover assignment and erstwhile home of Bernie, the morose bison head hanging over her desk—when the door opened, letting in a gust of January cold. Irena Fane walked in, bundled in a hip-length red coat that set off her dark hair and pale skin. I stared at her, Pepsi can halfway to my mouth.

"Dmitri said you will be my bodyguard," she announced simply.

No apology for running out on me Saturday, no explanation for the hail of bullets, no "glad to see you're all right." I turned a growl into a cough as I tossed my can toward the trash.

"Oh, and I need my cell phone back." She held out a gloved hand.

"Darn," I said with spurious apology. "I left it at home." I'd ransacked the phone for texts and phone numbers yesterday. All the texts and voice mails had been deleted, but I'd found a couple of numbers under RECENT CALLS that I intended to check out. "I didn't know I'd be seeing you today. Where did you disappear to?"

"Would you like some coffee?" Gigi offered.

For the first time, I noticed a new coffeemaker on top of the file cabinet. I sighed inwardly, wondering how long this one would last.

"Thank you," Irena said. She shook hands with Gigi. "I am Irena Fane."

"Gigi Goldman," I finished the introductions as Gigi rose to fill a star-decorated mug. "My p-partner." I still stumbled over the P-word on occasion. A brilliant idea hit me. "She'll be your bodyguard."

Gigi swiveled toward me, astonished, sloshing coffee over the mug's lip.

"You're Dmitri's mother?" Kendall asked.

"Yes." Irena smiled, although her jaw remained tight with tension.

"I think he's the best pair skater *ever*," Kendall gushed.

That earned a more natural smile. "Me, too."

"So, where did you run off—go Saturday? The police wanted to talk to you."

"I was scared," Irena said, giving a theatrical shiver. "You're probably used to getting shot at—"

Oh, yeah, it happened every day. A PI's life is one long shootout.

"—but it terrified me. I spent most of the afternoon and evening in the mall—I felt safer surrounded by people—and then called Dmitri from a pay phone. He said he'd met with you and that you would keep me safe until this blows over." She offered a tentative smile.

"You poor thing," Gigi said, pulling forward a chair for the woman to sit on. "Of course we'll take care of you." She gave me a meaningful look, urging me to reassure Irena.

I wasn't falling for it. Irena's story left several hours unaccounted for: Where had she been between mall closing time and eleven thirty or so when she got hold of Dmitri? "How did you get here today?" I asked.

"Dmitri loaned me his car. He said he would borrow one from a friend."

I looked out the front window; sure enough, the Mustang sat in the lot beside Gigi's yellow Hummer, not even a dent on the fender where he'd hit me. Clever, I thought. Dmitri obviously realized the police might now be searching for his car, so he'd foisted it on his mom. "He ran me down Saturday night, you know."

"He was sorry for that," Irena said after a tiny pause. "He thought you might be working for the men who are pursuing him, but then he realized his mistake. He asked me to apologize for him."

Hm. Her face was guileless, her tone appropriately apologetic, but something seemed off.

"Why didn't you tell me he was working with the feds?"

Irena played with the top toggle on her coat. "It's hot in here. Is there somewhere I can hang this?"

I indicated the coat rack by the door, and she shrugged out of her coat, revealing a terra-cotta sweater over black leggings that made her look tiny and fragile.

"The feds?" I prompted when she returned to her chair.

"Oh. Well, Dmitri told me that was confidential. He was very upset with me for telling you as much as I did."

"Charlie, can I speak with you a moment? In private?" Gigi asked, giving me another of those meaningful looks.

"Sure." Since our choices for privacy were the tiny bathroom or the sidewalk in front of the office, I headed for the great outdoors.

"I don't know anything about being a bodyguard!" Gigi wailed as soon as the door closed behind us. Traffic hissed by on Academy Boulevard, and clouds scudded the sky, hinting at the snow forecasters had predicted for this afternoon.

"There's nothing to it in a case like this," I reassured her. "The easiest thing to do is take the bodyguardee to a place no one expects them to be and sit on them."

"Sit on them?"

"Babysit her," I said impatiently. "Make sure she doesn't make any phone calls or open the door to strangers. You can scare her a little by closing the curtains and telling her not to make a target of herself in front of the windows."

Gigi gnawed her lower lip doubtfully. "Should I take her to a hotel?"

"Only if she springs for it," I said. "I was thinking your house might be a good place. No one would think to look for her there."

"Couldn't you—"

"Negatory." I shook my head firmly. "I've got too many leads to follow up on today. It could be dangerous for her to trail around after me."

"Why can't we recommend she go to a hotel and stay put?" Gigi asked.

"You've heard the saying 'Keep your friends close and your enemies closer'?"

Her blue eyes widened. "Is Irena our enemy? She seems so nice."

"Let's just say I'm not convinced she's a friend." Her disappearance after the shooting and her reappearance now seemed a bit hinky to me. As did her seeming acceptance of Dmitri's criminal proclivities. Plus, it struck me that as Yuliya Bobrova's sister, she came from the same crime-loving background that Bobrova did, so maybe Dmitri was genetically programmed to embrace a life of crime. Was there such a thing as a criminal gene? "She's our best chance of finding Dmitri again; clearly, they're still in touch. I've got her cell phone. If you keep her cooped up at your place and she uses your phone to call Dmitri, we'll have a record of the number and can maybe track him through that."

"If it's not a cell," Gigi pointed out.

I had to admit that the proliferation of cell phones had complicated the PI's life in many ways. "True." I caught a glimpse of Irena peering out the window at us. I waved in a friendly way, and she withdrew. "Load her into your Hummer and leave Dmitri's car here," I suggested. "That way, she'll have to rely on you for transportation."

"That's smart," Gigi said. I reached a hand to open the door, but she stopped me. "If I'm going to be a bodyguard, I should probably get my gun out of the safe, don't you think?"

Hell, no! Only if we wanted Irena to be more at risk from her bodyguard than from Dmitri's enemies. The hint of eagerness in Gigi's voice reminded me of the day she'd first shown up in the office, waving the gun around, convinced it was a PI's most necessary accessory. She'd been disappointed to realize I didn't take mine out of the safe more than three or four times a year. "How about the Taser?" I suggested. "That has plenty of stopping power."

Gigi looked stricken. "I'm so, so sorry—"

"Forget it," I said magnanimously, mindful of Dan's words. "Accidents happen."

<hr />

Having explained the plan to Irena, gotten her car keys off her for good measure, and seen the two women and Kendall off in the Hummer, I heaved a sigh of relief and called Sally Peterson, who said she could give me fifteen minutes between classes if I came to her office. Accordingly, I set off south on Academy Boulevard and made the right on Austin Bluffs that would take me to the University of Colorado in Colorado Springs. I was at her office within twenty minutes.

"Come," she called when I knocked on the half-open door.

She stood over her desk, reading glasses slipping down her nose, stuffing a pile of papers into a soft-sided briefcase. Other than a cleared semicircle on her desk, every square inch in the place was devoted to posters and photos of Dara. Dara with Dmitri, Dara with some pre-Dmitri partner, Dara with trophies, Dara with sports commentators. Strangely enough, there didn't seem to be any photos of Dara with Sally or Dara in jeans relaxing or hiking or with a prom date. It was as if Dara had no identity apart from that as skating phenom. Whew.

"Have you heard from her?" I asked with a nod at the room's decor.

"Oh, hi," she said absently, buckling the bag and shoving her reading glasses atop her head. "Walk with me—I'm running late for class."

I stood aside, and she exited past me, the tail of her royal blue cardigan snagging on the door's handle momentarily. She twitched it free and kept going. I fell into step beside her. An overachieving heater made the halls stuffy, and students of varying ages and ethnic backgrounds bumped us as they headed for their classes.

"She called this morning," Sally said. "Said she was fine. Wanted to know if we'd found Dmitri yet." She gave me a questioning look.

"Found and lost again." I gave her the details of my encounter with the elusive skater. "I wanted to make sure you knew that a friend of his was murdered Saturday—"

"A skater?" Sally looked horrified that it might be someone she knew.

"No, a co-worker from the catering company. Someone shot at his mother and me, too." I hesitated, not sure how she would take what I needed to say next. "Dara might be in real danger. She should contact the police—they're looking for Dmitri now. You probably need to accept that he's not going to be back in a skating rink anytime soon. He's admitted to credit card theft and seems to be mixed up in something worse and definitely more dangerous. If the police catch up with him, he may end up in jail, and if they don't . . ." I trailed off, not wanting to spell out that a dead partner wouldn't enhance Dara's chances for a gold medal.

"Then you'd better find him first," Sally Peterson said in a steely voice. "That's what I'm paying you for—to find him. If there's someone threatening him, find out who and get them off his back. Turn them in to the police . . . whatever it takes. Wherever Dara is, she's safe, and I'm not going to advise her to contact the police and get involved in the publicity storm that would generate. The Olympic Committee doesn't like adverse publicity for its athletes."

Did an obituary count as adverse publicity? I didn't ask.

We stopped at a classroom door, and the hubbub of chatting students drifted into the hall. "My class," Sally Peterson said. "Look, you find Dmitri and set it up so I can talk to him. I'm sure I can persuade him to do the right thing."

As I watched her stride into the classroom, announcing a pop quiz to a chorus of groans, I wondered what her definition of "the right thing" was. I had a sneaking suspicion it had more to do with ice-skating than with crime and justice.

—⁓⁓—

Returning to the parking lot to find my car unticketed—yes!—I slotted the key into the ignition as my phone rang. Montgomery.

"What've you got?" I answered.

"Interesting news. I reached out to the feds, and no one admits to running Dmitri Fane."

"He lied to me."

"Yes. But the guy I talked to at the FBI, who happens to be a poker buddy, mentioned that a week ago Friday they got a call from a man who claimed to have knowledge of an identity theft ring operating from Colorado. A ring that provides new identities to wanted criminals and sometimes illegals. You can guess why the fibbies were interested."

I whistled softly. "Terrorists?"

"That possibility made them eager to talk to the guy. He promised to send them proof that he had the goods, and they set up a meet for this past Saturday. They got the package—my buddy was pretty cagey about the contents—but the informant never showed and hasn't called back."

"They couldn't track him down? Surely they use caller ID."

"Disposable cell. They recorded the call, of course."

"Do you think it was Dmitri?"

"You tell me."

"Did you tell your FBI friend about him?"

"Of course," Montgomery said, a hint of impatience in his voice. "I had no choice."

Of course he didn't. *If* Dmitri was the FBI's mystery caller, and *if* he knew anything about terrorist identities, the FBI could bring a lot more resources to hunting him than the CSPD could. My mind wiggled its way back to last night's conversation with Aaron Wong. He'd said someone at Dellert House had pointed him toward Tattoo4U as the source of fake IDs. Could there be a connection? There had to be several groups, gangs, or individuals providing fake IDs in the Colorado Springs area—our population of illegal immigrants from Mexico and points south would provide a solid customer base, I figured. I knew of nothing that connected Dmitri Fane to Dellert House or Tattoo4U.

"Charlie? You still there?"

"Just thinking," I told Montgomery.

"Anything I should know about?"

"I don't want to waste your time with speculation," I hedged. "Let me poke around. If I come up with something concrete, you'll be the first to know."

"I'd better be." Montgomery hung up.

25

Irena Fane paced the long, narrow length of Gigi's Broadmoor living room, stopping only momentarily to look out the wall of picture windows before resuming her pacing. She was giving Gigi a headache. The woman was like a caged cat, Gigi thought, eyeing her nervously from the camel-colored leather sofa in front of the fifty-inch television. Not a big cat like a lion but something smaller and sleeker. An ocelot, Gigi decided. She'd warned the woman, as Charlie had suggested, about exposing herself at the windows, but Irena had paid no attention, saying she got claustrophobic in a room with no natural light.

"We should go out and look for Dmitri," Irena said for the sixteenth time since they'd entered the house forty-five minutes earlier. Kendall had run up to her bedroom as soon as they'd arrived. "Sitting here . . . we are wasting time."

"Your son was worried about your safety," Gigi said. "You're safest here. Charlie's looking for Dmitri. She's the best."

"How long have you been a bodyguard?" Irena demanded, hands balled on her hips. "Where did you go to bodyguard school?"

"I don't think there is a bodyguard school," Gigi said, considering it. "It's something you learn on the job." She didn't admit that her learning had just started.

"Then how do you know I'm safer here?"

"That's pure common sense. Why don't we bake cookies? I've been meaning to make a batch and take them to our new neighbors at Domenica's."

"Cookies! My son's life is in danger and you want to make cookies?" Irena snorted contemptuously. When Gigi rose from the sofa and headed for the kitchen, the smaller woman followed reluctantly, looking around. "The private investigator business must pay well," she observed, gaze lighting on the designer stainless steel appliances and granite countertops.

"Your son probably pays more for a skating costume than I make in a month," Gigi said, pulling flour from a cabinet. She didn't want to go into the whole situation about Les running off with Heather-Anne, leaving her and the kids to fend for themselves with nothing except the house, the Hummer, and the half interest in Swift Investigations to keep them off the street. He'd emptied all their checking accounts and cashed out their investments. None of that was Irena Fane's business.

Seemingly resigned to inactivity, Irena hoisted herself onto the bar stool at the kitchen island and watched as Gigi sifted flour, baking soda, and salt together. "Do you like being an investigator?" she asked.

"Most of the time," Gigi said. "It's not at all what I thought it would be, but I enjoy it. There's something new every day—it never gets boring."

"You do not seem like the investigator type," Irena said, eyeing her.

"I don't think there is a 'type.'"

"Of course there is. It's a man's career, really. You need to be tough, strong." She flexed a bicep.

"I can be tough," Gigi said, half offended. She stroked her upper arm surreptitiously, pretty sure a bicep lurked under the coral-colored angora sweater she wore. Why, she'd made it halfway through her *Arms of Steel* DVD yesterday, using the pink three-pound dumbbells Les had bought her four Christmases ago—and she'd only gained four pounds during the holidays, a personal best.

Irena laughed. "You are soft and kind. Not like that Charlie Swift. Now, she's tough. You should have seen her yesterday. Before I even realized someone was shooting at me, she slammed the door closed, dragged me up the staircase, and helped me get onto the roof."

"Then you deserted her," Gigi put in tartly.

"These things happen," Irena said obscurely. She pulled a cookie tin toward her and began rolling dough into balls and smushing them on the sheet. Within ten minutes, the cookie sheets were in the oven, giving off a tantalizing aroma of warm sugar and vanilla.

Gigi considered her uninvited guest, wondering what to do with her now. The blinds needed dusting and the bathrooms needed scrubbing—now that she could no longer afford a maid service, the basic household tasks went neglected for weeks—but she couldn't see inviting Irena to pick up a toilet bowl brush and start scrubbing. A phone rang, and Gigi looked around, confused. With a start, Irena pulled a cell phone from her jacket pocket, looked at the display, and said, "Yes?"

Gigi berated herself inwardly for not having considered the possibility that Irena might have acquired a new phone after handing hers over to Charlie at Dmitri's condo. She knew

Charlie would confiscate this phone, saying it was for the client's safety, but Gigi didn't feel comfortable snatching it from the woman's hand. What would she do if Irena mentioned that she was at Gigi's house? She fidgeted from foot to foot as Irena talked.

The thirty-second conversation from Irena's side consisted of yeses, nos, and a few ums, accompanied by sidelong looks at Gigi. "You, too," she said in a wrapping-it-up tone, adding, "I'm at—"

"No!" Gigi yelled, leaning across the counter to swipe at the phone.

Irena reared back, astonished, as the timer on the oven went off with a loud, droning *beep*. She swayed on the stool. The phone clattered to the floor.

"You can't tell anyone where you are," Gigi said over the beeping. She hurried to the oven and punched at the timer button. Sliding a mitt over her hand, she pulled the cookie tin out.

Irena slid gracefully off the stool and retrieved the phone. "He's gone," she said, snapping it shut. "I can tell my son where I am, I think. He does not pose a threat to me."

"That was Dmitri?" Gigi's eyes widened. "Do you know where he is?"

"He is taking care of a few things," Irena said, lids half-shuttering her eyes. "He says we will not have to worry anymore after tonight."

Gigi thought about trying to wrest the cell phone from Irena to check the phone number of the last incoming call. She couldn't quite work up the nerve to tackle the smaller woman, especially since she was a guest in her home. Flinging one's guests to the floor and forcibly removing their communications devices didn't fit the southern notion of hospitality Gigi had grown up with.

"Since it seems like I'm going to be stuck here most of the

day, what will we do?" Irena looked at Gigi as if expecting her to produce a first-run movie or a chamber ensemble for her entertainment.

Gigi disappeared into the walk-in pantry, emerging a moment later with a mop and a feather duster. "Mop or dust?" she asked.

26

I flipped a mental coin to decide whether I should revisit Czarina Catering first or head for Dellert House to check it out. Czarina Catering won, so I headed downtown, planning to swing by Dellert House afterward. Parking in the lot behind the champagne-colored Victorian, I entered Czarina Catering by way of the kitchen and found Gary Chemerkin pouring ingredients into an industrial-sized floor mixer that was almost as tall as I was. The door closed behind me with a quiet *snick*.

"Be with you in a moment," he said, not looking around. He coughed as the huge bag of flour he was spilling into the bowl poofed up a white cloud.

"That's one heap big mixer," I said.

He turned to look at me. His round glasses showed a hint of condensation, and sweat sheened his forehead. "Sixty quarts. What can I do for you now, Ms. Swift? I'm shorthanded and busy, so I don't have a lot of time." He wiped his hands on the white apron he wore over tan slacks and a pale green shirt with the sleeves rolled up. Shiny cordovan-colored loafers showed a film of flour. He didn't look like he'd come to work planning to slave in the kitchen.

"I'm still looking for Dmitri," I said, leaning back against one of the stainless steel counters. "I don't suppose you've seen or heard from him?"

"No," Chemerkin said shortly, "and I don't expect to. I've had it with that prima donna. He's fired." He flipped a switch, and the mixer started doing its thing.

"Dmitri being gone and Edgerton being dead must put quite a hole in your lineup."

He shot me a sharp look. "Boyce's death is a tragedy. We'll miss him here at Czarina. We're donating a cake for the post-funeral reception. Very tasteful. White cake and icing with real lilies for decoration. The family is still deciding on the text they want—probably his name and the dates."

Like a headstone. I shuddered at the thought of cutting into such a cake. "I suppose the publicity about Boyce's drug dealing hasn't done your business a lot of good."

"No one can convince me that Boyce was a dealer," Chemerkin said. He passed a hand over his neat beard. "He smoked a little weed now and then, sure, but dealing? No way. The police told me, of course, that they found a stash in Boyce's apartment, but that doesn't prove Boyce put it there."

"You think he was framed?" I considered the idea. "By whom?"

"How would I know that?" he asked testily.

"Dmitri?"

"Don't be ridiculous."

The idea intrigued me, and I was silent for a moment, thinking. Maybe Dmitri wasn't the victim here. Hell, he'd admitted to credit card fraud. Could he and Edgerton also have been in the drug business together? Had he disappeared because he thought Chemerkin or the police were on to them? That didn't explain the exploding cabin, though, or a shooter raining bullets on Irena and me. A few stolen credit card numbers or a drug stash small enough to hide in a toilet tank wasn't worth murdering over. I scrambled some of my assumptions. Maybe the drugs were a sideline or, as Chemerkin suggested, for personal use only. Perhaps Dmitri and Edgerton were part of a more sophisticated theft ring, one that used the catering business as a cover to systematically steal credit card data and used the stolen numbers to buy valuables that were later sold via eBay or Craigslist. I knew a lot of stolen merchandise got fenced on those sites. Or, since Dmitri had copped to transporting fake IDs . . . I thought about it: What kinds of data might be available in someone's kitchen, easily snatchable by a crooked caterer? I kept my bills and bank statements in a tray by the phone on the kitchen counter, and I had friends who kept all their paperwork on built-in kitchen desks. Some people even kept laptops there. Was it possible that Dmitri and Boyce could've carried out such thefts over the long term without Chemerkin noticing? I studied the man with his graying blond hair and slight paunch.

"I suppose Dmitri's credit card thefts would be even worse for business, if word got around."

His face flushed a brick red. "If you dare even *hint* at such a thing, I'll have you in court so fast your head will spin."

I found it interesting that he didn't outright deny Dmitri was a thief. I held up a placating hand. "I'm not planning to mention it to anyone, even though Dmitri told me he's been stealing credit card data from your clients for several months."

"You talked to Dmitri? Recently?" Interest sharpened Chemerkin's tone.

"Last night." Chemerkin's reaction seemed too intense, and I tried to read his expression, a mix of surprise, avidity, and something else I couldn't define.

As if aware that he'd aroused my suspicions, the man made a disgusted noise, turned back to study the mixing bowl's contents, and said, "If you see him again, tell him he's fired."

"Sure," I said, still trying to figure out his reaction. "Do you have a copy of your client list from the last year?" I thought it might be worth checking to see if any of Czarina's clients had reported being victims of identity theft.

He gave me a "fat chance" look. "Of course, but I'm not sharing it with you. My clients have a right to their privacy."

"Oh, come on," I said. "It's not like you're a lawyer or a therapist."

"Nevertheless."

Recognizing a stone wall when I ran into one, I shrugged. "Thanks for your time. If Dmitri does show up here"—I didn't think it likely—"will you give me a call?" I handed him my business card.

He took it reluctantly. "I don't expect him." An undertone of hurt colored the words, and I wondered suddenly if Chemerkin was in love with Dmitri. He was reacting more like a spurned lover than an irate boss.

"Nevertheless."

He expelled a sharp "heh" that might have been a laugh and tucked the card into his apron pocket. Wending my way around the steel counters, I had almost reached the door when a thought occurred to me. "Is Fiona around?"

A scowl corrugated his brow. "She's the reason I'm short-handed. She didn't come in this morning."

His words made me catch my breath. Fiona had described Dmitri as her best friend. Had she become a target for whoever was intent on teaching Dmitri a lesson, the people who had attacked Bobrova, killed Boyce, and shot at me and Irena? Fiona had a young daughter . . . "Where does she live?" I asked sharply.

"Beats me," Chemerkin said. "She moved apartments a few weeks ago, and I don't have the new address."

"Cell phone?"

He hesitated, sighed, and rattled it off from memory. "If you get hold of her, tell her to get here yesterday or she's fired, too."

The way Chemerkin flung the F-word around, he might be auditioning to replace Donald Trump on *The Apprentice*.

I thanked him and headed for my car, punching Fiona's number into my phone. It rang once and went straight to voice mail. Worried about the young woman, I backed carefully out of the lot and headed down Tejon, wondering how long it would take me to come up with an address for someone with the common last name of Campbell. I was about to call Gigi and put her to work on it when I spotted a slim figure in dark jeans and a teal sweater walking fast on the other side of the street, shoulders hunched against the chilly wind. Relief melted through me. Making a U-turn, I pulled the car up beside her, earning a wary glance and a quickened pace until I buzzed down the window. "Fiona!"

Fiona halted briefly, then kept walking. "I've got to get to work," she said as I kept pace with her, earning a honk from the car behind me.

"I'll give you a ride." Pushing open the passenger door, I invited her in.

Obviously torn, she finally slid onto the seat. The faint odor of cigarette smoke came with her. "I'm really late," she confessed. "I had to take the bus. Gary's going to be PO'd."

"He'll get over it," I said, confident that the man who'd lost two employees in the last week couldn't afford to fire a third for being tardy. Since she was clearly perfectly okay, I wondered if I should warn her that she might be in danger because of her association with Dmitri Fane. I decided to approach the topic obliquely. "Have you heard from Dmitri since we talked?" I asked.

She pulled at a strand of gelled hair. "Did you hear about Boyce Edgerton?"

Something in her expression and the way she ducked my question convinced me she'd been in touch with Dmitri. Wait a minute . . . "Why did you have to ride the bus today?" I asked.

"Car trouble."

"You loaned your car to Dmitri, didn't you?" Irena had said Dmitri had borrowed a car "from a friend" when he loaned her the Mustang.

"No! I'm still mad at him."

Right. She probably *was* still mad at him, but that hadn't made her turn down his request for her vehicle. I felt a new spurt of anger at Dmitri; he knew his friends were being attacked, and yet he'd put Fiona and her daughter in danger by getting in touch.

Running the palms of her hands up and down her jeaned thighs, Fiona slanted a look at me. "He only needed it for a day," she said.

I pulled to the curb a block shy of Czarina Catering and pivoted in the seat to face her. "Fiona, Dmitri's mixed up with some bad people. I don't know exactly what's going on, but you and your daughter might be in danger."

"That's ridiculous," she said, but the words lacked conviction, and she looked over her shoulder at the cars coming up behind us. Her clavicle bones stood out, thin as bird bones, and she seemed young and vulnerable.

"Do you have someplace safe to stay?"

"Tanya and I moved in with my folks a month ago," she said. "It's a gated community."

At least she had people around. "Did Dmitri say anything about where he might be going today, what he was doing?"

She shook her head, the wispy ends of her pixie cut dancing around her ears. "He called last night and asked if he could borrow my car for a day or so. I met him at the Arby's down the road from my folks' house, and he drove me back. I told him I really needed the car back by tomorrow, and he said it shouldn't be a problem, that after tonight things would get back to normal."

"What's happening tonight?"

She shrugged one shoulder. "He didn't say. I told him Tanya missed him, and he said maybe we could drive up to Dave and Buster's with her weekend after next."

I compressed my lips. Either Dmitri was living in la-la land or he was deliberately misleading Fiona. I couldn't see any way he'd be gallivanting up to a family fun center in Denver next weekend, not with criminals and the police on his tail. "Don't tell anyone at work you've talked to Dmitri," I cautioned.

"All right," she agreed, opening the door. "I've really got to get in there before Gary shits a brick."

Delaying her with a hand on her arm, I asked, "Do you think you could get hold of the company's client list? Say, the names of the people you've catered for over the past year?"

"Piece of cake," she said.

I passed her a business card with my fax number and e-mail on it. "Punny."

She stared at me a moment, then giggled. Putting a hand to her mouth, as if to stop the unfamiliar sound, she said, "I'll call you when I've got the list."

"Be careful," I said as she strode away. She didn't respond, and I watched until her petite, straight-backed form disappeared around the corner of Czarina Catering.

—*mm*—

Giving Gigi a quick call to make sure nothing disastrous had happened with Irena Fane, I told her I was going to Dellert House.

"Why?" she asked.

"To see if there might be a connection between Dmitri and someone at the halfway house. What did you say was the name of the guy who runs the place?"

"Roger Nutt," Gigi said, dismay in her voice, "but he can't be mixed up in this. He's much too nice, and he really cares about those boys. I'm seeing him tonight." Her voice dropped to a whisper. "Ant-cay alk-tay ow-nay."

"What?" I stared at my cell, thinking something had interfered with the connection.

"Ig-pay atin-lay," she said, still whispering.

"Oh, for God's sake, Gigi! If you're worried about someone— Irena or the kids—listening in, go to another room."

I heard the muffled sounds of a brief conversation and some footsteps before Gigi came back on the line. "Irena was right there," she said. "I figured that someone born in Russia wouldn't speak Pig Latin. I'm outside now."

Gaagh.

"You know, I'm wondering if maybe Irena is spying on me. Every time the phone rings, she's right there, listening in, and I know she already talked to Dmitri at least once today."

Hm. "You could be right, Gigi," I said, considering it. "Maybe Dmitri set up this whole bodyguard thing to get a spy into our camp, keep him posted on what we're doing."

"You think she's really a spy?" Gigi squeaked. "What should I do?"

She sounded ready to call the CIA or Homeland Security. "Let me think about it," I said. "Go on doing whatever you're doing. I'll let you know if I think of some way to turn the tables on Mata Harirena."

"Say hello to Roger if you see him," Gigi said.

From her tone, I knew she was gaga about the man. I hoped he didn't turn out to be the villain Dmitri was mixed up with.

27

~mm~

Dellert House was quiet and seemingly deserted when I arrived twenty minutes later. The snow that had been threatening all morning had started to fall, soft white flakes that were already sticking to grassy areas and trees. I eyed the sky warily, hoping it quit before making the roads slick enough to foul up traffic. No one answered when I knocked on the door of the dilapidated house, so I turned the knob.

"Hello?" I called, walking into the foyer. A threadbare rug and a wall sconce with a sad little twenty-five-watt bulb were the only things that greeted me. "Hello? Anyone here?" I called louder.

Taking the silence and my continued solitude as an invitation to explore, I poked my head into the room on my left, deducing from the long table and mismatched chairs that it was a dining room. It smelled vaguely of sauerkraut. Trekking back across the hall, I discovered what had once been a formal parlor back in the house's heyday but now contained only a couple of scuffed sofas—undoubtedly donated—and a rickety bookcase filled with paperbacks, most of them sci-fi, horror, or action thrillers. Man stuff. Back in the still-empty foyer, I debated my options: the stairs leading—probably—to the bedrooms, a hall straight ahead that I guessed led to the kitchen, and another hall to my left. I went left, drawn by the copy machine against the wall halfway down; with any luck, I'd find offices that way. Checking the copy machine's trays as I passed—nothing—I peered into the first room on my right. File cabinets and taped-up boxes stacked four or six deep against the walls. Promising, if I had more time and had the slightest clue what I was looking for. The open door across from the storage room held a desk with a laptop, a chair with a heavy parka thrown over it, and a row of thriving violets in four-inch pots on the windowsill. The glowing screen of the laptop drew me like a flame tempting a moth, but I hadn't taken more than a step toward the desk when a man's voice asked, "Can I help you with something?"

His tone was more "What the hell are you doing here?" so I turned with my most reassuring smile. He was short and sixtyish, with a graying beard and mustache and a shiny bald head. Shrewd eyes surveyed me with a hint of hostility. From the way he rubbed his hands on his black suit pants, I deduced he'd been in the bathroom.

"Looking for Roger Nutt. Is that you?"

He nodded warily. "Who's asking?"

"I'm Charlie Swift," I said, holding out my hand. He shook it reluctantly. "Gigi Goldman's partner. She said to say hi." This was a first—invoking Gigi's name to soften up an interviewee.

He didn't quite smile, but his expression lightened. "She mentioned you."

I felt a moment's impulse to ask "In a good way or a bad way?" but I repressed it, telling myself it didn't matter what

Gigi thought about me. "I wanted to let you know we found Kungfu," I said, "in case you were worrying about him."

"Really?" Nutt stepped past me to his desk and closed the laptop screen. "Around here?"

"Yes, he was still in town," I said.

"He's all right?"

I nodded.

"I'm glad to hear it. We've got room for him, if he wants to come back here, and we've still got the stuff he left."

"He's found a safe place to stay," I said, carefully not mentioning Father Dan or St. Paul's, "but he asked me to pick up his things. He's working today or he'd've come himself." It was a tiny white lie; I figured Aaron would've asked me to pick up his things if he'd known I was coming to Dellert House.

"Sure," Nutt said.

He led me across the hall to the storage room. "I've got a funeral to attend"—he indicated his black suit and white shirt with a sweep of his hand—"and I don't want to get all dusty, so if you wouldn't mind . . ." He pointed to a stack of boxes and nudged the second one from the bottom with his shoe.

"Of course," I said, stooping to shift the taped boxes, which didn't weigh much. A spider scurried to hide under a different box. I shuddered. Spiders—ugh. "I'm sorry for your loss."

Nutt sighed sadly. "One of our volunteers was murdered Saturday. It's been a huge shock to all of us here."

A frisson scuttled up my spine like a spider, and I jerked, almost dropping the box I held. "Murdered?" My voice came out as a squeak.

Nutt didn't seem to see anything odd in my reaction. "In his apartment," he said. "The men who bunk here, some of them have been homeless; they're used to sleeping with one eye open, never feeling safe. Boyce, on the other hand . . ." He shook his head. "I'm sure it never crossed his mind that an intruder would break into his apartment."

Boyce Edgerton had spent time here as a volunteer. That fact clanged in my brain, almost drowning out Nutt's next words.

"I packed this up a couple days ago, right after Gigi was here."

"Is all this stuff from teens—men—who stayed here?" I asked, looking at the dozen or so boxes, most labeled with four or more names in black marker.

"Um-hm," Nutt said, sinking to his haunches and slicing a pocketknife through the tape. It gave with a ripping sound.

"They just go away and leave it here?"

"Sadly, yes. We keep it for a few weeks—in case they come back for it—and then we donate it to Goodwill or turn the clothes over to needy men staying with us."

That gave me a thought. Maybe Aaron's brother had left his effects here when he disappeared. I decided it might be worth revealing part of Aaron's story to Nutt on the chance it would net us Nate Wong's stuff. "Did you have another Asian kid staying here?" I asked. "About a month ago?"

Nutt looked up from the box he was digging through. Items seemed to be encased in labeled plastic bags, and he had a slippery pile of them beside him. He surveyed me for a long moment without speaking. "What are you after, Ms. Swift?" he finally asked.

"Kungfu wasn't really a runaway," I said. "He was searching for his brother. The last time the boy's mother heard from him, a month back, he was staying here."

Pinching at his lower lip, Nutt debated whether to tell me anything. "What was the kid's name?" he asked. "We get a few

Asians through here, not too many. It's mostly whites and Hispanics."

"Wong," I said. "Nate Wong." Was there the remotest chance Aaron's brother had used his true name?

Something flickered in Nutt's eyes.

"What?"

"I remember him," Nutt said slowly. "He had a military-looking buzz cut and called me 'sir' every time he opened his mouth. I figured him for an army guy, maybe even a deserter. Real nervous. I don't know if we'd still have his stuff here or if it's already been donated."

I couldn't fault the man's instincts. He pointed to a stack of boxes in the corner, and I unstacked them until I came to one with ALLEN, NAVA, BUSSEY, NAUMAN, WONG scribbled on the side.

"That one." He hesitated. "Shouldn't I be giving Wong's effects to Kungfu? I don't really know that you're authorized to take them."

"You're on the verge of giving them to Goodwill," I pointed out, fairly dancing with impatience. "What does it matter if you give them to me instead?"

For answer, he slit the tape on the box and pulled out the bulky plastic bag on top. "Here." He handed it to me and slid it across the bag marked KUNGFU from the other stack. "You'd tell me if there was something going on I should know about, wouldn't you?" he asked. "These boys are my responsibility while they're here, and I take that seriously. If there's something illegal, or dangerous, going on . . ."

He trailed off and looked a question at me.

"Not that I know of," I said honestly. I didn't *know* anything, and I wouldn't have confided in Roger Nutt if I did. He seemed harmless, caring even, but that didn't count for much. I cradled both plastic bags awkwardly and said good-bye. Nutt walked me to the foyer—almost as if he didn't trust me not to snoop around on my own—and opened the door for me. The snow on the porch was deeper, and I eyed it with dismay.

"Tell Gigi I'm looking forward to this evening," he said with a smile.

"I will," I said, wondering if he really liked Gigi. If so, maybe he'd marry her and she could go back to being a housewife instead of a PI . . . Okay, it might be a bit early to speculate about marriage, but two dates was practically a long-term relationship in my book. "Thanks for your help."

Walking to my car, parked on the street a block away, I wished I'd worn my snow boots. Snow squished over the sides of my low-heeled pumps, and my feet were soaked by the time I climbed into the car. Cranking the heat, I shucked off my shoes and knee-highs, wiggling my bare toes in front of the vent. With dry feet, I tore at the masking tape sealing Nate's bag. I wondered fleetingly if I should let Aaron do this but decided time was of the essence. The bag yielded pitifully little. One pair of cargo shorts, two T-shirts, a pair of socks, a webbed belt, and a thin wallet containing a photo of a young brunette, a military ID card in the name of Nathaniel N. Wong, and three dollars. Holding the wallet in my hands, I felt real uneasiness. Who would voluntarily go off and leave a wallet? I tried to tell myself Nate had ditched all remnants of his former identity when he got his new identity papers and headed for Canada, but the uneasiness remained. I slid the photo out of the plastic sleeve, and a slip of paper fell into my lap. Flipping the photo over, I read, "To Nate, Love Alisha." A girlfriend. Aaron hadn't mentioned her, and I wondered if Nate had met her at his military base.

I fished the scrap of paper out of my lap and unfolded it. A telephone number. Alisha's? No area code, so I didn't know if the number was local or for California or somewhere else. On impulse, I punched the numbers into my cell phone and let it ring. Finally, a harried voice answered. "Czarina Catering."

I hung up without saying anything, a shiver that had nothing to do with the cold traveling down my spine. Here was a concrete link between Dmitri Fane and Dellert House. For some reason, Nate Wong, a young man looking for a new identity, had Dmitri's number in his wallet. Well, it wasn't actually Dmitri's number; it was Boyce's, too, come to think of it. I tamped down my excitement and put the car in gear, driving barefoot. What did I really know?

One: Dmitri Fane was a credit-card-stealing crook mixed up in couriering fake IDs for unnamed Mr. X. Two: Mr. X and/or other parties wanted something from Dmitri badly enough to beat up his coach and shoot at his mother. Three: Nate Wong told his mother that he was at Dellert House and knew where to get fake identity papers. He didn't mention Dmitri or Tattoo4U, but he had the Czarina Catering phone number in his wallet. Four: Aaron Wong arrived at Dellert House, let it be known he wanted a new identity, and someone directed him to Tattoo4U. Five: Boyce Edgerton volunteered at Dellert House. He was my candidate for most likely note leaver. Six: Someone, possibly Dmitri Fane, called the FBI and said he had evidence of an identity theft ring in the area providing new IDs for criminals and other undesirables.

The car swerved on a slick spot as I got off I-25 onto Woodmen, and I slowed to a crawl. A line of cars trailed back all the way from the intersection with Academy. Damn snow. I realized, sitting in the traffic jam, that I had no solid connection between Dmitri Fane and anything. I didn't know that the

Wongs' search for new identities was linked to Dmitri at all, although it seemed likely. The closest thing I had to a link was the phone number in Nate's wallet—maybe he wanted to order a cake, or maybe he and Boyce had struck up a friendship. If that had been the case, though, wouldn't Boyce have given Nate his home number? I couldn't see Montgomery getting a court order to search either Tattoo4U or Czarina Catering for evidence of identity theft based on this thin web of almost-connections I had. I might be working two completely separate cases or they might be tied together. I blew an exasperated raspberry as I finally edged into the parking lot at Swift Investigations.

A Pepsi took the edge off, and having the office to myself went a long way toward restoring my equilibrium. I sank into my chair and looked around, appreciating the peace, even though the scent of coffee lingered. No Kendall, no Gigi, no clients. Perfect. I'd become somewhat reconciled to Gigi in the months since she'd been foisted on me—she had decent computer skills, and clients tended to like her—but I missed my solitude and missed the simplicity of my undecorated, uncoffeed office. As I drained the Pepsi and clanged the can into my trash can, the fax machine beeped and began to spit paper.

Reaching for the first page, I realized Fiona had come through: It was a list of Czarina Catering clients. I skimmed it, not expecting to recognize any of the names. I trailed a finger down the page: ENT Bank, Mr. and Mrs. Robert Emmons, SAIC . . . I flipped the page and kept reading. Emily Stevens, Tanner Industries . . . I was about to pitch the list into the trash when two names I recognized caught my eye: Dellert House and Trevor Anthony.

28

Half an hour later I walked through the doors of St. Paul's Episcopal Church looking for Aaron Wong. I'd brought his brother's belongings with me. I knew the church administrative offices, including Dan's, were to the left, so I headed right, toward the sanctuary. I'd be just as happy not to have to talk to Dan. I peered into the church, dimly lit by the snowy sky showcased by massive picture windows behind the altar, but saw no one. Rows of empty pews lined either side of a central aisle, and the brassy pipes of a serious organ glimmered to my right. I sometimes heard the organ playing when I jogged past the church on a Sunday morning, and the glorious music almost tempted me in to the service. Almost.

Stairs led downward across from the sanctuary, and I descended, finding myself in a hall lined with meeting rooms, a nursery, and Sunday school classrooms. One room had a bright yellow ark on a table with wooden animal pairs marching toward it. My mind flashed on my mother reading me the story of Noah's Ark when I was really little—three?—from the fat board-book kids' Bible that had been one of my childhood treasures. I had an impression of her frizzy light brown hair falling across her face, me clutching my blankie, her finger underscoring the words as she read. "Two of every kind of animal boarded the boat . . ."

I didn't have many memories of my mother doing anything maternal—braiding my hair, kissing me good night, spritzing Bactine on skinned knees—and I couldn't place the memory. Had we been at Grandy and Gramps' house in Washington? Or had it happened earlier than that? I shook it off, uncomfortable with it. I left the Sunday school room and traipsed down a long hall, following the faint sound of hip-hop music. I found Aaron scrubbing an oven in a kitchen attached to a community gathering area, singing along with the radio.

"Aaron?"

He jumped at the sound of my voice, bumping his head. He backed out of the oven, rubbing the sore spot. "Charlie. What are you doing here? Did you find something?" He looked past me as if expecting to see his brother standing there.

"No, but I checked at Dellert House, and they gave me this." I passed him the bag with Nate's clothes and wallet. "He left them behind. I've got your stuff in the car," I added.

Aaron held the bag gingerly, turning it over in his soapy hands. Setting the bag on the counter, he rinsed his hands in the sink. His back was stiff.

"It's only clothes," I said, "and a wallet."

Aaron turned to face me, his dark eyes grave. "That's not good."

I shrugged. "Hard to know. His military ID's in there, along with a photo of a girl named Alisha."

"Alisha? Doesn't mean anything to me. He must have met her at basic." He sorted through the bag's contents quickly, holding the wallet for a moment before opening it.

"There was also a phone number for Czarina Catering," I said as he studied Alisha's photo. "Do you know the business?"

"No. Do you think she might know where he is?" He indicated the photo.

"It's possible," I said.

He flung the wallet at the counter, where it hit a canister and ricocheted to the floor. "It's a stupid idea. We have no way of finding her—no last name, we don't know where she's from. Stupid!"

I put a hand on his shoulder and squeezed but didn't say anything.

Footsteps warned of Dan's approach a split second before he appeared in the doorway. "Aaron, I thought we might grab some lunch—" He caught sight of me. "Charlie." He stepped forward until he was standing inches in front of me, his height and bulk blocking Aaron and the kitchen from view. I stared determinedly at the eye-level button on his black clerical shirt.

Dan said, "I'm sorry about what I said last night. It was uncalled for and none of my business. Forgive me?"

I felt his eyes on me, and I looked up to find his blue gaze fixed on my face. He looked like my forgiveness really mattered to him. I heaved a put-upon sigh. "Of course. You weren't entirely wrong. I can be a little . . . sharp, on occasion."

"On occasion?"

He cocked an eyebrow, and I socked his arm, the feeling of oppression that had weighed me down since last night lifting.

"Why don't we all go to lunch?" he suggested, looking around to include Aaron in the invitation. "We can run over to Zio's if the snow's not too bad."

"I don't think so, thanks," Aaron said. "I think I need to call my mom." Clutching Nate's wallet, he slipped from the room.

Dan watched him go, concern in his eyes, and I explained

about finding Nate's stuff at Dellert House. "That's not the worst of it," I added. I told him about Roger Nutt being a Czarina client and what Dmitri had said about being forced to become a courier of fake IDs.

"Let's talk upstairs," Dan said, leading the way up a back flight of stairs to a hallway near his office. The secretary's desk was deserted, and I figured she was at lunch. Grabbing a snow shovel leaning against the door leading from the office area to the front parking area, he handed another to me.

"I liked the lunch idea better," I grumbled, following him out into the snowy day. What the hell—my pumps were already wet, and I could change shoes at home when we were done. Since the temperature hovered only slightly below thirty, the snow was wet and heavy, and I felt the pull in my shoulder muscles as I scooped a shovelful from the walkway and heaved it aside. Dan worked beside me, his strong arms and back shifting easily triple the snow I was. "Does the church pay you extra for snow-clearing duties?" I asked, blowing on my cold fingers.

"I think this falls under 'other duties as assigned,'" he said with a grin. The physical labor agreed with him; he looked more relaxed after a few minutes of heaving snow around. I leaned on my shovel and watched him. "So," he said, nudging the last clumps of snow off the walk, "let me get this straight. You suspect Roger Nutt is the mastermind behind this identity theft ring, or whatever you want to call it, because he hired Czarina Catering to cater a party for him last August?"

"It fits," I insisted, hearing doubt in his voice. "His job gives him the perfect opportunity to find—or hide—people looking for new identities."

"I don't know Roger well," Dan said, "but he's got a good rep in the nonprofit community, and we've collaborated to find work for a couple of the Dellert House boys. Are you going to give his name to the police?"

I kicked at a snow clod and watched it disintegrate in a puff of white. "I don't know. As you point out, all I have right now is suspicions. I can't see the police being able to do anything with the information. I need something more concrete before I talk to them. Trevor Anthony was a customer, too; I can't forget that."

"Who's he?"

"A skater with a grudge against Dmitri and Dara. A twentysomething punk with an ego as pronounced as his abs."

"So what's your next step?"

My phone rang, and I held up a finger to Dan, spotting Gigi's number. "What's up, Gigi?"

"She's gone!" Gigi cried, her Georgia accent heavily evident, as it always was when she got emotional.

"Irena?" I sighed heavily. "Oh, well, she's a grown wom—"

"She stole my Hummer!"

Oops.

"She's been hounding me and hounding me all day to go out and look for Dmitri. I explained that that's what you were doing, but she kept insisting. I went upstairs for a moment, and when I came down, she was gone. I couldn't believe it at first, and I searched the whole house for her. I went outside, thinking she might have gone for a walk—she was that stir-crazy—and that's when I noticed my Hummer was gone." She sounded close to tears.

"Did you leave the keys in the car?"

"In my purse. She went through my purse," Gigi said, sounding almost more affronted by this invasion of her privacy than by the car theft.

"Did you call the police?"

"No, I called you."

"Okay. I'll get hold of Montgomery and tell the police to be on the lookout for your Hummer. Did she give you any hint of where she might be going? Where she might look for Dmitri?"

"Nothing," Gigi wailed.

A thought came to me. "Hey, aren't you going out with Roger Nutt tonight?"

"Yes, to José Muldoon's, but—"

"I'll be at your house in an hour. No, make it two. Don't go anywhere."

"As if I could."

I hung up and met Dan's inquiring gaze. "There's more than one way to skin a skunk."

29

I passed on lunch, went home to change into warm socks and waterproofed boots, scooped up some equipment I preferred to keep at home rather than in the office, and headed back out. The snow had tapered off, and the sun fought with a thinning layer of clouds. If it came out strongly for a couple of hours, I might get away without having to shovel my walks and drive-way. Of course, if it melted the snow and we had a hard freeze tonight, the roads would be an ice rink.

Speaking of which . . . I pointed the car south on I-25 and headed for the World Arena, intending to have a chat with Trevor Anthony. I'd reached him on his cell, and he'd told me he could spare a few minutes from his practice with Angel. They were practicing in the World Arena proper, rather than the Ice Hall, in preparation for Nationals, which started on Tuesday. "You didn't find Dmitri, did you?" he'd asked, clearly hoping the answer would be "No," or "Yes, at the morgue."

The World Arena is a large event venue, on another scale completely from the Ice Hall. Tiered rows of seats descended toward the ice, which looked somehow more remote and grander than the Olympic rink at the Ice Hall, even though it was the same size. I knew Colorado College played its hockey games here to near-capacity crowds of eight thousand or so, but I'd only ever been here for a ZZ Top concert. Somehow, standing at an unmanned entrance that led from the concourse to the seating areas, I felt the excitement of Nationals in the air. Coaches called to skaters on the ice, and a handful of spectators—reporters? parents? friends?—sprinkled the auditorium. The air crackled with tension, and I couldn't begin to imagine how it would feel to the skaters on Tuesday when the competition kicked off.

The stale smell of the ice hit me as I started down the steep steps from the concourse to the rink, a totally different scent than the marijuana fumes that had pervaded the place during the ZZ Top event. A *chr-chr-chr* sound attracted my attention to the far end of the rink, where a man worked on a Zamboni. Several skaters twirled and glided and jumped on the ice, but I had no trouble picking out Trevor and Angel as I drew level with the rink. He wore what looked like runners' leggings topped by a thin shirt that showed every line of his abs and bulge of his pecs. Her blond hair floated behind them—okay, angel-like—as they zipped around the rink. They did some sort of crossover thingy and then she was floating above him, held aloft by his one hand, her arms outstretched in a "look, Ma, no hands" sort of way. As I watched, his front skate stuttered and he lurched. Angel teetered and fell toward the ice, arms and legs flailing. Trevor recovered enough to throw his arms around her waist and haul her almost upright so she landed awkwardly on one foot before sprawling on the ice.

"Damn it, Angel," Trevor said, jumping over her to avoid running into her, and coming to a halt. "Your center of gravity wasn't—"

She burst into tears, clearly shaken by the near catastrophe.

"Hey, you tripped, man," another skater said, sliding to a stop and helping Angel up. "Are you okay?" he asked her.

She tested her weight on her ankle. "I think so. I'll have some ugly bruises." She tried a laugh, but it was thin. "Trevor, let's try it again from—"

"The damn ice is too rough," Trevor snarled. "I'm through until they get the Zamboni fixed." He said it loud enough for the mechanic to hear, but the man made no response. Without another word to his partner, he zipped toward the gate, noticing me when he was halfway across the ice. Immediately, a smile erased the scowl. "Hi, PI lady," he said, changing direction to intercept me. "Come to watch the next Olympic pairs gold medalists in training?" He tossed his head to fling golden hair off his brow. The look in his blue eyes implied I'd come to watch him.

"I'm working, actually," I said, "although I enjoy watching the skating more than I thought I would. Looks like Angel took a hard fall."

"She's tough," he said dismissively. "So, you're still looking for Dmitri? Let's face it—he ran off because he couldn't take the pressure. Let him stay lost. Like I told you before, I've got no idea where he—"

"Actually, I wanted to ask about the party that Dmitri's company catered for you last August," I said.

He stopped sliding his feet back and forth and frowned. "What? Hey, do private dicks moonlight as bill collectors? The cocktail shrimp were off—some of my friends got sick—and the mini cheesecakes were soggy. I'm not paying ano—"

"I'm not here about your bill," I said, taken aback. "What was the party for? Where'd you have it? Did anything unusual happen?"

"Oh." He calmed down, passing a hand over his hair. "It was for my twenty-fifth birthday. My folks wanted me to celebrate in style, so they set it up and sent me a check to cover it. They were on an Alaskan cruise."

He'd cashed the check, spent half of the money on a big-screen TV or a weekend at Steamboat, and screwed Czarina Catering on the bill. What a charmer.

"We did it at my loft downtown," he said. "Two hundred of my closest friends. Hey, you want an invitation to my next party?"

I pulled my hand back from the railing when he laid his on top of it. "Did anything out of the ordinary happen?"

"Not unless you count half a dozen people tossing their cookies," he said, grinning as if there were something engaging about drunks throwing up.

"Was Dmitri there?"

"Oh, yeah," he said, not even trying to hide a triumphant smirk. "He was there. He had to work. Poor Dmitri." He gave a theatrical sigh. "He bartended all night. I don't think he even got a break to visit the john."

It was clear Trevor Anthony got off on the memory of putting Dmitri in his place, of making him work while his friends partied. Trevor might take second place on the ice, but he was determined to show himself as Dmitri's superior off it. It seemed clear Dmitri hadn't had much of an opportunity to steal financial data at Trevor's place, not with Trevor keeping an eye on him to gloat. I couldn't quite see the shallow, spiteful Trevor as the mastermind behind the fake ID ring, anyway. What wanted criminal or terrorist would feel comfortable dealing with this overgrown frat boy?

"Why do you want to know about my party?" Trevor asked. "What's it got to do with Dmitri?"

"Come on, Trev," someone yelled from across the rink.

"I'm thinking about having a party"—yeah, when I made a profit of more than thirty-two cents a month with Swift Investigations—"and I wanted to know if you were satisfied with the job they did."

He looked unsure, but his friend called again, and Trevor said, "Okay. Well, send me an invitation."

Before he could skate away, I said, "You told Kendall that you thought Dmitri was splitting with Dara. What made you think that?"

He gestured to the rink. "They're not here, are they?" His tone was flip, but a watchful look came into his eyes.

"No," I conceded. I played to his vanity. "Come on, Trevor. You're smart enough to pick up on things that other people would overlook. What do you know?"

Glancing sideways to make sure no one was within hearing distance, he leaned close enough that I felt his breath on my ear and smelled the damp sweat on his skin. I fought the urge to pull back as he whispered, "Let's just say I overheard him making reservations to the Cayman Islands. One-way reservations—and it's not like there's a lot of ice-skating in the Caymans, you know?" With a wink, he spun and skated hard toward the other side of the rink before I could ask if he'd managed to overhear a departure date.

I pondered Trevor's claim as I climbed back to concourse level. I figured "overheard" was Trevor-speak for "eavesdropped on." I had no trouble envisioning the jealous Trevor listening in on Dmitri's conversations and figured he was right about Dmitri making plane reservations. However, a trip to the Caymans might merely be a vacation, not a permanent move. Maybe the ticket was one-way because Dmitri didn't know how long he wanted to stay. It was wishful thinking on Trevor's part, I decided, that made him assume Dmitri was abandoning competitive skating for a surf-and-sun lifestyle in the Caribbean.

I focused my mind on Roger Nutt and Dellert House's party. He could have caught Dmitri stealing credit card data during the party and forced him to help deliver the identity packets. With any luck, Gigi might be able to find out more on her date this evening.

—*mm*—

"You want me to do what?" Gigi's waxed and tinted brows rose toward her hairline, and she fanned herself vigorously.

"Wear a wire," I repeated patiently. Well, sort of patiently.

"You mean like the Mafia informers wear to trap the don into confessing to murder? Or undercover cops wear for a drug deal? The kind the bad guys always find and rip off, right before shooting the poor cop?" Her blue eyes widened.

"That's movies," I said dismissively. "Not real life."

We were sitting in Gigi's swanky living room, a symphony of cream fabric, pale blue leather, velvet drapes, and exotic wood floors. Clearly a decorator's work since there were no heart-shaped throw pillows or puppy-printed curtains or glass swan bowls filled with M&M's. A layer of dust coated the silk flower arrangements and filmed the gilt-framed mirror over the hearth. Looming in a corner, a treadmill struck an out-of-place note, and I wondered if Gigi was working out.

"I can't." She shook her head, fanning her beigey-blond hair across her cheeks. "It wouldn't be right. Besides, I wouldn't know what to say or do, or how to act."

"Act normal," I said. "Say you're having a party and ask if he can recommend a caterer."

"But I always use the Food Designers," Gigi said. "Or, I did before Les left. Now I can't afford—"

"Pretend."

"You mean lie?"

I sighed. Gigi was going to be seriously handicapped as an investigator if she couldn't get over her hangup about lying. It was one of the PI's most useful tools, I'd found. As were its relatives: misleading, prevaricating, fibbing, and creative manipulation of the truth. "Don't think of it as lying," I said. Before she could object, I added, "Remember, we're talking about someone who has killed at least once, beaten up an old lady, and shot at yours truly."

"Not Roger," Gigi said, setting her mouth in a mulish line.

"Maybe he didn't do it himself," I said, "but you've got to admit there's a pretty solid circumstantial case against him." I took her through the evidence again. "All you have to do is wear this pin." I pulled out the crystal-encrusted pin, the remnant of a joint operation with an agency that shall remain nameless where I'd spent a tense evening in a bar chatting up an arms dealer, wearing the pin and the shortest, tightest dress I'd ever had on.

"Ooh, pretty," Gigi said, touching one of the green crystals with a finger. "Where's the wire?"

"It's wireless."

"Then why's it called a wire?"

I ignored the question. "It's state of the art. Digital. It'll record your conversation, and we can download it later. With any luck we'll get Nutt on tape saying something that Montgomery can use to get a search warrant."

"I'll flub it up," Gigi objected.

"Why don't you go get dressed and I'll drive you back to the office to pick up Irena's Mustang."

The prospect of driving the silver Mustang perked Gigi up, and she went upstairs to don her dress without further comment. She came down half an hour later, wearing a ruffled pink satin and tulle confection that made me think some ballet company must be missing its Sugar Plum Fairy costume, and an armful of sparkly bracelets. She was way overdressed for José Muldoon's, but I didn't say anything. I helped place the pin on her dress.

"I thought the shoes would match the pin," she said, sticking out one plump calf so I could admire the mint green high-heeled peep-toe pump.

"Can you walk on those?" I asked. "In snow?"

She gave me a pitying look. "Of course."

I'd never been one to suffer frostbitten toes for the sake of fashion, but Gigi clearly thought it was worth it. As we reached the airy foyer of her house I looked around, realizing I hadn't seen or heard either of her kids since I'd arrived an hour earlier. "Where are the kids?"

"Dexter's out with friends"—her expression said she didn't much like them—"and Kendall's in her room sulking. I haven't seen her since we got back with Irena. She got miffed when Irena said she was too young for Dmitri—which, of course, she *is,* besides the fact that Dmitri's gay." She sighed. "I don't know how to break it to her."

"Say, 'Dmitri's gay,' " I suggested.

She gave me a look that said I didn't understand the difficulties of communicating with teenagers, grabbed a full-length fur coat from the closet, and opened the door to a blast of wintry air.

30

This isn't so hard, Gigi thought an hour later, spooning up the tasty chicken tortilla soup she'd ordered as an appetizer. Roger didn't seem to suspect he was being recorded as he chatted about a Broncos game he'd been to over the weekend.

"Did I tell you you look lovely this evening?" Roger asked, dabbing at his mouth with a napkin. "Pink suits you."

Gigi beamed. It had been a long time since anyone—a man— had told her she looked nice. Not since Les. Well, not Les, either, she thought, not for several years. Had the pin microphone picked up the compliment? Maybe she should be sitting beside Roger instead of across the table from him. "You know," she said, rising, "it's a little drafty in this spot." She resettled herself on Roger's right, then realized the pin was above her right breast, farthest away from Roger. Should she move again? No, that would look suspicious. Maybe if she sort of turned toward him. She shifted in her chair, and her foot brushed his under the table. Oh, no! Now he would think she was coming on to him.

Roger smiled. "I met your partner today. Did she tell you? I can see what you mean about her."

At the thought of Charlie listening to the recording later, Gigi gasped and turned it into a cough.

"Are you okay?" Roger asked, pounding her back.

"Um-hm," she murmured, gulping some water.

"Did you find anything interesting in Nate Wong's effects, anything to help you locate him? Charlie told me about his brother being Kungfu and that he was really in town to search for Nate." He broke off a piece of bread and buttered it.

Roger sounded genuinely concerned about Nate, Gigi thought, but maybe he was just trying to find out if they knew anything that incriminated him. "I don't think there was anything too useful," she said. "I was working a different case today."

"Tell me about being a private investigator," Roger said, smiling warmly. "What attracted you to that kind of work? You don't seem the type, if you'll pardon me for saying so."

Gigi was tired of hearing that. "What type? The smart type?"

Roger drew back, brows raised. "No, not at all. Sorry. I meant the snoopy type, the type that enjoys pawing through people's secrets."

"Is that what you think we do?" Gigi asked.

"Isn't it?"

She shook her head.

"Educate me."

Roger seemed genuinely interested, so Gigi told him about Les's departure with Heather-Anne and the need for her to find work since he'd taken all their money with him. Through the salad and halfway into her main course, Gigi chattered about her first couple of disastrous cases, the drudgery of serving summonses, and how good she was getting at investigating via the computer. "Mostly, I do background checks for employers—stuff like that," she said. "Routine."

"I can tell you like it," Roger said, a slight smile denting his cheeks, "and I'm sure you're good at it because you're so easy to talk to."

"Am I?" Gigi felt herself flushing. The way the pendant light reflected off Roger's smooth head was really kind of sexy. She'd never found bald men particularly attractive before, but there was something about that expanse of skin . . . With a guilty start, she realized they were almost up to dessert and she hadn't managed to work in a single reference to Czarina Catering or fake IDs or anything.

"You know," she said, "I've been thinking about having a party. You don't have a catering company that you like, do you?"

A line appeared between his brows. "I thought you just told me money was tight since your husband left?"

"Oh, yes, right! I mean, the party would be for the business, for Swift Investigations." She talked faster, forgetting to breathe. "To see if we can't attract new clients."

"Oh." Roger nodded as if that made sense, and Gigi took a deep breath. Stupid! Why had she let Charlie talk her into this? "We do an annual fund-raiser for Dellert House," Roger said, "and that's always catered. The caterer we used to use went under a couple years back, and this past year we had a new company. The service was good, but I thought the food was only so-so. Soggy cheesecake."

"I hate that! What's their name?"

He gave her a puzzled look.

"So I don't call them by accident, I mean."

"Something Russian," he said. "Started with a C. I'm sorry, but our director of development arranges that sort of thing, not me."

This was getting her absolutely nowhere, Gigi thought. A change of topics was in order. "You know, I think Charlie said she found Nate Wong's military *ID* card in the stuff he left at Dellert House. Doesn't that seem strange to you, that someone would leave their *identification* behind? What can he be using for *ID*? I mean, like for when he wants to buy some beer or cash a check?"

A sad look drifted over Roger's face. "Many of the men who stay with us are anxious to leave their former selves behind," he said. "It's not uncommon."

The server came by to take their dessert order, and Gigi dithered between a flan and fried ice cream. Finally opting for the flan, she asked, "Do they just make up a new name? Like a pen name?"

Snorting a half-laugh, Roger said, "I don't think it's that easy."

He added something else, but Gigi didn't hear it because a mariachi combo had launched into a Spanish song only feet away from their table. Would the microphone pick up anything with the guitars so close? Gigi scooted her chair nearer to Roger's. "Sorry," she said, making sure her right breast was pointed at him, "I didn't catch that."

"I said that generating fake IDs is big business, or so I hear. A good driver's license is not something the average runaway can whip up with a copier and a laminating machine."

"Do you have someone you recommend?"

"It's not like a catering company, Gigi; it's illegal." Roger stared at her, distrust settling over his features. "What is this about?"

"About? Nothing! I mean, it's very interesting. Who hasn't wanted to re-create themselves at some point in their lives, start over as a new person?" The thought had tremendous appeal, she realized as she said it. No debt to pay down, no surly teenagers to cope with, no broken marriage to haunt her. What name would she choose? Amanda? Juliana? She'd always wanted a frillier name than Georgia Maude. Why did her mother's best friend have to be named Maude?

"A tabula rasa, as it were?" Roger asked, looking intrigued by the idea and less suspicious. "What would you do differently?"

What *wouldn't* she do differently, Gigi thought, wondering what a tabula rasa was. "How did you end up running Dellert House?" she asked.

A reminiscent look settled on Roger's features. "I drifted into the nonprofit world by accident," he said. "I have degrees in social work and civil engineering—"

"You must be smart," Gigi said, thinking of her own beauty school certificate.

"—and I started out working as an engineer for the state. Highways." He made a face. "That proved less than fulfilling, so after my divorce I—"

"You're divorced?"

"Yes. Is that okay?" He gave her a quizzical look.

"Of course! I mean, I'm divorced, too. Isn't everybody?"

"I hope not everybody," Roger laughed.

Gigi blushed and scooped up another bit of flan, savoring the texture and flavors on her tongue. The mariachis finally moved on, and the quiet was a relief.

"I got a job as a probation officer, but I was still working for the state, and it felt too stifling."

Gigi started. A probation officer! Hadn't Charlie mentioned

that whoever was involved with the fake ID manufacturing probably had an in with a prison or a halfway house so he could meet people who wanted new identities?

Oblivious to Gigi's sudden distress, Roger continued, "So then I got involved with an organization called Greccio here in town. They're a nonprofit that provides housing for low-income families. I worked there for six years as a leasing agent, and when the director job came open at Dellert House, their board contacted me about the position. I applied, they hired me, and here we are, five years later. I finally feel like I'm doing what I'm supposed to be doing, like you with the PI business, I bet." Scraping his fork across his plate, he licked the last of the peach goo from it.

"Oh, no, I—" Gigi cut herself off. She did like being a PI, but she wasn't sure it was her passion. She'd only gotten into it because she needed to put food on the table—and pay ice-skating coaching fees and Dexter's insurance on the BMW—after Les left. "Was it scary—working with murderers?"

"Very few of my probationers were murderers," Roger said with the air of someone who has answered the question a few hundred times. "Although my best friend did time for murder."

Gigi started, and a drip of flan plopped onto her pink satin bodice. "Oh, no!" She snatched up her napkin and scrubbed at the spot, making the stain larger.

"Here." Roger handed her his napkin, which he had dipped into his water glass.

"Thanks." Gigi rubbed some more, sure the dress was ruined. Her favorite Betsey Johnson. She wanted to burst into tears. Flagging the waitress down to ask for some club soda— Was it club soda or tonic water that worked on stains? Was it only wine stains or would it remove caramel?—Gigi joggled the brooch. Loosened by her tugging on the fabric, it clipped the table's edge and tumbled to the floor.

Gigi froze in horror.

"I'll get it," Roger said, leaning over.

"No!" Gigi bent at the waist and clunked heads with Roger.

"Ow." Roger returned to an upright position, rubbing at his forehead.

Ignoring the pain, Gigi felt around on the floor until her fingers brushed the brooch. She emerged from beneath the tablecloth with it clutched in her hand, flushed and perspiring. "Got it."

"I wasn't going to steal it, you know," Roger said edgily.

"Oh, no! I didn't think— Of course you wouldn't—" Her fingers were trembling too much for her to repin the brooch on her dress.

"Here, let me."

"No!" Gigi batted away Roger's hand.

He drew back, staring at her.

"I'm sorry," she whispered. "I'm afraid it'll fall off again. I'll just put it in my purse." She was done with the stupid listening device. She didn't care if Roger confessed to identity theft, fiddling his taxes, and cheating on a fifth-grade science test. She slid the brooch into her satin handbag and clicked it closed. Roger must think she was a lunatic . . . or worse. It made her want to cry because even if he was involved with identity theft and murder, she liked him. "So," she managed a fragile smile. "You were saying about your friend the murderer?"

───※───

Having seen Gigi off on her date with Nutt, I got into the rental and pointed it toward Old Colorado City. It had occurred to me earlier that maybe Aaron Wong had the right idea: A snooping expedition at Tattoo4U might yield some interesting data. I didn't know exactly what kinds of materials or supplies were necessary for producing first-rate fake IDs, but I figured a computer, high-quality color printer, scanner, camera, laminating machine, some art supplies, and the like would be necessary. The mental list loosed a memory—hadn't I seen a laminating machine at the Estes Park cabin before it went ka-blooey? I couldn't see the setup being at Dellert House with all the men and boys coming and going at strange hours. If Roger Nutt was in on this, they might be at his house, but I was betting that they were at Tattoo4U. It struck me that this operation was a bit like counterfeiting—an artist was key to its success—and the only "artist" whose name had come up was Graham, the tattoo artist. Anyone who could replicate intricate scenes on human flesh could surely do the background on an Idaho driver's license, a green card, or a Social Security card, especially with stolen documents to work with. If I didn't find evidence at Tattoo4U, maybe I could get a line on where Graham lived and poke around there.

I'd taken the precaution of calling Tattoo4U and was satisfied when no one picked up and a recording told me the hours were ten to six. Since it was now past eight and it had been dark for two hours, I figured the time was right for a little reconnaissance. I'd be less conspicuous now, I thought, than if I waited till the wee hours. Still, it paid to be cautious. Parking in the lot across from the shop, I noticed the lights were out and the CLOSED sign was up. I boldly crossed the street and walked smack up to the door, trying the knob like a customer frustrated that the shop was closed. "Graham?" I called.

No response. No hint of sound from within. Hiding my satisfied smile, I returned to my car and drove off, circling back to park a couple of blocks behind the shop. In jeans and a black turtleneck, I was virtually invisible—I hoped—as I strode down the street, bolt cutters held close to my right leg with a gloved hand. After a car passed, I ducked into the alley behind Tattoo4U's block, spooking a gray cat that dashed away from the trash can it was investigating. With the frigid wind lapping at my face and adrenaline pricking at me, I skated on the thin edge between total alertness and fear. Breaking and entering was not something I did lightly, since it carried a prison term if I screwed up.

At Tattoo4U's back door, I risked a quick squirt of light from the miniflashlight on my key chain. The padlock was secured, just as it had been when Aaron tried to break in. A quick glance to left and right, wrenching pressure on the bolt cutters, and the lock gave way with a metallic snap. Slipping the hasp free, I finagled the doorknob lock with a bent paper clip and a rarely used credit card, vowing to find someone to teach me how to use the picklocks Gigi had acquired via eBay. With a deep breath, I pushed the door open just wide enough to sidle through it.

I was barely clear of the door when my foot snagged on something solid angled across the floor and I staggered. I managed to stay upright by grabbing what felt like a counter or shelf but knocked against something that rolled in a clunky way and then dropped with a resounding thud. Great. I felt about as stealthy as a sumo wrestler in a lingerie shop. Steadying myself with one hand, I flicked on the small flashlight and pointed it at the ground. Oh, shit.

The suddenly shaking beam traveled up a jeaned thigh, across a blood-soaked shirt with two bullet holes in it, over a tangle of ginger beard, to a staring eye. The eye startled me so much I jumped and almost dropped the flashlight. A split second later I realized the eye was filmed and unmoving. Automatically, I squatted and searched for a pulse on the man's neck, the wiry growth of beard feeling alien under my fingertips. Graham was slightly chilled and most definitely dead.

37

My phone vibrated, and I jumped. Still staring at Graham's body, I pulled it out. Gigi. I debated not answering it, not wanting to tell her what I was up to since she was almost as opposed to breaking and entering as she was to lying, and she'd certainly freak if I told her about Graham, but I picked up before it went to voice mail. "What?"

"I slid off the road and wrecked the Mustang! The on-ramp was so slick. I can't—"

The hysteria in Gigi's voice sounded way out of proportion for a fender bender, and it stopped my own shaking as I focused on her panic. "Are you hurt? Did you call Triple A?"

"I'm fine. It's not me, it's her!"

Her? Had she hit someone? My muscles tensed.

"She's with her. They're meeting Dmitri. Oh, my God, my baby!"

"Calm down, Gigi," I said, utterly confused. "Who's with who?"

"Kendall," Gigi gasped. "With Irena. Well, she's not *with* Irena, but she's in the Hummer."

"Irena kidnapped Kendall?" Surely not. Who in their right mind would voluntarily snatch a sullen fourteen-year-old? Better question: Who would pay good money to get one back?

"I don't know if she kidnapped her, exactly," Gigi hedged. "It's possible Kendall might have . . . invited herself along."

"Good God!" I wanted to say more, but my imperative was to get out of Tattoo4U before a cop ventured along to ask awkward questions about the body on the floor. "I'll call you back in a min—"

"They're at the World Arena." Gigi sounded close to tears. "Kendall heard Irena tell Dmitri she'd meet him there and they'd 'finish it.' She's scared."

"Where is she?" I didn't need this, not while I was hovering over a dead body.

"Still in the back."

"Of the Hummer?"

"Uh-huh." She paused. "Under a blanket."

"She stowed away." I closed my eyes. Kendall must have seen Irena rifle Gigi's purse for the Hummer keys and figured she'd get in on the action by stowing away. Maybe she even hoped to be the one to find Dmitri, confounding Gigi and me. Whatever, now she was in the midst of something that had already resulted in at least two deaths. "Tell her to stay in the car, no matter what Irena does."

"I already did," Gigi said. "I don't know if she'll listen to me."

Fat chance.

"She's not answering her phone now, Charlie!" Tears choked her voice.

"I'm on my way," I said. "Hang up now and call Triple A, Gigi."

I clicked off. After a moment's hesitation, I picked up Tattoo4U's phone and dialed the nonemergency police number to report a body in Tattoo4U. As I spoke, I trailed the flashlight's beam around the room, hitting at least four computers, a printer, and a professional-looking camera on a tripod in front of a blue backdrop. I felt little satisfaction in the discovery now. I hung up on the startled officer, hoping I'd slowed the response enough to get clear before the cops arrived. Slipping out the way I'd come, I jogged back to my car without seeing anyone. Inside, I took a deep breath, held it for a moment, and let it out. I started the car and cranked up the heat.

As the finding-a-dead-body jitters subsided, I pointed the car toward I-25 and tried Montgomery's cell. Voice mail. Leaving a terse message about my destination and the situation as I understood it, I cut the connection and thought about calling 911. Deciding to wait until I'd had a chance to assess the situation in person—What was I going to say? According to a fourteen-year-old, an ice-skater and his mother were maybe meeting some bad people at the rink?—I skidded slightly getting off at the World Arena exit and went with it, glad there were no other cars around. I drove as fast as I dared, then cornered into the World Arena's vast, empty parking lot. The building, its domed bulk set above the lots and wide stairs leading up to it, a Parthenon of entertainment, squatted in the middle of an asphalt landscape. The dim security lights didn't quite reach to where a lone vehicle was parked at the far edge of the lot. I raked it with my headlights: Gigi's yellow Hummer.

Figuring that surprise wasn't really an option, I drove to the Hummer and stopped with the car's lights aimed into the vehicle. I could tell the front seat was empty as I braked. Leaving my engine running and my door open, I liberated my flashlight from the glove compartment and drew my gun from its holster. Cautiously approaching the Hummer, I confirmed that there was no one slumped in the front seats and peered through the windshield into the back. No one. I circled the car, trying to peer in the back window, but could see nothing through the tinted window. On the passenger side of the Hummer, the back door was closed but not securely latched, as if someone had been in too much of a hurry to close it properly. Whispering, "Kendall?" I worked the handle with my gloved fingertips.

No answer. Easing the door wider with the flashlight, I announced, "I've got a gun." When that didn't elicit a response or a bullet, I stuck my head in, hoping it didn't get shot off. No one crouched in the footwells of the backseat. "Kendall, if you're in here, now's a good time to come out," I said a little louder. When I got no reply, I ducked my head around the backseat to the cargo area, spotting a rumpled zebra-striped blanket, a Snickers wrapper, and what looked like oil drippings on the carpet. No Kendall.

Letting my breath out in a long *whew*, I aimed the flashlight beam at the stains, which glinted red and wet.

Turning off the rental's engine and shutting its door, I debated my next move, unsure what I faced. My fingers wrapped around the gun were tingling with cold, and I wiggled them. At the very least, I figured Dmitri, Irena, and Kendall were inside, along with whoever was after Dmitri. Whether that was a lone operator or a team of desperadoes, I had no idea. I wished they'd parked in the lot so I could estimate a head count, but Gigi's Hummer was the only vehicle in sight. I tried Montgomery again with no luck. With an inward sigh, I called 911 and told the operator where I was and that I'd found blood in a car—no need to mention it was just a few droplets—and had reason to believe someone was in danger inside the World Arena.

"Are you being threatened right now, ma'am?" the calm voice asked.

"No, it's—"

"Please stay where you are and—"

Screw that. I flipped the phone closed, silenced it, and headed into the World Arena.

32

I tried three sets of doors across the front of the World Arena before finding one propped open with a folded wedge of paper. I wondered how Dmitri had gained access but figured if he'd been skating here for years, he probably knew his way around and/or had managed to score a key at some point. The concourse curved blankly to either side of me, the areas closest to the glass doors very dimly lit by the ambient light from outside, the rest obscured by darkness, which I did not find reassuring. I'd been hoping for a security guard or two and a little illumination, at least. The last two times I'd bumbled around in dark buildings I'd found bloodied bodies: Bobrova and Graham. I devoutly hoped I wouldn't find Kendall in the same condition.

The thought of the teenager and of Gigi's worry spurred me on. Slipping through the door, I crossed the concourse to swinging doors that opened into the auditorium, moving from almost dark to I-might-as-well-have-my-eyes-closed dark. I paused to listen and thought I heard the low murmur of voices coming from below me, in the direction of the rink. Hugging the wall, I slunk around the door and peered down. Nothing but darkness. It was like standing on the lip of a volcano crater at night. I could feel the presence of other people, though; I was not alone.

"Fane!"

The voice was a bellow not far in front of me, and I instinctively dropped to my haunches behind the back row of seats. A faint reddish glow from the exit sign above me was the only light—useless.

"Fane! I am through playing games. We deal now or I will hunt down everyone you ever cared about and kill them."

I didn't recognize the voice. It was deep, with a Mexican accent.

"I'm here. Keep your shirt on."

Dmitri. His voice came from the far side of the rink. He was trying to sound calm, but I heard a slight tremor behind the flippant words. Apparently, so did the other man, who laughed.

"It is good for you to be scared," the man said.

"You have the money?"

"Right here." He thumped on something that might have been a suitcase. "You'd better have the data."

"It's in the center of the ice. Walk out there, leave the bag with the money, take the disk, and go."

"What is this shit?" the man grumbled. "If this is some kind of trick . . ." His voice receded, and I could hear footsteps as he tromped toward the ice.

Where the hell was Kendall? Where was Irena, for that matter? My eyes had adjusted somewhat to the darkness and I slipped my shoes off to silently descend the steps, grateful now for the inky blackness. I prayed the lights would stay off since I was all too shootable on the stairs. The fibers of my socks stuck to bits and smears of gum or congealed sno-cone syrup, and I could feel threads pulling away. Nearing the ground level, I slowed, feeling my way with my toes so I didn't trip on the last stair.

At the bottom, I hunched low and duck-walked to the wall surrounding the rink. I poked my head up, scanning for either of the women. The ice gave off a dim glow of its own, probably the reflection of exit lights on the oval surface. I caught a flicker of movement to my left; someone crouched, half hidden in the aisle between the seats. Kendall? A faint whiff of musky herd animal and coconut drifted to me. Kendall was definitely nearby. I wondered briefly if my sense of smell was compensating for my eyes' lack of usefulness in the dark. Staying low, I edged my way along the wall.

I was almost there when a light sliced through the darkness and made me fling a hand in front of my eyes and drop flat on my stomach. When there was no outcry, I raised my head cautiously. A spotlight, the beam of pure white light tracking from far above the rink, illuminated a circle in the middle of the ice where a packet the size of a CD lay. A husky man with brown hair crouched over the packet, duffel bag in one hand, gun in the other. I'd never seen him before, although the brown hair and pudgy physique made me wonder if he was the guy Angel saw with Dmitri at the grocery store. When the light blazed on, he spun around, pointing the gun wildly, trying to evade the spotlight, which followed him as he moved. "What is this?"

"Leave the suitcase and go, Aguilar," Dmitri called. "Or should I say 'Belcaro'?"

His voice was close, so I knew it wasn't him operating the

spotlight. Irena? Everything outside the circle of light was darker than it had been, cavern-in-the-bowels-of-the-earth black, and I blinked rapidly, trying to restore my night vision. I edged forward again, but a movement to my left caught my attention. I squinted, making out a vaguely human shape, but it was a man, not Kendall, and he was crouched, forearms braced against the wall, sighting a pistol toward the middle of the rink.

I froze. Whose side was he on? Since he hadn't shot Duffel Man when he had the chance, I guessed he was gunning for Dmitri.

By this time, Aguilar had pocketed the packet and dropped the duffel bag in the circle of light. He called out, "This better be the end of it, Fane. Don't expect any referrals from me."

"I'm retiring," Dmitri called back. "Open it."

With the air of someone humoring a child, the man bent, flipped back the duffel's straps, unzipped it, and flung it open. Bundles of money lined the interior, and several spilled onto the ice as the man nudged the case with his foot contemptuously. "Want to count it?" Aguilar taunted.

"I trust you," Dmitri said, his voice jauntier now. "Just go."

The man turned toward me, the spotlight at his back now, and shuffled toward the gate in the wall between the gunman and me. The spotlight trailed him, glancing off the still Zamboni parked by the gate. He would pass within an arm's length of me when he came off the ice, so I sidled to my left, hoping he wouldn't spot me in the dark. As he passed through the gate, he muttered, "Kill him," to the hidden gunman and trotted up the stairs. A slight creak fifteen seconds later told me he'd pushed through the swinging doors leading to the concourse.

Silence settled on the rink. Not a peaceful silence, but the uneasy silence that comes a split second before an avalanche when all the birds and critters still, intuiting the rending of the snow crust before any human can hear it. I'd been skiing the backcountry near Steamboat once and *felt* that silence just before the ground heaved and a wall of snow hurtled down the mountain. The hiss of skate blades across ice broke the silence. Dmitri? I debated calling out, but the growl of an engine startled me, and I flinched as the Zamboni trundled across the ice. I could vaguely make out its hulking outline as a darker shape in the dark. Who was driving it? The gunman, figuring he didn't have much of a shot with no light? I'd have given six months' fees to know where the light switch was.

Even as I had the thought, the spotlight flared to life again, its beam skidding across the ice. I saw Dmitri standing in the middle of the rink on skates, the suitcase at his feet. The glare bleached his skin white, and his mouth was pulled down in a snarl of concentration. It glinted off the gun in his hand before moving on, finally illuminating the Zamboni. I followed the light beam up and made out Irena crouched behind the spotlight far above the rink, using it to steady her aim as she pointed a gun at the Zamboni coming from my right. She fired, and a bullet pinged off the metal. Just then, the overhead light blazed on, illuminating the strange tableau. The dark-haired man steering the Zamboni with one hand ducked and tried to level a silenced pistol at Dmitri. I swung my H&K up. I wanted desperately to find Kendall, but I felt some compulsion to keep the shooter from killing Dmitri.

"Look out, Dmitri! He's got a gun!"

Kendall's clear young voice rang out, and suddenly there she was on my left, surefootedly running across the ice toward Dmitri, pointing at the gunman. As if Dmitri could miss an armed assailant chugging toward him on a Zamboni. Startled, Dmitri swung his gun in Kendall's direction. With a look of grim satisfaction, the dark thug's finger tightened on the trigger.

With no time to think, I fired at the man on the ice cleaner, hitting him midtorso so his shot went wild, digging into the ice mere feet from Dmitri. In slow motion, the man toppled off the far side of the Zamboni, which continued toward the far end of the rink, where it lodged against a colorful travel agency ad on the rink wall, chirring uselessly. As I watched, Kendall flung herself at Dmitri, almost knocking him over, and exclaimed in the voice of a movie heroine, "Thank God you're safe! I got here in time."

Dmitri threw an arm around her to keep from falling but quickly disentangled himself. Her expression of bliss turned to one of consternation as he grabbed her by the ponytail, jerking her head back, and lodged his pistol under her chin.

"Drop it," he said, gaze fixed on me, "and come here."

"Dmitri, what—?" Kendall began.

"Shut it, Kendra," he snapped.

"Kendall," she and I corrected him.

"Don't think I won't do it," Dmitri said meaningfully to me, jamming Kendall with the pistol hard enough to make her whimper.

"Easy," I said, carrying my H&K loosely in my raised right hand as I bumped the gate open with my hip. After a moment's hesitation, I stepped onto the ice, feeling the cold and wet immediately through my socks. Dmitri motioned toward my gun again, and I stooped to place it on the ice. As I straightened, I said, "You're stressed, not thinking right, because of what's happened. We're no threat to you." All the missing pieces were falling into place, and I was very, very scared for Kendall. Dmitri was clearly not the victim he made himself out to be, but I had to make him think I still saw him as the coerced, unwilling participant in this whole charade, at least until I figured out how to get Kendall away from him.

"Yeah, right," Dmitri said. Without taking his eyes off of me, he said over his shoulder, "Mom, get the money."

I'd been dimly aware of footsteps descending the stairs, and now Irena appeared, lithe figure tensed, gaze darting around the rink, gun gripped tightly in a white-knuckled hand. One foot skidded when she stepped on the ice, but she recovered. She ignored Dmitri's order, stopping a foot from where he held Kendall. "How'd you get here?" she asked Kendall, eyes narrowed, tapping the gun against her thigh.

"I stowed away when you stole my mom's car," Kendall said defiantly. "I wanted to help find Dmitri."

She tried to smile up at him, but the gun jabbing into the soft flesh beneath her chin made it impossible for her to turn her head. For the first time, she looked nervous, even a little scared, and I thought maybe the cluebird had landed. About time. Some people need a gun pointed at them before they'll open their eyes.

Irena and Dmitri exchanged a glance. "She knows, then," Irena said. "Graham."

"When?"

"On the way here."

"I don't know anything," Kendall objected.

Irena had killed Graham, I deduced from their cryptic exchange, and Kendall was a witness. Not to the killing itself, probably, or she'd be looking a lot more scared, but she could undoubtedly place Irena at the murder scene at the right time, having been riding in the back of the Hummer all evening. I wondered if I'd missed them by hours or only a few minutes. At least an hour, I figured, remembering the clammy chill of Graham's flesh.

"Get the money," Dmitri ordered.

Irena strode past the blond shooter's body without sparing it a glance and picked up the suitcase from where it rested near the far wall. "I have it," she said, pulled a little off balance by the bag's weight.

"And his gun," Dmitri said.

"Why?" She looked from Kendall to me. "Oh." A small, hard smile curled her lips, and she started toward the body. Almost there, she slipped. She didn't fall, but she spilled several bundles from the duffel onto the ice. With a muttered curse, she bent to retrieve them.

Kendall began to plead with Dmitri, her tone conciliatory at first but moving rapidly toward hysteria.

I knew that whatever their plan had initially been, their revised plan called for shooting me and Kendall with the dead man's gun, making it look as if he'd killed us. I didn't know what kind of story they'd spin for the cops, but if Kendall and I were dead, there'd be no one to contradict it. Anger flamed in me. Not only did I not want to die, but I didn't want Dmitri free to compete for an Olympic medal, spewing his "I was forced into this" story to a credulous media eager to spread the tale of an athlete's heroic efforts to save Kendall and me and bring down a villainous identity theft ring. Gag me.

Something different about the sound from the Zamboni's engine caught my attention, and I slid my gaze sideways in time to see it back away from the wall, ram into it, then slowly reverse and begin chugging toward Irena. Who—? A glimpse of pink huddled behind the steering wheel gave me hope. Irena, preoccupied with fitting the money bundles back into the bag, didn't look up. Kendall's voice in Dmitri's ear, and her wiggling efforts to free herself, kept him from noticing the machine's movements immediately. I focused on him, waiting for that split second when he noticed the Zamboni headed for his mother. I did what I could to distract him.

"So everything you told me Saturday night was a lie?"

He smirked. "Not everything. Shut *up!*" The latter comment was apparently meant for Kendall, who quieted and stilled when he jabbed the gun's barrel viciously into the soft flesh under her chin. "That's better. I really was just lifting credit cards until Graham caught me when I paid for Dara's tattoo with a stolen card. It was a stupid mistake. Then—"

Shit. I'd wasted a lot of investigative energy by assuming someone caught Dmitri stealing a card. I'd never considered the possibility he'd been nabbed using one. Maybe I should consider another line of work.

I wrinkled my brow, trying not to let my gaze slide to the Zamboni, now going backward in a big circle behind Dmitri and Irena. Who knew I should have set Gigi up with Zamboni driving lessons in addition to surveillance classes and computer training?

"—then, once we teamed up, we got into identity theft and making false identities in a big way. We expanded the business, you might say. Boyce and I provided Social Security numbers, bank account numbers, other financial data, and IDs that we found while catering, and Graham provided artistic and ID-manufacturing expertise, you might say. He'd been doing it for years in Australia before he emigrated here." He grinned cockily, and his gun hand sagged away from Kendall's chin slightly. The girl's eyes flitted to me, and I gave her a reassuring smile that said "don't do anything stupid but be ready when I make my move." It's hard to convey all that with a facial expression, but I tried.

"With Mom's connections from Russia—lots of her family's

friends have come to the U.S.—and others we found by getting the word out quietly at halfway houses and prisons and the like, we were cleaning up. There's a healthy balance in my offshore account."

The Zamboni straightened out and headed for Irena again where she squatted, strapping up the duffel bag. "So, what happened with the feds? You got an attack of conscience and called them, then chickened out."

His brows slammed together. "That was Boyce. Stupid fuck. He told me Friday night, after the party where that stupid chick accused me of selling marijuana, that he'd had enough, that he had called the FBI and was going to meet with them this past Saturday. He was warning me, giving me time to get out." An expression of sadness or regret flitted across his handsome features before he firmed his mouth.

"So you killed him and set him up."

"Not me. I told Graham."

Irena noticed the Zamboni first, straightening with the dark man's pistol in her hand to find the ice-smoothing machine only fifteen feet away. "Hey!" she yelped, firing both guns at the metal behemoth bearing down on her. Bullets zinged off the metal and ricocheted around the rink. The sound was an assault, multiplied by the building's acoustics, which were designed to amplify a band's music to bone-vibrating levels.

Dmitri's head swung toward his mother, and he whipped the pistol toward the Zamboni, hauling Kendall around with him. In that moment, I leaped, pushing forward with all the strength in my legs. The ice stole some of my traction, but I slammed into the pair of them with a satisfying thud, tearing Kendall from Dmitri's loosened grip and shoving her across the ice before I landed—*bam*—on my elbow and shoulder, the ice scraping my cheek. Pain zinged through my right butt cheek and tailbone, still sore from when Bobrova tripped me. Dmitri skated backward, still on his feet, gun wavering indecisively between me and the Zamboni. Irena, apparently out of bullets, flung her guns at the Zamboni and turned to run, taking only one step before Gigi clipped her with the Zamboni's front corner and sent her sprawling on the ice, out cold. The Zamboni's ice-shaving blades snagged on the duffel bag and dragged it, spewing money all over the ice.

"Mom!" Dmitri started toward his mother, but I had half crawled, half slid forward until I could reach his ankle. Wrapping my forearm around it, I jerked.

He toppled, the gun sailing out of his hand, as loud voices shouted, "Police! Freeze! Put down your weapons."

"Are you okay?" I asked Kendall as she stalked toward me. The girl was part penguin, I decided fuzzily, to be able to stay upright on the slick ice.

Ignoring me, she stopped beside Dmitri and launched a small foot into his rib cage.

"Oof."

"You tried to shoot my mother! And you didn't even know my name!"

He stared up at her, confused by the vision of petite, blond, scorned fury, as police officers swarmed him, flipped him onto his stomach, and cuffed his hands behind him, letting Kendall kick him a couple more times before gently pulling her away. When an officer yanked him to his feet, Dmitri flashed his engaging smile and started explaining how he was working with the feds to stop an identity theft ring. Two other officers enthusiastically began collecting the money that coated the rink's surface like a papery lichen.

Gigi dismounted awkwardly from her metal steed, still wearing the pink dress, which looked considerably the worse for wear, like an '80s bridesmaid gown battered in a mosh pit. Her champagne-colored hair was mashed flat on one side, and a bruise discolored her cheek, a souvenir of her fender bender, I guessed.

"Kendall!" Southern accent wringing at least three syllables from the name—"Kay-en-dall"—she kicked off the green pumps and staggered toward her daughter, who hurtled into her mother's arms and promptly burst into tears. "Are you hurt, baby? Are you okay? Where does it hurt?"

It wasn't Kendall who was hurt, I realized, feeling a dull ache spreading from my right buttock. Cold seeped through my jeans, numbing my thighs where they contacted the ice. I reached a hand down to my hip, and it came away streaked with blood. Damn. I'd been shot. And it hurt.

"There, there, baby," Gigi said, stroking the girl's blond hair. "I'm so, so grateful you're all right. Because I am going to kill you for making me worry like that!" They moved toward the side of the rink, paying no attention to me. No one cared that I'd been shot making sure the spoiled teenager didn't get a bullet through *her* perky posterior. I poked out my lower lip and indulged in a little pity party.

I had about decided I needed to make an effort to get up, because the ice beneath me was melting and I was soaked from shoulders to ankles, when Montgomery appeared above me. I stared up into his face in a detached sort of way, thinking how handsome he was, even upside down.

He stretched down a hand, and I reached up with an effort to put my hand in his. His fingers closed over mine, strong and hard and warm. "Are you going to nap there the rest of the evening, Swift?" he asked, a smile slanting across his face. "Come on, get your lazy ass up." He tugged on my hand, and I let out a yelp.

"Wha—?" He stared at the smear of red that became visible on the ice when I shifted. "You're shot! Why didn't you say—? Medic!"

33

I'd have gotten more rest at a Blue Man Group percussion concert than I got in the hospital that night. I lay awake after the surgery to patch up my derriere, gritting my teeth with pain and trying to sort through the events that led to the shootout at the ice rink.

"You'd feel a lot better if you'd take your pain meds," a sickeningly cheerful nurse said, opening the blinds the next morning. I squinted as the sunlight striped my face. I lay on my left side facing the door, some sort of bolster behind me propping me up so I didn't roll onto the butt cheek with the bullet hole in it.

"I hate drugs," I muttered. "They make me feel all . . . not me."

She muttered something that might have been "And that's a bad thing?" as she checked my vitals and scratched notes on my chart. "Breakfast'll be here in a minute," she chirped on her way out, "and I'm sure Dr. Tuckwell will be by before long."

"When can I get out of here?" I called after her, but she was gone. I sipped water from the plastic tumbler on the swing-arm tray beside the bed and discovered the TV remote. I aimed it at the TV, turning my head at an awkward angle, hoping to find some news related to last night's happenings. Nothing but traffic updates, an *Everybody Loves Raymond* rerun, and a yoga class. I clicked it off.

A brief knock sounded on the door, and I looked up, expecting to see breakfast—probably a bowl of soggy cereal and that orange juice that comes in little plastic cups and leaves a funny aftertaste. I didn't suppose there'd be a Pepsi on my tray.

"Charlie, you're awake. How can I ever thank you?" Gigi came in with a bright smile, hair recoiffed to stiff perfection, bruise minimized with makeup, royal blue velour pants and matching jacket replacing the pink dress. She bore an arrangement of yellow and white daisies tucked into a smiley-face mug, which she placed on my tray table. "Kendall, say thank you."

Only then did I notice Kendall behind her mom, glowering. "Thanks," she muttered with all the enthusiasm of a child expected to be grateful for a heaping plateful of boiled eggplant. "Everything was copacetic—I was going to rescue Dmitri and he was going to be so grateful—"

"I'm not sure Dmitri needed rescuing," I said wryly, "and I missed the gratitude. Did he thank us before or after he shot at us?"

"He was only pissed off because you got him arrested," she flashed. "Besides, he didn't shoot! All the shooting was Dmitri's mom and that other guy, the one trying to—"

I stared at her. Last night she'd been kicking him, but today she was defending him? The teenager's capacity for self-delusion, or for sticking to a position in complete disregard of all evidence, awed me.

"Kendall!" Gigi said in a much sterner tone than I was used to hearing from her. Apparently, it was new to Kendall, too, because she stopped with her mouth open and stared at her mother. "Wait in the hall."

The girl left, scuffing her pink boots over the hospital's shiny linoleum.

"I'm glad I wrecked his car," Gigi said when Kendall had gone, giving a decisive nod.

That surprised a laugh out of me.

"Well, I am," she said defiantly. "When I got to the rink—I got the Mustang started again, but it was making a really ugly grinding noise—and saw him aiming that gun at Kendall, I froze. I couldn't scream or move or anything. Then I saw the Zamboni and . . . well, it seemed like my only shot, so I snuck out of the tunnel and climbed onto it. Then—"

"Tunnel?" What was she talking about?

"There's a tunnel from the Ice Hall to the arena that brings you out at ice level," she explained with a "you didn't know that?" expression.

"That would have been useful to know," I said, figuring Dmitri and Irena probably accessed the World Arena through the tunnel and then opened the door I'd come through from the inside for Aguilar and his minions to use.

"I thought Dmitri was going to shoot my baby, but then you pushed her down and saved her life, and I will be grateful to my dying day." Gigi sniffled, and I gestured at the tissue box on the windowsill.

"I don't think he would've shot Kendall on purpose," I said. "She startled him." Irena, however, was a whole 'nother kettle of fish.

"Well, dead is dead whether it's on purpose or not, and I'll never forget you saved her, and got shot doing it. I'll take care of everything while you're in the hospital and convalescing. You don't need to worry about a thing. And I've got a good mind to make Kendall come to your house every day after school and run errands for you until you're up and about."

I blanched. I didn't know who'd hate that more—me or Kendall. "I plan to be up and about by tomorrow," I said, "so don't worry about it. Did Kendall tell you how she came to be at the rink?"

"I'm not deaf, you know," Kendall called from the hallway. She edged back in, leaning against the jamb. "Mom refused to look for Dmitri even though he was in *danger,* so when I saw Mrs. Fane taking the Hummer keys, I jumped in the back and covered up with the blanket, thinking she might need my help. She did, too," she said self-righteously, jutting out her lower lip. "If I hadn't been there, at the rink—"

"Where did you go before the World Arena?" I cut into her heroine fantasy. Squeaking wheels and the scent of scrambled eggs announced the arrival of the breakfast cart. An orderly walked past the door bearing two trays.

"I'm not sure where all we went," she said, "because I was afraid to look half the time, for fear Mrs. Fane might see me and . . . and misinterpret. She drove around for a while—I'm not sure where—and then stopped at some restaurant for dinner," Kendall said. "In a strip mall. It took her, like, two hours to eat. I was freezing in that dumb Hummer and starving, too. All I had to eat was a stupid Snickers bar." She glared at Gigi as if it were Gigi's fault they didn't have food stashed in the Hummer for stowaways. "Then I know we went to Old Colorado City, because she got out there and I was able to sit up and look around. It was dark, though, so I couldn't see much."

"Where did she go?" I tensed and then clenched my fists on the blanket as pain zinged from my ass all the way to the sole of my foot.

"Some tattoo place," Kendall said.

Gigi leaned down and whispered in my ear, "The police found a body there. Shot."

Shocker. Irena tidying up loose ends. I wondered if it had, indeed, been Graham who killed Boyce, as Dmitri implied, or if his mother had, once again, stepped in to keep Dmitri safe. No, it couldn't have been Irena, because she was in Detroit when Boyce was murdered. The police would figure it out.

"I think it's really cool that someone that old would get a tat," Kendall said, looking at Gigi with an expression that said her mom would never do anything half so cool. The girl's eyes lit up. "Mom, can I—?"

"No."

The sullen look clouded Kendall's face again. "Well! You could at least say we'll talk about it."

"No."

I gave Gigi an encouraging smile; she was getting the hang of using the N-word.

Then she went and spoiled it, crossing to the teen where she slouched in the doorway. "Honey, you're beautiful just the way you are. Why, I know dozens of girls who would kill for your lovely skin." She cupped Kendall's face in her hands.

"Where did Irena go after that?" I interrupted before Kendall harangued Gigi into driving her to the nearest tattoo parlor.

"She went to the hospital."

"Memorial North?"

Kendall nodded. "I got out and did a few jumping jacks to keep warm . . . she was in there maybe twenty minutes."

So she'd gone to see her sister. The suspicious side of me wondered if she'd gone to comfort her or tie up another loose end. Either way, I guessed Bobrova was still alive since neither Gigi nor Kendall had said otherwise. I bit my lip, thinking. An orderly sidled past Kendall, tray held high, and laid it on my table after moving the flower, tissues, and tumbler to the windowsill. "Breakfast," he announced.

"Can I get a Pepsi with that?" I asked, peeking under the metal dome at eggs, toast, and applesauce.

He laughed, thinking I was joking, and left.

"We'll go so you can eat," Gigi said, hooking her pink leather tote bag over her arm.

"Wait," I said, in no hurry to eat the rubbery-looking eggs. "Did Irena go anywhere else?"

Kendall shook her head. "She got the phone call pretty much as soon as she got back to the car after visiting the hospital and we went to the World Arena. She drives like Dexter," she added in a noncomplimentary tone, "and she almost wrecked making the turn into the lot. My face banged against the seat, and I got a bloody nose."

That explained the blood droplets in the Hummer's cargo area.

"Poor baby," Gigi said, brow crinkling.

Kendall had gotten off pretty lightly, in my opinion. I thought about what might have happened if Irena had discovered her, and got the shivers.

"What you did last night—trying to warn Dmitri—was brave," I told Kendall. Stupid, but brave. I remembered the heroine daydreams I'd invented at about her age—fantasies of helping people exit an airliner after a crash, or single-handedly tackling an armed bank robber to save the hostages—and I empathized with her desire to impress someone, anyone, but preferably the object of her crush, Dmitri. Who had been markedly unimpressed.

She flushed at my words, crossing and uncrossing her arms over her chest. Her eyes met mine for a fleeting second. "Come on," she told Gigi. "We'll be late. I've still got to do my makeup

276

and get my costume and skates, and you know I like to be at the arena a couple hours before I skate."

"Are they going ahead with Nationals at the World Arena?" I asked, surprised.

"Duh," Kendall said with an eye roll. She tugged at her mom's sleeve and headed impatiently for the door.

With a waggle of her fingers, Gigi followed her daughter into the hall.

After forcing myself to eat half my breakfast, I lay back against my pillow. I must have dozed off, because when I opened my eyes, Dan was sitting in the chair at my bedside, studying me. His bulk shrunk the hospital room, and I was damned glad to see him, even though his presence made me conscious of my undoubtedly ratty hair, my unbrushed teeth, and the skimpy hospital gown that was sagging down my shoulder.

"I'm not that bad off, am I?" I asked by way of greeting. "Last rites bad?"

He smiled. "I brought you this." He held up a can of Pepsi.

"You're a god," I said, taking it from him. I guzzled half the can and let out a satisfied "Aah."

"Some clothes, too." He hefted a bulging plastic grocery bag.

My eyes lit up. "Can you bust me out of here?"

"Absolutely. I'll track down the doc while you dress." He leaned forward to brush a lock of hair off my face. "I'm glad you're okay, Charlie."

The emotion behind his words made me flush. To hide my discomfort, I said, "Okay? I've got a hole in my cheek that's going to make sitting down pretty damn difficult for the next few weeks."

"Good thing you're not much of one for sitting down, then, isn't it?" He grinned and rose to find the doctor.

Getting dressed was more difficult than I had anticipated, even though Dan had—smartly—brought a skirt instead of slacks. Pulling myself to a sitting position via the bed's hand-rail, I inched my body to the side of the bed and swung my legs off, letting out a whistle of pain. Standing would be problematic, so I untied the strings of the hospital gown and let it puddle around my waist before slipping the skirt over my head. Shifting so I was propped on my left hip, I worked the skirt down over my hips and let the hospital gown slide to my ankles. My posterior felt like someone was flicking a lighter somewhere inside my glutes. I was starting to think I might have been too hasty in rejecting the last dose of pain meds.

I was barely decent before Dan returned with the doctor in tow.

She took me through some rigmarole about meds, signs of infection, and PT and finally signed the release papers. "You'll be back here within forty-eight hours," the doctor predicted with a sigh.

"Why?" I was mildly alarmed. Was I injured worse than she let on?

"Your kind don't do what's good for them," she said. Spinning on her heel, she strode down the corridor, lab coat flapping behind her, a tiny dove with a raptor attitude.

"My kind? What did she mean by that?" I asked a chuckling Dan as he pushed me in the mandatory wheelchair down to the entrance.

"I have no idea," he said, laughing louder.

34

Having caved in to Dan's demands and taken my pain pills, I slept for a couple of hours on the couch in my living room, totally wiped out, as tired as the first and only time I'd run the Pikes Peak Ascent, a half-marathon up the mountain. The getting shot thing was worse than the getting-tased thing, I decided, as I drifted off. I awoke to a pounding on the door and Montgomery's voice calling, "Charlie!"

"Stop scaring the wildlife and come in," I yelled, glad I'd brushed my teeth and hair before lying down on the couch. I shoved myself to a sitting position, gritting my teeth.

Montgomery strode in, bristling with energy and an outdoorsy scent, stopping inches in front of me. His dark eyes traveled the length of me before he proclaimed, "You look like shit."

"Tha—" I started, only to find his face suddenly even with mine. Bracing himself with his hands on the back of the couch, he leaned in and kissed me thoroughly. In my weakened and drugged state, I made no attempt to break away, even savoring the feel of his mouth on mine, the clean cedary scent of him, the blood thrumming through my veins. Every inch of me tingled, but I put it down to the drugs. It was a good thirty seconds before he drew away, and I had trouble catching my breath.

"That's your good-night kiss from the date I suppose is now postponed," he informed me, lowering himself carefully to sit beside me. "I've never met anyone who would go to these lengths to avoid a date with me," he said, mock-sadly.

"Get over yourself," I said tartly. "It's not all about you."

"You know you don't mean that."

"What do you want?" I asked grumpily, wanting him to kiss me again but not wanting him to know I wanted it. "I'm tired, and my rear end hurts."

"I could kiss it and make it all better," he said, a mischievous look in his eyes.

"You're not the kiss-ass type," I said. One of the things I liked about him.

"I can make an exception . . ."

"Want a Pepsi?" I asked, way too aware of the heat in his eyes and the muscled length of his thigh pressed against mine on the couch. I shifted away. "There's some in the fridge."

He rose and fetched two sodas. "Nice place," he said when he returned. "It suits you."

"What was in the packet?" I asked as he settled in the couch.

"Right down to business. You're nothing if not consistent, Charlie." He smiled as he said it, though, and took a sip from his can. "The feds say the man we picked up outside the arena is a drug dealer, Jesús Aguilar, medium big, who disappeared from Oaxaca six months back, days before they were going to arrest him in a joint operation with the Mexican police. The

CD had photos of him preplastic surgery and with his new face, along with copies of documents related to his new identity as Randall Belcaro. He's not talking much—lawyered up immediately—but our best guess is that Fane knew he was a big fish, and decided to blackmail him, threatening to publicize his new identity, if he didn't fork over big bucks. A quarter mil, to be precise, minus a few bills that some lucky concertgoers or janitors will discover under the World Arena seats some day."

"What does Dmitri say?"

Montgomery leaned back. "Ah, that's where it gets interesting. Mr. Fane repeated the tale he told you, about being forced to become a courier when Duncan Graham caught him using a stolen credit card to pay for a tattoo for Dara Peterson. Graham is not in a position to verify this, due to the bullets in his chest, fired, in all probability, by Irena Fane. The bullets match the gun we took off her at the World Arena, and Gigi's daughter can place her at Tattoo4U around the time of death. We're still waiting on ballistics results for Edgerton."

I stared at him. "Irena was still in Detroit when he got shot."

Montgomery got that superior look that irks the hell out of me. "*Au contraire.* Her name doesn't show up on any airline manifest in the last month. My guess is she drove here a couple weeks ago, possibly when Fane got the brilliant idea of blackmailing Aguilar so he could retire from his criminal life with a nice little nest egg, and has been with her son off and on ever since."

That explained why she had no luggage at the airport. I hated having to admit that Irena Fane fooled me, even for a short while. "So Dmitri says he was forced to become a courier— that doesn't explain why he disappeared and how he came to be blackmailing your friend Mr. Aguilar. Dmitri's in this up to his lying blue eyeballs."

"I tend to agree with you," Montgomery said, leaning back against the couch and laying his arm casually over my shoulders, "but we have no proof. Fane's gun hadn't been fired recently, so he's not on the hook for Graham's death or your injury, and a bullet from your gun put Aguilar's enforcer in the hospital with a collapsed lung and assorted other damage."

I'd already ascertained from the hospital staff that he was going to live, and I was glad. Killing someone—even in self-defense or to save someone else's life—is a heavy burden. I didn't need another death on my conscience.

"It gets worse—or better, depending on your perspective. Fane kept a list of the identities he delivered, complete with copies of the IDs and such that are allowing a slew of criminals and other undesirables to start over again. He's trading that list to the feds for immunity."

"What?" I bolted upright, then grimaced as my ass objected to the strain on the stitches.

"I knew that would make you happy." Montgomery gave me a rueful smile. "It doesn't exactly thrill me, either, but it's a done deal."

"So he's going to walk away?"

"Skate away is more like it. I understand he and Dara perform their short program Thursday."

I growled.

"I understand how you feel, Charlie," he said, easing himself off the couch. "But you know how the game is played. The feds really want that list. They'll bring down some much bigger fish than Fane once they get a look at it. They've already located two pedophiles and a murderer who escaped from custody in Alabama. The greater good and all that."

"Screw the greater good," I said. An image of Dmitri jabbing his gun under Kendall's chin was seared into my brain. "I can't believe he gets to compete in the Olympics as if nothing has happened."

"He's got to win at Nationals first, as I understand it," he said, looking down at me. "I've got to go. Big powwow with the FBI, my chief, and assorted others to decide how we're moving forward with Fane's list. You get some rest." He bent to press a warm kiss on my lips and then drew back, his face still so close to mine I had to cross my eyes slightly to focus on him. "I could get used to that."

Truth be told, I could, too, but I flapped my hand at him as if his kiss hadn't lit up my skin from the inside. "Go away. Catch some criminals. Make the taxpayers proud."

When he'd left, I threw off the afghan tangled around my legs, reached for my cane—Dan had loaned me a handsome wooden one with the handle carved into a griffin's head so I didn't have to use the utilitarian metal one the hospital gave me—and hobbled to the kitchen. Downing my meds and a large glass of milk, I stared into my yard, feeling some of the tension ebb as chickadees and a mountain blue jay pecked at my suet feeder and a breeze sifted snow off the evergreen branches. A lot of people—Gigi, for instance—find the winter landscape dull, but I love the winter palette of grasses and shrubs that range from pale tan and dull gold to reddish brown and mahogany with splotches of green from pines or juniper. As my gaze fell on my hot tub and I mourned not being able to soak in it until my wound healed, the doorbell rang.

I called, "Coming," and limped toward the door, irritated by how the gunshot wound slowed me down. Checking the peephole, I raised my brows. I pulled the door wide, inviting my guest in. "I guess you got word that it's safe to come home," I greeted Dara Peterson.

The girl looked as fit and confident as the day she breezed into my office, and considerably less tense. Her dark hair spilled out from beneath a red tam that flattered her clear skin, and her white teeth gleamed as she flashed a smile. "Yeah. I called home, and my mom let me know."

"Where were you?"

"Austin. With a friend who's at UT. He was cool with me hanging at his place for a few days."

I gestured her toward the easy chair. She flopped into it, swinging one Ugg-booted foot in a carefree way that told me all was right in her world now that she and Dmitri could compete at Nationals and, one presumed, the Olympics.

"I just stopped by to thank you for finding Dmitri, even though I fired you. My mom told me she hired you again, so that all worked out. We're skating our short program Thursday and our long program on Saturday. So we have a couple of days to train, although it won't be the same without Coach Bobrova. Dmitri told me what he's been going through the last few months and I can't believe it!"

"That's probably the right reaction," I said drily. I remained standing—it was easier on my tush.

Her brows twitched together. "What do you mean?"

Dara had paid me to find Dmitri Fane, and I figured her retainer bought her the truth at least. So I filled her in on Dmitri's criminal activities, from credit card fraud to stealing identity documents and helping Graham produce new IDs so some seriously bad guys could go on being seriously bad under new names.

She bit her lip as I wound down. "Well, he shouldn't have

taken those credit cards, but that Graham guy forced him to help with the identity stuff, after all—and he didn't *hurt* anyone."

"Oh, come on," I said, disgusted. I banged the rubberized tip of my cane onto the floor, realizing as the impact reverberated through my hand that it was a Bobrova-ish gesture. Dara might be only nineteen, but that was old enough to make some hard moral calls. "He might not have beaten Yuliya Bobrova to the brink of death himself, or killed Edgerton and Graham, but he was *directly* responsible for those deaths. If he'd gone to the police when Graham caught him out—never mind not stealing credit cards in the first place—those people would still be alive. As it is, they're dead, and Dmitri, with your help, is free to skate his way to an Olympic medal."

Dara jumped to her feet, face flushed. "That is so not fair! Don't think I don't see what you're trying to do. You're pissed that Dmitri's not going to jail, and you want me to punish him by refusing to skate with him. Well, it's not all about Dmitri, is it? It's about me and my dreams, too. And my mom, who has sacrificed for years so I could compete in the Olympics. And it's about America and bringing home the most medals from the Olympics. Dmitri and I are the nation's best hope for an Olympic gold in figure skating, you know. Japan will get the women's gold, Canada or Russia will win in ice dancing, and we don't have a man who will finish in the top five." Unshed tears glittered in her eyes, and she dug a hand into her jacket pocket. "I came over to give you tickets to our performances, but I guess I shouldn't count on seeing you there." She flung the tickets at me, and the light cardboard rectangles swooped and spun before settling on the floor.

"Dara—" I didn't know what I was going to say, but it didn't matter, because she blasted through the door and slammed it behind her. I flung the cane to the floor in frustration and then had to hop on one foot, jouncing pain through my torn muscles, to retrieve it from where it rolled to a stop against a table leg.

I handled that with all the finesse of a grade schooler lying about undone homework, I thought. Dara had figured out what I was hinting at practically before I knew I was doing it. She was right on all counts: I was PO'd that Dmitri wasn't facing a jail term, and I thought it would be fabulous if he got his comeuppance some other way. Despite the negative publicity surrounding him, no one from U.S. Figure Skating or the Olympic Committee was making noises about denying Dmitri the opportunity to compete. Aguilar, the Mexican drug lord who should be mightily annoyed with Dmitri, had other things on his mind—like cutting his own deals with the DEA and Mexican authorities—besides sending a minion out to stomp Dmitri. As for Dara . . . well, it didn't look like Dara was willing to sever their partnership and leave Dmitri to skate a pair routine solo. I resolved to try to let it go, although the injustice made me burn. Lord knows I'd dealt with many cases where justice wasn't served, either in a courtroom or outside it.

Wednesday, Bobrova regained consciousness and identified Aguilar's thug, the one I'd shot, as her assailant. The police matched the bullets found in Dmitri's condo with a gun hidden in the thug's rented SUV, and a recently stitched knife wound in his left arm seemed to indicate he was the man Dmitri slashed at the Estes Park cabin. He admitted to tossing his lighter into the gas-filled cabin but denied knowing I was in it at the time. I actually believed him.

Thursday, I decided a walk was in order so my muscle tone wouldn't deteriorate completely, but I barely made it a quarter mile before pain forced me to turn around. I spent most of the day in bed, exhausted by my attempt at exercise. While I snoozed, the district attorney filed formal charges against Irena Fane for the premeditated murders of Duncan Graham and Boyce Edgerton—I guessed ballistics matched her gun to the bullet in Boyce—and Peterson and Fane landed in a tie for third after their short program. Angel and Trevor were sitting atop the leaderboard or whatever they call it in figure skating.

Friday, Aaron Wong burst through my door, a smile as wide as the Mississippi River splitting his face. "Mom heard from Nate!" he crowed. I demanded all the details and learned that Nate Wong, now calling himself DuShawn Morton, had indeed scored a new driver's license and Social Security card through Graham at Tattoo4U.

"DuShawn?" I queried, arching one brow.

Aaron winced. "Yeah, I know. His new name's the least of it. He left here, hitched back to the East Coast, and married that Alisha girl whose photo was in his wallet. Her parents were against it—"

"They didn't want their daughter to marry an eighteen-year-old unemployed deserter living under a false name? You amaze me."

With a grin, Aaron continued, "Yeah, especially since she's only sixteen. So they eloped and have been hiding out from her parents and the military ever since, moving from motel to motel in the Carolinas until they ran out of money. When they couldn't pay their bill, they offered to clean rooms at the last fleabag motel they landed at, but the owner called the cops on them, and the cops called Alicia's parents, who apparently want to string up Nate—"

"DuShawn."

"—and have him drawn and quartered. They're accusing

him of statutory rape, kidnapping, and I don't know what all else. My mom's flying in here tonight, and we're leaving for South Carolina in the morning to see if we can help straighten this mess out." Having expelled his news on a single breath, he paused to suck in air.

"Good luck," I said, thinking that the army ought to realize they were better off without Nate-DuShawn in uniform and drop all charges on the condition that he never take up a career that would allow him access to heavy artillery or even a slingshot.

Saturday night I sat lopsidedly in an ice-side seat at the World Arena, Gigi beside me, as the last five pairs couples warmed up to skate for the national championship and the right to represent the United States of America at the Olympics. The Arena was a bit more than half full, and the bright lights, hum of conversation, and music playing over the loudspeakers made it seem like a different building entirely than the one I'd been shot in Monday night. As the skaters leaped and spun and glided, Gigi tore off and ate fluffy bits of aqua cotton candy the same color and texture as her bulky mohair sweater.

"Roger called me," she said with a sidelong look. "For a date."

"Congratulations," I said, wondering if it would be premature to suggest that February—okay, May—was a lovely month for a wedding. After which, she could resign from the PI business . . .

"I didn't think he would," she admitted. "Not after last time when I behaved like a loony with that stupid spy brooch. And I'm okay with his best friend being a murderer—"

"Huh?" I stared at her.

"—since it was a drunk driving accident *years* ago and he's paid his debt to society and been sober for decades." She nodded her head emphatically.

"Was Kendall happy with eighth place?" I asked. The junior women's competition had wrapped up earlier that day. Despite my throbbing derriere, I'd come to watch at Gigi's request and been seriously impressed with Kendall. The petite blonde had seemed to float across the ice, making double and triple jumps look easy and only falling once on a tricky combination. The way she scrambled back up and continued on, a smile glued to her face, made me realize she was built of tougher stuff than I had imagined. Which didn't mean I wanted her working at Swift Investigations ever again. Still mad at Dmitri for not knowing her name or for threatening to kill her—I wasn't sure which rankled more—she had refused to come to tonight's competition.

"She's ecstatic," Gigi said. "That's eleven places up from last year. By the time the next Olympics rolls around . . ." She left the thought unfinished and sighed.

"What?"

She sighed again. "Kendall had been making noises about wanting to quit, but now she's all fired up again."

"Isn't that good?"

"It's expensive," Gigi said simply, "but if it gives her joy, I'll have to find a way to scrape up the money."

I sat silently, thinking about the three mothers of skaters I'd spent time with this week. All had made sacrifices so their kids could excel. Irena went so far as to murder people who might derail her son's career. Sally Peterson seemed, if anything, more committed to her daughter competing at the Olympics than Dara was, and I wondered where their relationship would go when Dara retired. Gigi, surprisingly, seemed to have the sanest approach, supporting Kendall's aspirations without getting her own identity all tangled up with her daughter's success. "I hope Kendall appreciates what you're doing for her," I said.

Gigi smiled gratefully. "Want some?" She thrust the gooey blue mass at me.

"No, thanks," I said, shuddering.

The lights dimmed and a hush settled over the crowd as the announcer called out the names of the first of the last five pairs to skate. Angel and Trevor, in first place after the short program, skated second and earned their all-time highest score, according to the announcer.

"Dara and Dmitri will have a hard time beating that," Gigi murmured. She tried to explain the beyond-complicated scoring system to me, which seemed to require a PhD and a Cray computer to comprehend, but the woman behind us shushed her as the next skaters took the ice.

Finally, the announcer boomed, "Peterson and Fane," and the couple skated to the center of the ice, their plain black and white costumes in stark contrast to the fiery reds and sequined blues of other competitors. An expectant hush fell over the crowd as the first notes of Tchaikovsky's *Swan Lake* sang through the speakers. Any faint, unadmitted hope I might have had that Dara would leave Dmitri standing alone in the middle of the ice, or better yet trip him as he skated past her, died as I caught her expression of fierce concentration. She was here to win.

Their blades bit into the ice, and they opened with what Gigi murmured were side-by-side double axels. From that point on, I was caught up in the tension and grace of the program, the contrast of his dark strength with her fragile beauty, barely conscious of Gigi commentating. ". . . look at the height on that throw triple salchow . . . perfect synch on their flying camels . . . tricky footwork . . . such speed . . . Oh, my God!" She dropped the cotton candy onto her lap.

The whole arena gasped as Dmitri whirled Dara up into a lift where he supported her arched figure with one hand while gliding on one foot. She spun and he flipped her back to the ice so her skate touched down as lightly as a dragonfly on water. They concluded with a death spiral, and I found myself on my feet with the rest of the crowd, clapping as loudly as I could when they struck their final pose exactly on the music's last note. Applause echoed around the arena for a good two minutes as Dara and Dmitri bowed and waved to the fans, Dara's face shining, Dmitri pumping a triumphant fist.

With the crowd still clapping, they skated toward what Gigi called the kiss-and-cry area, Dara gracefully retrieving flowers and stuffed animals tossed by fans on the way. As she straightened from scooping up a carnation, our eyes met. I beamed at her, wholly caught up in the power and pathos of their performance. Dmitri might be a criminal, but man, could he skate. I made a mental note to ask Dan why God—if He existed—gave a dirtball like Dmitri the ability to move so many people, to bring them close to tears and yet leave them feeling totally uplifted. Dara's lips curved in an answering smile, and she raised the carnation to me before following Dmitri off the ice to await their scores.